TALES

 ## from

THE BOOK

(Part 1)

Kristina Chase

ISBN 978-1-0980-0746-1 (paperback)
ISBN 978-1-0980-0747-8 (digital)

Christian Faith Publishing, Inc.
832 Park Avenue
Meadville, PA 16335
www.christianfaithpublishing.com

Art work by Ben Lefler jflerb@gmail.com and Shawn P. Petersen

Printed in the United States of America

Mothers. Fathers. Sisters. Brothers. Aunts. Uncles. Nieces. Nephews. Cousins. Grans. Steps. Friends. Best Friends. Pen Pals. Great Coworkers. Good Jobs. Great Supervisors. Good Leaders. The Grand Canyon. Electricity. So-so Jobs. Time Off. Paid Time Off. Robins. Church. Home. Porches. Macadamia Nuts. Beryllium. Porches With Fans. Daisies. Guitars. Tennessee Walkers. All Dogs. Cats Of Course. Birds. Honey. Lightening. Glass. The Road That I Have Traveled. Whales. Seaweed. Corn. Hills. Icebergs. Rice. Dentists. Trees. Crappie (The Fish). Redwood Trees. Basil. Dogwood Trees. Evergreen Trees. Magnolia Trees. Bluebirds. Grass. Boron. Lemon Grass. Gold. Clown Fish. Tape. Lemon Balm. Lemons. Oranges. Grapes. Pineapples. Mango. The People Working Patience In Me. Neon Tetras. Boiling Points. Moonlight. Planets. Maple Syrup. Stars. Peanuts. The Sun. Greens. Diamonds. Peanuts. Finches. Blues. Peppermint. Blacks. Yellows. Lemon Curd. Whites. Fluorine. Coyotes. Reds. Day. Soap. Catnip. Night. Budgies. Fishing Piers. Summer.

Crickets. Bumblebees. Breeze. Quarter Horses. Cauliflower. Manatees. Cashews. Ponds. Elephants. SALVATION. Rosemary. Giraffes. Deer. Gravity. Penguins. Ink. Paper. Butterflies. Pitch. Sound Waves. Cabbage. Lake Waves. Light Waves. Celery. Sweet Potatoes. Diamonds In The Rough. Ferries. Springtime. Tug Boats. Begonias. Sheep. Carbon. Wool. Lentils. Platinum. Hereford Cows. Guinea Pigs. Rubies. The Moon. Plutonium. Donkeys. Piano. Woodpeckers. Quarter Horses. Rhododendrons. Bilberry. Some Bugs. Goats. Mimosa Trees. Loud Toucans. Hydrogen. Large Sail Boats. Kayaks. Eggplant. Canoes. Timber That Become Lumber Or Toilet Tissue. Xenon. Concrete. Butterfly Bushes. Lithium. Clean Hot Water. Indoor Plumbing. Math. Organic Chemistry. Lanthanum. Inorganic Chemistry. Oregano. Seashells. Crabs. Goldfish. Cumin. Neodymium. Pepper. Rock Salt. Tuna. Pachysandra. Caterpillars. Barracuda. GRACE. Actinium. Speech. Oxygen. Snowshoe Hare. Samarium. Striped Bass. Wide Mouthed Bass. Peaches. Swans.

Light Bulbs. Water. Fireflies. Pews With Book Holders On The Backs. Ample Parking Space. Wild Horses. Helium. Parking Lot Attendants. Barium. Crows. Lettuce. Sheds. Hummus. Radium. Car Shades. Numbers. Ebb Tide. Security Guards. Broccoli. Bridges. Beaches. Peppers. My Thorns In The Flesh. Iodine. Squash. Melting Points. Jersey Cows. Air Bubbles. Lavender. Thyme. Sage. Antimony. Appaloosas. Coriander. Leeks. Lakes. Artichoke. Asparagus. Nitrogen. Brussel Sprouts. Wind. Pistachios. Ruthenium. Rhode Island Red Chickens. Rutgers Tomatoes. Spinach. Rhubarb. Radishes. Drums. Creeks. Turnips. Pumpkin. Potato. Tellurium. Peas. Soup. Sundays. The Alphabet. Rafting. Flagstone. Cana Lilly. PEACE. Hermit Crabs. In The Wild. Kosher Salt. Molybdenum. Soft Pillows. Helium. Geese That Cross Streets Safely. LOVE. Pearls. Neon. Sodium. Clocks. Acids & Bases. Sleep. Quiet. Magnesium. Skunks At A Distance. Aluminum. Silicon. Ice Cream Sandwiches. Zirconium. Lantana. Slate. Moss. Strawberries. Phosphorus.

For Veanna Mae Jackson and Mary Lee Andrews. Yes, ma'ams, I was listening.

Contents

Introduction

The Word says that the Lord Jesus taught so many things that the entire world could not contain them all if they were written. I often wonder what someone in the crowd hearing Him saw and thought. *That* guy. (Or, *that* gal!) What was his (or her) life like before and after meeting Jesus? So I have written short fictional vignettes, some from the vantage point of average unknown persons. I wish to impress upon the reader that we have a tremendous advantage of living at this particular point in history. The personalities in the Bible, many of whom we think of as heroes, may not have been feeling heroic while they were in the midst of their own stories. They may have been uncertain, confused, or perhaps frightened not knowing how their circumstances would turn out. Some of them may have wavered in their decision to trust God to go with them through their experience. For better or worse, all of them are examples for us! God loves to use every day people who make themselves available to Him! Let Him prepare you! Whatever it is that He tells you to do, He will equip you for the task.

My hope is that you make yourself available to God for the work, which He has for you. Just show up; He'll show out!

Acknowledgments

Thanks to the people living and working in and around Greensboro, Georgia, who live every day to honor God. Thanks to the saints of Hills Chapel Baptist Church for every little thing back in the day. Thanks to the First United Methodist Church on the lake for your support and friendship. Your kindness is genuine. Thanks to the saints of New Birth Missionary Baptist Church, Atlanta, Georgia, for being the hands and feet of Jesus to so many. Many thanks to my Virginia associates who keep me encouraged along the way. Thanks to Grove Avenue Baptist Church for walking with me through a difficult season, The Village Church, for being seriously mission oriented. Thanks to Mrs. Judy Gattis Smith. You are a beautiful soul. Thank you for teaching children about God and saying, "May you see the mystery and love of God today!" Thank you, The Church at Brandermill, for your love of the Lord. It is evident in every one of you, and thank you, City Church, you keep me focused. Big sis, Carol V: ¡Eres la mejor! John Boito Sr., Sir, you have such a godly heart. Thank you all for your input and feedback. Thank you, publishing staff, for your guidance.

The Meeting
(Gen. 2:7–20)

Warm. He felt warmth on his face. His eyes saw on a bed of deep rose, circles of oranges, greens, and pinks. His eyelids fluttered and then opened. A soft smile crept across his lips as he gazed into the warmth. His eyes wandered, soaking in images in brilliant greens, whites, yellows, and reds. He fixed back on the warmth. "You are my father. You are... God!"

I Am.

"Who...am I?"

You are Adam. I made you from this clay.

Adam looked down at the lifeless ground, then, with two fingers, rubbed his forearm. He looked back at his Father, then bent over to touch the ground, picking up a few grains of dirt allowing it to sift through two fingers. Adam smiled. There would be more questions on this, but for right now, he said, "I know you, but tell me about you."

I Am. I have always been and will always be. I am Creator of all things. Nothing has come into being without Me. I Am.

"I...feel—"

What you are experiencing is love. I am love, and I impart love into my creation. You are my child. I love you.

"I...love you? I love you!" Adam sat hunching his back, flexing, and wiggling toes, very satisfied with his constructed declaration. Something settled lightly on his shoulder. It's wings hosted complex bands of shape and color which looked like a large set of eyes staring hard at Adam all the while fanning his cheek. "Well, what's that?" Adam laughed.

It's a creation. I have a great many to show you. Would you like to begin?

"Aahhh…yes!"

The Creator stretched out His hand toward Adam. Adam stretched toward his Father. He put his hand in the palm of the Father's and grabbed hold. He felt that warmth again throughout his body—the warmth said *safe, loved* and *home!* The ringed black eyes fluttered away from his shoulder. The Creator helped Adam stand up. Adam stretched. He turned his torso as far as he could in one direction, looking behind him and then turned in the other direction. He stood on the tips of his toes with palms stretched skyward. He tried to stretch his arms out so that his fingers on the right hand were as far as they could possibly be from those on his left. He bent over dusting his hands with the red earth—which he was named for—flexed his toes up, and dug the ball of his left big toe into the dirt. Satisfied with his self-discoveries, he looked at the Father. Hands outstretched again, Adam took his first steps gracefully. He grabbed hold of the Father's hand, gasping in elation over this new skill of ambulance.

They strolled—the man as a child seeing everything new, mind sharp and absorptive, questioning endlessly and the Creator, a patient loving father, wanting a world of love for His child.

Hmm, Adam thought aloud, *well, who are they?*

My servants. You may call them angels. There are a great many of them, and they are each individuals. They each have responsibilities.

"What about the big one over there. He seems unhappy. Why would he be unhappy?"

He has chosen poorly. Beware of treachery. I give admonition and choice to my servants. Be sure to test all things. If you are ever uncertain, ask ME. *You must have freedom in order to choose, to love, yet your freedom is in bondage to Me.*

"What?"

Beware of the false tongue. Test all things. Whatever you hear that has not come from Me is not truth.

For a moment, Adam studied the figure which was sulking at a distance. Then he turned to focus on the beauty and busyness of the garden.

"So it seems like everything has a job: the grass has a job, the trees have a job, even the flowers work. All of these creatures, even the tiniest ones, work. It's like they all work together even though they're not really working together. One is doing one thing so that another can do its job. Is anyone here not working?"

Yes, you, but that just changed!

The Creator laughed a laugh like a song that absolutely delighted Adam! Inside, Adam felt like leaping with happiness. He sat on a large boulder and listened intently as the Creator explained his newly appointed duties. Work! Adam watched the animals around them, furnishing endless inquiry with respect to them.

Would you like to name them?

"Why...yes!" Adam answered, quite astonished by the invitation.

The Creator brought many animals to Adam. The man observed them and gave them names with their behavior or characteristics in mind. Adam enjoyed birds the most because of their abilities of flight. He loved horses because their communication is so subtle, dogs for their devotion, and, of course, the ants for their cooperative industry.

Always keep foremost in your mind that I love you and that I have the best for you. There is much which you do not see and even more that you don't understand. When things grow loud, listen well for my voice. Do not allow distractions to take your thoughts from me. Maintain control of your mind and you will control your heart. Your heart will control the rest of your body. Test all things. If you do not know, ask ME. *I speak life to you.*

As they walked, the man explored, learned, and loved his home. "I love how everything is so thought out. Trees make shade, provide food, homes, goats mow the grass down, worms break down their droppings, ants tunnel the soil, bees pollinate, wind spreads seed. Everything is so amazing! And they're all so content to do what you made them to do, and look at them, how nicely they're paired to their mates—the buck has a doe, the stallion has a mare. The rooster has a hen. The ram has an ewe. All of creation is a wonder!"

Yes, and now, my child, you must sleep awhile.

And He Made Them
(Gen. 3)

Remorse (2 Pet. 2:4)

S cene: Mostly quiet, occasional barely audible background sounds of discomfort emit. Light is so dim that protagonist's outer silhouette is visible but no features. Smoke permeates the environment, a bitter brimstone fume that forces the eyebrow into a chronic furrow. Drifting masses of fume intermittently obscure view of protagonist's silhouette. Protagonist is writing a diary on the ground, scratching letters through ground bits of rock and ashes with a stick. Occasionally, he stops and looks back at the length of his writing, which extends several hundred feet. One can sense the futility in his effort as parts of the journal are washed over by a shallow ebbing tide or a shadow in the distance aimlessly trudging past, dragging right through the inscriptions. Regardless, the protagonist turns his head back downward to continue writing. It is evident that the protagonist scratches in the ground to stave off inevitable boredom. Occasionally, the writing stick wears down, and the protagonist stops to search out a replacement. He returns to write:

> *Most Unfortunate Me,*
>
> > *Constrained by the perpetuity of forever and the condemnation of my being for the most heinous and despicable of acts wherein I willingly sinned against the Great Father, I remain confined, awaiting only the bleakest of futures. I dare not address myself*

"Dearest Me," for I have not been dear, not in many ages but envious, spiteful, most contemptible, loathsome, vile, and, not least of all, evil. These are my accomplishments, the heritage I leave, thankfully, to no one: that is my sole consolation. No inheritance for the future, no posterity behind. I have only time to reflect on the past, "the act," and the precipitating circumstances. Angry? Certainly. Unfortunately, the blame points true toward self, and oh, that is tiresome to revisit. For the sake of diversion, I direct it elsewhere, but with the exhaustion of such wasteful efforts come the fundamental, oh how I hate this word, truth, and therein lies everything. Just as the true compass ever points north. The whole and fact of the matter is that the thought, the crime, the act, and the punishment are all mine to claim. That, is the truth.

For the sake of nothing, anything, no one, for who will hear me, I reflect on the time before. Time was quieter then. Quiet but explosive as He created all matter. Sonic booms of light, wind, incalculable volumes of pressure—every descriptive played when He fashioned stellar bodies, entire systems of energies. It is difficult to describe. I suppose that I might think about it more and attempt it again. After all, I have nothing but time. The creations were progressively more remarkable to me. To us. All of us. He created me as I was, not as the loathsome fragment to which I have degraded. Even we were young at one time, although not in the human sense. We grew, but we did not have to "grow up," in a physical sense. Not at all, as we are spirit creatures, not flesh. We were created in our state of fullness, if I might so phrase it. Our growing—we grew to love Him more, learn more about Him, and marvel at Him. And He did love us. And we all knew it all of the time. So why? Why the despicable wickedness? Yes, indeed, why? I can offer no good answer. No logical one. Only the most unfortunate succession of choices and most wretched consequences to face. I dare say that to some degree, this has happened to everyone but the degree, that is the point of difference. In fact, we have all fallen off the mark but some in deliberate act and continuous engagement. That is the point of difference. Back then, back in time, before the emergence of evil, there was love and reconciliation; but let me speak of where it began on Earth.

God made a garden. Not a garden like you or I or any of the most skilled gardeners you may know would build. Oh, no, friend. God built a showplace, a masterpiece and you've never seen anything like it! This was a garden! It was tall and short, thick and spacious enough to stroll in, ordered and wild, shady and sunny, flowered and overflowing with food. Beautiful, stately but cozy enough to call home, and that's where He put the man—at home. He set the man to work there, pruning, hedging and harvesting. The man was both delighted and exhausted, so God gave him help, the helpmate. They shared the pleasure of God's creation together, and God came to walk and talk with the man every afternoon. Yes, God loved this special creation man very much, and so, it became the special target of a certain enemy.

Story: Eve, the helpmate, climbs a few feet up to a large flat-ish stone. She sits on the rock, legs dangling, toes wiggling, smiling at the warm dapple of sun on her back. The sitting rock makes the perfect lookout spot to observe man, beast, and all that flutters by. She inhales a mixture of hydrangea, hibiscus, and rose intermitted by an occasional breeze of lemongrass. A gentle wind shakes the grass, inciting desire for a bit of a nap. Eve is not aware that she is being observed from a distance. In order to avoid suspicion, the observer searches for a guise or rather a disguise, by which to approach Eve. Every creature that the observer approaches flees his presence, except for one. A lumbering snake, in a moment of indecision racked with curiosity, hesitates for an unfortunate moment. The observer inhabits the snake, which immediately finds itself unwitting prisoner in its own body, no longer in control, now yielded to its intruder. The snake, having short legs and a new operator, presently waddles to sitting rock where Eve relaxes. It gives Eve a long courteous nod and climbs onto the stone to sit adjacent to her. Unable to manipulate the brief legs, the snake sits awkwardly, legs straight out, front legs moving about impersonating arms as if they are new appendages with kinks still to be worked through. Eve turns her attention to about hip level in order to observe this creature. It doesn't stand out as wrong but of noticeably different behavior from anything she's seen thus far, and no one has said anything overtly about a snake. Or a talking one. It looks directly ahead, gives its tongue a long slow flicker and then a very long sigh.

SNAKE. (*Sighs*)

Another long slow flicker and a very long sigh.

SNAKE. (*Sighs*)

Again, a long slow flicker and a very long sigh.

SNAKE. (*Sighs*)

EVE. (*Endowed with patience*) You okay, fella?

SNAKE. (*Responds slowly, as one lets line out to a great fish one has just hooked. Slowly. Presently, he responds, still staring out straight ahead, avoiding eye contact with Eve.*) Oh, I suppose it's just such a waste. You must be hungry!

EVE. (*Feeling confused*) What'd you mean?

SNAKE. (*Sighs*) I mean…all that food and nothing to eat. Me, I haven't eaten since…why, it must be since yesterday! Or maybe the day before. It's hard having to scavenge…

Now, if Eve were here in this day and age, she would be known as The Cat Lady. Everyone knows one—a person who brings home all things furry and fawns over them all. So, hearing about some creature not having eaten in 3 days, she puts everything else on the back burner. Eve gives her full attention to this creature with the odd motions.

EVE. Oh, there's plenty to eat. Look over there. That's the vegetable garden. That's where Adam is now, somewhere in there! We've got tomatoes, squash, peas, potatoes, all kinds of melons, berries, a fruit tree orchard next door. Oh, lots of stuff to eat. I don't know all the different names yet! There's plenty to eat.

SNAKE. (*Flickers and sighs*) But there's something you *can't* have here, isn't there?

EVE. There's zucchini, pumpkin, green beans, stringy beans, crowders umm yumm. Okra, if you like that kind of thing. Sweet yams, collards. I haven't figured out what to do with those leafy greens yet: kale, collards, turnip greens. Think on that! Potatoes come in several colors. The herbs and the spice plants back over there, Oh my goodness!

SNAKE. But there's something that you *can't* have...*isn't* there?

Eve finds this a rather somber way to look at things, but in the name of friendship, she continues to chatter.

EVE. Can't have...can't have... Umm, um, well, sure! (*Eve looks around the garden.*) There! Over there, in the middle, there's that big tree. We're not to touch that one.

Silence for a few minutes. Long flicker and a sigh.

SNAKE. So now, did He *say* that?

EVE. Yeah.

SNAKE. No, no, I mean, did He actually say, actually...that?

EVE. *Yeah...*

SNAKE. Well, then, that settles it. You're not getting it.

EVE. Getting *what?*

SNAKE. Governance, my dear, oh, governance!

EVE. Come again?

Snake, now appearing to have control of the upper limbs, turns to face Eve, pointing a digit in her direction.

SNAKE. Look, what makes you special?

EVE. Umm, special?

SNAKE. Yessss, yes, child. What makes you *so special*, so different? So different from everything else around here?

Eve is baffled by the conversation she's fallen into and neglects the caution that she first expressed, not having found any other creature thusly engaging. She has clearly thrust caution aside in amusement of this curious exchange.

EVE. Umm, dunno. What'd you mean?

SNAKE. Just look around you.

Eve looks around, notices nothing unusual, and returns her attention to him.

SNAKE. Well, look at all these creatures. You just named them!

EVE. Adam did.

SNAKE. Whoever. Look at that there—a lion, a tiger, oh my goodness, and that big thing over there, the one that squawks…

EVE. That one's the elephant, and *squawk* isn't the word we were thinking of, something bigger, perhaps. A bigger word. It makes a big sound. Bigger…

SNAKE. Whatever. Is there anyone out there like *me*?

A pause ensues, and Eve concedes.

EVE. Umm, no, not that I've come across so far. You're kind of, I dunno…s…

SNAKE. Sssophisticated, I'm *sophisticated.*

EVE. I was thinking, "suspect," but okay. But you're a weird egg, sort of, Snake.

SNAKE. Gifted. I'm uniquely gifted. And so are *you!*

EVE. Right, umm...okay. Uhhmm, what'd ya mean?

SNAKE. Who did all the naming? You did, right?

EVE. Adam did. I wasn't here.

SNAKE. Not here? Well, where were you just then?

EVE. Uhmm. Nowhere?

SNAKE. Whatever. *Who*ever! Well, who is thinking of a big word for the *selephas*?

EVE. *El-e-phant. El-e-phant, el-e-phant. el-e-phant!* *And he* is, really. I'm his helpmate.

SNAKE. Whoever! Am I lisping? *You* could have invented the *ele*...oh, whatever, if you really had put it to your mind.

EVE. I wasn't even here yet.

Snake continues bridging the lost moments to help his victim along the trail he's set for her.

SNAKE. You're brimming over with untapped potential! You don't know it, because *someone,* doesn't want you to know. (*Very slowly Snake says*) Why, you could have built your own garden, and even better than this one. Look at the pale color on these flowers here. Oh what...a...pity... (*Head hung low in dejection, snake turns facing forward again as if he doesn't want to share the grief of his observation.*)

Eve, who shows herself less than intuitive but ever supportive, seeks to console her new "friend."

EVE. Oh, no no! He doesn't make mistakes! This place is perfect. It's a great place, and we love it! And there's plenty of food! Maybe if you just eat something, you'll feel better!

SNAKE. Sure, sure, of course (*sighs*)…but what if there's an *even better* place to live than this, but you don't know about it and you're stuck like a bad mortgage right here on a depreciating lot?

EVE. There you go talkin' crazy again!

Snake detects her derailment, tries to get Eve back on his track.

SNAKE. It's an idea I'm working on for later. But look, suffice to say there's something better, and you can have it for yourself, for you and for Adam. Now wouldn't he like that? Wouldn't he be *so* happy when you come home and say, "Honey, I built us a better garden over there!" (*He points a digit off to the right, to nowhere in particular. Eve finds herself momentarily turning off in that direction as well, visibly lost to the conversation.*) Wouldn't he be so proud of you?

EVE. What's "better"?

Snake detects a weak point.

SNAKE. It's what you're missing.

EVE. How come I'm missing?

SNAKE. Not *you're* missing. You're missing *it*!

EVE. The "better"?

SNAKE. Exactly…

EVE. How do I know that? How can I tell?

SNAKE. Because I'm *telling* you. *He* wouldn't tell you. He'll *never* tell you. Has He told you *yet*?

Eve pauses but isn't quite certain what to ponder. She is only certain that she hasn't ascertained—something. She continues the dialogue in the hope of comprehending whatever it is that she seems to be lacking.

EVE. Well, umm, no. I mean, let's think this thing out: If I'm not missing out on anything, then He wouldn't have to be telling me about "it," because there wouldn't be an "it", so I haven't heard about "it," so—

SNAKE. Unless He doesn't want you to know! Oh, it's just as I figured! Just as I feared! (*Sighs*) just as I told you. Sorry, I had to be the one to tell you, but I'm your friend and you can trust me. He's keeping you so busy with this *useless* second-rate garden that you'll never get around to moving on to something better.

EVE. There's a lot of good food around here. I wouldn't call the garden useless. Can you smell the hibiscus?

SNAKE. Whatever. There are worlds out there, and you could be conquering them, ruling them, making your own rules, being your own, well, woman! Not just, 'the help'.

EVE. I like things here fine.

SNAKE. Out there's *better. I'm just sayin'...*

Eve stands up on the rock, then takes a knee to get not eye-to-eye but much closer than before, perhaps a foot away from the snake's face.

EVE. Look, little, whatever you are—

SNAKE. I'm a snake.

EVE. Okay, little snake guy. Things are good here. *Just fine*. I don't know how to "conquer" or "governance" or "mortgage" or half these other things you're telling me, and you're starting to make me itchy. That's bad, so let's just change the subject.

SNAKE. Okay, *okay*.

There is silence for several minutes as they both sit on the stone, just staring ahead, at nothing in particular. Momentarily, they turn to look at each other, and then resume looking straight ahead.

SNAKE. You know, that el—

EVE. LE-PHANT! Elephant!

SNAKE. Could never come up with a great invention.

EVE. (*Sighs*) Like what?

SNAKE. Like anything you could come up with if you were free to do what you want. Like anything I've done.

Eve feels a moment of inquiry.

EVE. And what have youuuu done?

SNAKE. You wouldn't understand the complexity of my thoughts and accomplishments, you being so bound, encumbered and all.

EVE. An accomplished snake, who'd a thought...

SNAKE. Jest if you will. I think big thoughts. You see that cumulus cloud up over there?

EVE. Yeah?

SNAKE. Mine.

EVE. Get out!

SNAKE. Mine. Makes nice shade, eh?

EVE. God made everything good.

SNAKE. So you think. And why do you think that?

EVE. 'Cause He told us so.

SNAKE. And why do you think *that?*

EVE. What? Why do I think *that?* Because He *told us that!* And *that's* enough of that!

SNAKE. I'm just saying…mine—

EVE. Can you prove it?

SNAKE. You can't not prove it…

EVE. So if you made the nebulous, why did God say He made everything?

SNAKE. Exactly.

EVE. Exactly…

SNAKE. You're being had. You can achieve highest goals. You can achieve the clouds. You can be just like Him, only He doesn't want you to know it.

EVE. (*Sighs*) And why wouldn't He want me to know it?

SNAKE. Because you'd be just like Him. Then He wouldn't be the power broker. The big guy in charge. Who knows, *He* might even have to ask *you* for a favor sometime. You could be just like Him if you knew the secrets to His power, but since you don't, you'll just have to hang out here… with these su—

EVE. *zu-kee-ne, zu-kee-ne. Zucchini!* You're tripping over your tongue, aren't you, today?

SNAKE. (*Sighs*) I'm just so, so…. morose, over your state of affairs, being stuck here and all.

EVE. Well, I'm not really feeling stuck, or *mor-ose,* or anyways *disadvantaged,* even if you did make the nebulous.

SNAKE. Mine…and its *cumulus*…it's just a little water.

EVE. What's just water?

30

SNAKE. The cumulus. It's made of water.

EVE. What? Water up there? Why?

SNAKE. (*Sighs*) It's complicated. I mean, it's no big deal, but it's complicated. (*He makes a modest turn of the head away in a pensive moment and then a few moments of silence passes.*)

EVE. It's a cool idea.

SNAKE. I *know*... I have lots. I could share some with you, and then you could be like me.

Eve's eyebrows shoot up in sarcasm she didn't know that she had.

EVE. Eh, heh, heh...yoou'rrre a snake...

SNAKE. Only on the outside. Actually I'm quite attractive and talented on the inside. Don't let first looks fool you. Anyway, you could be like Him *and* me. Then everything will be a lot of fun! And you could do what you want.

EVE. What's that mean?

SNAKE. It's what I started to tell you about before about "governance." About *self*-governance. Nobody telling you what to do, where to go, which zukeens to pick.

EVE. You know, you have a speech impediment.

SNAKE. I do what I want, and you can to. It'll make you better than all the rest of the creatures here. You'll be the best!

EVE. Which is...

SNAKE. Better than "better."

EVE. I'm good, thanks.

SNAKE. But you'll be *better*.

EVE. The natural progression, no doubt. So look, what if I did decide to try out this "better," what'd I have to do?

31

SNAKE. It's simple. Not much at all really, and everything'll be great. Well, first, "better."

EVE. Yeah…?

SNAKE. Sure! Well, you know over in the middle of the garden—

EVE. The rhododendron, lantana, azalea, camellia, boxwood, snowberry, mountain laurel, dwarf myrtle shrub patch?

SNAKE. Eh…*no*. You know over—

EVE. The tulip, crocus, verbena, hyacinth, bluebell, poppy, yarrow, gladiolus, marigold, hyssop, celestia, columbine, iris, phlox, lavender patch? You know, there are seven kinds of iris there.

SNAKE. Emmm…uh…uh. There, where—

EVE. The rose, impatient, zinnia, morning glory, sweet alyssum, forget-me-not, delphinium, day lily, foxglove, sunflower, geranium, daisy garden? Oh, I think they're my favorites! So many colors and so vibrant! But I love the hostas too. And the cannas! Big as a tree! A small tree, mind you, like a cherry tree or peach or apple for that matter.

SNAKE. Yes!

EVE. What?

SNAKE. The tree, the tree over there in the center of the lawn, in the middle of the garden!

EVE. Um, well, no. Not really, 'cause God told us not to fool with that. So we don't go over there at all. That's the only thing off limits, and we have all this other stuff. We don't touch it, pluck it—nothing. Don't even look over there. He said no. He said we can have everything else, just don't mess with that. I think there's an "or else."

SNAKE. See…

EVE. See, see what?

SNAKE. It's the secret. The secret you're not supposed to know. If you do, you'll be "in." That's the "or else."

EVE. Well, that doesn't sound bad. I thought that "or else" was a bad thing. As a matter of fact, yeah, it was. He said we'd die.

SNAKE. That's what He *wants* you to think. That's how He stays in charge. He's the power broker. The only one in "the know"…

EVE. Know what?

SNAKE. That's what He doesn't want you to know.

Eve casts a long look at the snake.

EVE. (*Sighs*) Little snake, you're exhausting. And you're making me itch, and—

SNAKE. That's bad I know, I know. I heard you, but look at me. I'm your friend. We've been sitting here talking just like old friends. Has any other creature sat and chatted with you like this? You can trust me. He hasn't told you the whole story. The fact is, that if you go over there and take a piece fruit from that tree, it's gonna look so good, smell so good and taste deeevine! And if that isn't enough, once you've eaten from it, you're not gonna *die.* You're gonna be just like Him. You'll *really* be living! That'd be nice, wouldn't it? Now wouldn't your husband be so proud of you if you made your lot in life better? He'll be so happy he'll take you on a vacation—

EVE. What's that?

SNAKE. You'll see! Everything's gonna be great! Fun! And you're gonna be just like Him and have all the same good stuff. Look! You can go over there right now, may as well. Now is always the best time to have anything worth having. I don't see Adam, but you can tell him later. He'll be so proud of what you did. He'll be speechless! You're gonna change his day! And you'll both be *better*!

EVE. (*Eve turns over and downward to look at her reptilian company sitting on the stone with her. He looks up at her and smiles a long, slow very crooked grin.*) You know, you do talk a lot for a creature. I don't know of any other creature who talks like you.

SNAKE. Trust me, there aren't any. I'm specially gifted. Unique.

EVE. You're very…

SNAKE. Convincing.

EVE. I was thinking *suspicious*.

SNAKE. I'm your friend.

EVE. Hmm…

SNAKE. Can your zukin or your elehpts show such concern for you and offer such sound advice?

EVE. Zucchini and elephant—confound your slurry tongue!

SNAKE. I work around it. How 'bout it? It's time for "better," besides, it's time for lunch. Kill two birds with one stone.

EVE. What does that mean?

Snake clenches its entire body in exasperation.

SNAKE. It means go grab the fruit and eat it already.

Eve lets out a big sigh, as if she's thought a lot, gone in a circle, and found herself in the same spot of confusion. The one thing she is sure about is that her wily and talkative companion is right about lunch, so she considers making a go of it. Eve stands erect, stretches pensively and thoroughly as if an athlete ready to commence a disciplined event. She looks wistfully toward the center of the garden—panoramically around—stiffens up, and then begins to walk very slowly with the confidence of an uncertain resolution toward the center of the garden. The snake trots a few feet behind, ready to allay any hesitation on her part.

Eve surveys the large tree. Emerged from the soil, the massive trunk divided at about eye level. It seemed to split off into two trunks so that it looked like two large trees entangled. From the combined perimeter of the trunks there extended divergent branches which spanned the length between them as bridges. The branches grew into an entwinement of trunk, branch, leaf, and unparalleled beauty. There are taller trees in the garden, but this duet's combination of girth, height, span, and movement fettered by smoothly braided cables of thick vine finds no counterpart.

EVE. (*Sigh*)… Looks like…a tree. Like trees. There are a lot and a lot more trees around here. Could be any trees. They just look like trees…

Snake senses that although Eve doesn't want to take this action, she has allowed herself to be walked to the cliff's edge and needs only a gentle nudge to send her headlong, so he continues with subtle coercion.

SNAKE. Any tree, so why not this? One tree's good
    as another, right?

Eve isn't listening to her "adviser" anymore.
She has gone past the point of resolute decision
although she still has a hesitation. What is it?
Something inside her mind that tells her what
she already knows—that this is wrong. Where is
Adam? What is he doing just now? She wishes
she had paid more attention when he and God
talked every afternoon. Eve just stands for a while
under the thick canopy of tree branches, which
makes it seem darker like late afternoon. Her
gaze freezes at the dance of twisting trunk. Her
mind is searching back for archived data. The
voice inside her continues to shout, *No! Stop! Run
away! This is wrong!* The snake continued to make
persistent persuasions and eye contact, when she
would chance to turn her back to him, he moves
to her direct line of vision, maintaining some
distance to ensure her independence in action.
When her hand ventures up, as to touch the fruit
and then draws away as to quit the whole scene,
there he is in gentle persuasion with promise of
some yet unseen pleasure. This struggle ensues
for some moments Snake thinks best not to elon-
gate the scene lest some distraction interrupt.
He makes a delicate glance around to ensure
that Adam is nowhere about and then makes the
push. Meanwhile, Eve talks to herself quietly.

EVE. What *had* God said? What was it about
    this, this snake? It seemed to reason, it
    seemed a friend, it seemed much more
    knowledgeable than any of the other
    creatures. Conversational, and it keeps

talking about God. It must know Him. It must know some things that we don't. It wouldn't say the wrong thing. I mean, it's standing right here. It said that God said that all this tree business was not a bad thing. Maybe I misunderstood it all.

She looks back at the snake who is earnestly watching for the moment to step in with a last push.

EVE. It's…what is its name anyway? Well, it certainly seems to make sense in its own way. And I'll bet its right about this fruit making a good lunch. It's probably altogether right, and I'm just making too much of it all. But *(sigh)* I know what God said, at least I *knew* what God said. Talking on the inside of my head and listening to Snake on the outside, I'm not even sure what I know anymore. I wish Adam were here. Maybe I should go find him and ask—

SNAKE. Oh, no need for that! It's just a few bits of fruit, ya know… I…haven't eaten since yesterday…*(sigh)*…it would be so good…

EVE. That's true. I'll just try some, and if it's good, I'll bring Adam some. If not, I'll know not to try this tree again. Not a big deal, really.

SNAKE. Not. At. All…

EVE. Funny, I feel a little nervous, something in me. Maybe I'm just excited to try a new thing. Oh, I'm just making a big deal out of nothing.

SNAKE. Nothing. At. All.

EVE. I'll just a take a bite…umm, umm…and of the other…

SNAKE. (*Speaking quietly to himself*) Sooo…tell me again, what's so great about homo sapiens? Oh, right, nothing! I only had to help the fool a little bit. What a stupid invention. Totally manipulable. And they got a *whole planet*…the loveliest of all. Just. Not. Fair. But, whatever! Well, this makes a good day's work. Let's see what else I can *un*do…

Here, the protagonist stops writing and looks around, as if searching for someone. He utters a long deep groan. He groans and returns to his writing:

Snake walks away from the garden. After a brief few moments, Eve notices that she's alone. She would have offered her little friend some of the fruits, but…

EVE. The slippery little fella's gone away. No matter, I'll just save some for Adam. I'll see if I can find him now.

Eve meanders about and, after a time, finds Adam working in the garden as she might have supposed. She begins to tell him about her newly found friend who assured her that the central trees were a good thing. Adam listens quizzically to her tale. He is ready to take a break and hungry, so even though he hears Eve tell him where she got the fruit he heartily samples it. Adam begins to describe the hollyhocks and lantana he's found earlier in the day. They attract lots of bees, and when the bees finish feeding, he has followed some and discovers a delightful cove of honey. As Adam is telling his adventure, the words seem like they are sticking to the roof of his mouth. What is wrong? He feels fine—arms legs, toes—but aaach! He looks down and sees that he is completely naked! And worse, there is Eve. At that instant she realizes too, that they are both naked! Such an absolute absurdity to be out in broad daylight in nakedness. Well, to be sure, no one lives there aside from them and the animals, but God! Oh, God! He would come around and see them! He loves to spend time with Adam every day and He'd be here soon!

Adam: Aaach! What's happened? We can't let God see us like this. He'll be here soon. We've got to get covered!

The two scramble frantically with the concept of 'garments' but what is that, really? What do they have to make any? Nothing really. Finally, they reason their way to "sewing" fig leaves together to make some rudimentary coverings. Eve has the worse time of it to be sure, but they manage, and just in time as they hear God coming around calling Adam's name. Not proud of their handiwork, they hide as best they can. Perhaps they could skip today's visit until they could figure out what is going on and get a plan together. But everyone well knows, even as they did just then, that when God asks a question—any question—it isn't for the purpose of *His* edification. It's for yours. And when He calls you, it isn't because He doesn't know where you are. Face it; He's baiting you, and you will chomp hook, line, and sinker. What you may not know is that it is always in your best interest. Adam has loved the one on one time God shares with him every day. Then one day, God gives Adam, Eve.

That is His way. But now here, the two of them are so afraid they are shaking against each other. Hiding is not what Adam wants to be doing, so what is happening?

Adam, where are you?

ADAM. *Aaach, the bait! It's of no use. Don't His eyes roam to and fro over all the earth?*

The trembling duet are standing from their hiding place, shaking in fear. Adam is unable to step forward, eyes wide as if unable to blink, mind trying to process what things are happening too fast for him. He opens his mouth, and stammer falls out in effort to explain the garments and the hiding. Then silence. His heart is pounding so loud that his eardrums hurt, and Adam immediately feels that somehow, *it* is all over. Everything that he's known is finished, although he doesn't know exactly what that means. Just when he clenches his eyes shut, expecting to meet oblivion, God puts out the bait again in the calm, soft tempo that characterized Him.

Who told you that you were naked?

Isn't that the *aside*, as opposed to the *fact* that they are naked? But if anyone knows how to probe, it's Him. It makes Adam regret that he has not verified the authenticity of the situation and the perpetrator before he ate the fruit. He clearly heard Eve tell him her story, but he did nothing. Why didn't he put the brakes on the situation just then? Why didn't he just say no? Why didn't he just say, "We'll ask God when He comes around later." He has asked God about countless other things on their daily walks, about everything in fact. "But, wait a minute," Adam thinks.

"Why didn't *she* say, 'I'll ask God first?' This is her scenario; she knows what the Word of God is. And how many animals has she seen? Plenty! Well, maybe not as many as I, but which among them acted anything like this "snake"? Whose fault is all of this? Surely hers!"

Adam has not intended to disconnect from God, but now as God pronounced His judgment, he feels a cold separation, which he'd never known before. In his own defense, he begins to impute Eve as the cause of this onslaught of trouble. Eve, in turn, blames her slippery little friend who, as an aloof onlooker, has found himself frozen in his tracks, unable to escape while God then cast judgment upon him as well.

EVE. (*Thinking*) *Slippery little creep.*

Eve is not fully sensing the profound trouble they are now in. Adam knows better. As they are physically driven out of the garden, he let out a howl. The very agonized core of his being feels confusion, anger, injustice.

ADAM. Wait! I didn't *do* anything! Wait! You don't understand! It wasn't me. I'm innocent. WAIT! Wait, wait, wait...! This punishment is too much! I just want to go back to the way it was *just this morning*: everything was perfect, so normal. It was sweet. Now everything's horrible. It's gone mad, and there's a slippery snake to blame. Wait, oh Great God, source of my life's blood, wait, wait, oh wait...

The depth of his grief is immense, but the pain of separation from the father he loves is more than Adam could bear. At the garden's edge is a gate. Adam has never been past the gate, to the *outside*. Now his own legs force him through the gate, to the other side. *Outside.* From the heavens descend two cherubim, running and flying at the same time, each seems to be a soldier hewn of iron with faces like platinum. They race to the gate, execute an "about face," and post themselves, one on either side, resolute to let no one pass. Adam turns around, now facing the gate, intending to run back into the garden. He looks up to see the two huge beings. The newly posted soldiers simultaneously take a half step forward toward Adam, pointing drawn swords toward his heart. Adam, completely startled, falls backward, flat on his back. On the ground and fearful, he tries to scramble away backward with the palms of his hands pushing the dirt forward. Unseen pressure pushes down on his body, keeping him from rising or so much as dragging away through the dirt. A hollow droning sound—a swarm of bees, perhaps? No. Louder, deeper, frightening, now louder and closing in on his immobile state. Above him, clouds break, releasing an immense sword descending, just missing Adam's head. It posts itself at the gate in between the two iron soldiers. The sword is nearly Adam's height, one quarter thick as it is long, titanium in appearance, and visibly sharp on both sides. Alight with fire, it begins a slow, deliberate thirty-degree rotation, drawing a small circle through the air, it's sharp tip pointing outward. As the sword rotates slowly, its circumference widened until it lies flat at ninety degrees. The sword comes to a halt, the horrible drone of bee sound stops, the pointy tip facing Adam. Still grounded, Adam resumes his retreat, digging palms into the soil and pushing to propel himself backward. The great sword, which appears to manage itself, remains silent no more than a few moments. Once again in motion, the horrible mechanical drone recommences. It begins its rotation slowly, incrementing speed—faster, a little faster, until its movement is rapidly rotating in three dimensions. It rotates in every possible direction so fast that it seems much like a smooth ball of fire. The heat of its flame is too intense for the man to endure in close proximity. It sounds a pulsating metallic throb, which makes Eve cover her ears with the palms of her hands. Adam would have run through the gate to get back home if he could. He presses closer to the ground he is already pinned to. The heat of the sword is oppressive, as if a piece of the very sun is placed inside of it. Adam yells into the garden, back to God, his sound is lost in the phenomena at the gate. He shouts, begs, cries, and screams. For a moment, he lifts and turns his torso left and sees the snake coiled a safe distance from the heat, quietly observing his agony. In a rage, Adam grabs four stones and hurls them at the snake, only missing one time. Eve notices the snake isn't walking, but it sliding away now, on its belly, and then she sees it no more. Adam returns to his entreat; it is everything now to get back home.

Aaauuggghh! His shouting is useless, but he cannot stop. Everything rests on getting back in. Eve knows instinctively, although still lacking full implication of what has just transpired, she knows there is no going back. Hours later,

Adam has exhausted himself running from the east gate along the perimeter, finding the entire garden sealed off, the entrance impenetrable and the God with whom he has shared all his days, unresponsive. He feels a cold, vacuous, "lonely" settle on him like a heavy coat. He collapses to the ground from exhaustion, shock, and sorrow. Worn out, he soon falls asleep. Eve sits next to him and lifts his head in her lap. Her eyes bulge as a dam holding back the flood of tears about to break. She quietly strokes Adam's sweaty hair, picking out each grain of sand and clump of dirt. Her confusion, so heavily overlaid with guilt, leaves her speechless. She rocks him as he sleeps; the afternoon leads to evening and then darkness.

Adam wakes up slowly. His everything aches. Every inch of him feels dirty. He is. He is, in fact, filthy. Sweat has dried and crusted around his forehead. His toes are caked in between with grass and dirt. He's dug deep into the soil desperately running the perimeter of his home, no more. No more? Is this true or some wild nightmare? Recollecting yesterday's anguish, a familiarity comes to him. It must be true, all a fact. He finds himself lying on the ground, eyes drawing up toward a glowing light. There's the gate, that droning sound and those two iron cherubim soldiers still standing guard on either side of the sword. The heat of the sword, still flaming, still rotating, now acting as a torch lighting the darkness. Still in front of the gate. Still, the deep pulsating frightens him. Although he doesn't know what any of this means, it is still there and here he is still, on the outside. Eyes sore, hands sore, legs aching, misery revisiting him. God has made clothing of animal skin for them right before their eyes, part of the multifaceted shock of yesterday afternoon. Still, the softness of the animal skin next to his seems to be the only tenderness in his world. He sits up slowly, stretching, inspecting minor bruises on both arms and legs—only scrapes and scratches. Adam stretches his limbs and, sitting quietly, slowly comes to himself. Besides the metallic rhythm of the sword, the silence is unfamiliar. His heart beats a little faster as he thinks to stand up for a look-around. He has never been outside of the garden. His home was inside. *Inside!*

Adam tries to venture a few steps in any direction but the day is just coming to dawn—still too dark to explore. Thirty or so feet away, Adam could make out a hunched over mass—his wife. Sitting on the grass, her legs pulled in close, chin on her knees and arms wrapped around her legs; eyes open, fixed in a hard gaze, looking at nothing. Adam cannot see that her dark eyes run with red threads, sallow skin bagged all around them. Sleepless and tormented, she has cried nearly every drop of life out of herself. Adam does not speak, not yet. His eyes continue to survey the new landscape as daylight emerges. He makes out several beasts yards away. Something's different, though: there are none around him. Adam approaches a coney, which takes off so fast that he nearly jumps back in fear. He walks on ahead to a field sparse with trees. Crossing a creek up to his ankles, Adam sees a few small splashes as retreating fish abandoned their clam shells on the water's bottom. A snail on the bank debates on a swim or sun bath. Stopping at a date tree, Adam gently stretches out an index finger to a small gray starling. Like a panic, it flies away. A small herd of ibex keeps him in their line of sight, moving proportionately away as he moves closer. Finally, one bolts away and the others follows, leaving Adam standing alone.

ADAM. God, oh my Father! I don't see you. I can't hear you. Why won't you come? Why won't you come back to me? I *need* you. I'm so alone, yes. And I feel...*fear.*

The quiet frightens Adam. His garden has been alive, bright, breezy, overabundant with the songs of so many kinds of birds. Squirrels chase each other in helical ladders around tree trunks. Bees danced their wiggle dance. Oh, Adam has only just found their secret cache of sweet honey! Even the river has its song smacking the rocks along its curved paths lined with all manner of shale, stone, and thirsty water-loving plants hanging their sunny faces over the banks. Tadpoles frolick, frogs sing, beetles burrow in the damp soil. Now, nothing.

Adam's vision improves as the morning alights, but the landscape seems yet chillingly still. As an errant damselfly speeds along, Adam feels it touch the back of his head. Wandering a little further, he occasionally finds an animal or a few. Whenever he approaches, they retreat. He tried again—approach, retreat, approach, retreat.

ADAM. They're avoiding me. It's as if they know something's gone wrong. Everything is... *off,* somehow.

A deepening of his sorrow, if at all possible, wells within him. That is another *why,* for

46

another time. For now, Adam is still fleshing out his surroundings. What to do about home? Where to find God?

ADAM: He always came to me. Maybe I can just find Him and go talk to Him. He can't hear me and He won't listen to me, but I didn't do this. I mean, not like this. I don't know what happened or how, really. I mean, I know not to go to the middle of the garden, but what's going on? What have I done? What has *she* done? She did this, I didn't really. Oh, I don't know, and I'm sorry. I just, oh, please won't you talk to me? I'm so confused, and *I want to go home!*

Adam hears only silence. He looks up to the blue sky and smattering of clouds. For several seconds, he lets out agony, pain, and remorse in one shattering wail. His lungs flatten. The sound scrapes his throat, demands all of his breath, echoes up and out, and fades from his ears as it moves out across the earth. He sinks down to the dirt, resting his forehead on a barren patch of soil.

Sin separates God from man. The devil unleashes his evil reign on earth. But God has a marvelous plan...
Protagonist stops writing. Looking up, he sees no sky, only dismal sulfur and smoke. Brimstone scents the ambient atmosphere. An occasional fire kindles in the distance offering a moment of brightness in the murky atmosphere. He looks like he might utter a wail, but he has uttered many a wail to no one's advantage. He appears as one who has expended all of his tears and must now resign himself to his fate. He snaps the worn writing stick into thirds and the thirds into fourths. Staring down at the broken pieces in the soil then straight ahead into nothing, he rises and heads that way.

Male and Female
(Gen. 4)

She found her husband on the ground, dirty, dried tear-stained face again but not as before. His eyes fixed a vacuous stare a few feet away at nothing. He lifted them toward her with a blank look and then up to a beautiful afternoon sky, vaguely hoping for a sign—the wisp of breeze, which always preceded God as He made His daily constitutional walk through the garden to fellowship with Adam. Taking a knee, she extended a hand to him, Adam studying it for a long moment before accepting it. With tears streaming down his reddened cheeks still dusted with dirt, he rose.

There was no particular direction to go. They both knew now that they were at the beginning of something. Whatever or however, it was forward from here. They had yet to figure out what that meant. As a gentle hint, Adam's stomach rumbled. It was the first furtive smiles between them since the incident of their expulsion. They set about looking for food.

This simple endeavor became the largest part of their existence for weeks. First a date tree, then nuts, then saving them and a "where," a home. The simplest recourse was a cave—it was already there. His mind, still next to perfect, multitasked in earnest. Having so many immediacies, everything was an opportunity for an invention. Everything used or found became a cup, a bowl, a bucket. The man became farmer by necessity. It was, by far more difficult than his previous role as 'caretaker.' But a farmer needs tools, knowledge, and seed. All by trial as months passed and, little by little, the garden faded. The flowers first and with them many insects. Over years winds bent the trees until they could not stand erect, carried away their leaves and withered the shrubs. Lush canopy deteriorated, exposing sparse ground cover. Little by little, beautiful landscape fell to desolation, sand, wind, and stone until it was no more.

Adam largely left the gathering and storing details to his wife. God had provided each of them with a garment to wear. Although every day they felt farther from the God who created them, they did not understand that The Lord had a plan of redemption already in place, because His love for them was so great. Adam was far away from seeing the manifestation of this salvation. The couple's daily existence was mentally and physically exhausting, always. They became adept at finding a valuable resource in everything that they were able to accumulate, turning all into tools, containers, widgets, ropes, leads, straps, and hangers. He learned to utilize domestic animals for their strengths—a dog's nose and keen hearing, a mule's strong back. Eve mused over a use for the wool of sheep. Every evening was a reconstitution of the day—what happened and what could be learned from it. Their forward progress was scratched inch by inch. In the evening Adam retreated to the cave to review the day's events and make another decision to move forward.

The family moved east. The garden was largely a memory, a marshy field where only a few large trees remained. Mostly everything was gone, and so, the cherubim were gone. The Adams moved east to find a place more amenable to his fledgling farming skills. Eve had often asked God to forgive her for her seemingly terminal misjudgment. But God no longer walked with Adam daily, as He did back in the garden. At times, God dispatched angelic assistance to guide them with rudimentary essentials of shelter, gathering, growing, preserving, and the like, but it was nothing like in the beginning. At the first, God was a Father who loved the closeness with his children. Since expulsion from the garden, there exists a chasm between human and the Creator, which the couple did not understand or know how to breach. They just wanted to go back and do that day over, as of yet still failing to comprehend the significance of their fall.

But move forward they must. Everything was an immediate need—home, food supply. Everything that crossed Adam's line of sight became a tool, a cover, a carrier, a lifter, a box, a storage unit.

Need mixed with the need to know what was needed. Failure was pervasive, exhaustion ever present, days—endless. On good days, a stone became a hammer. Hammer mated peg and something came to be. On bad days, most days, ingenuity failed as mostly it does, with not even a furtive hint of progress. Thatch became a bed but then a refuge for ants. Cave became a dwelling but then overrun and home-steaded by some other species. Adam scratched a mark into the dusty surface of a great stone every evening since he had parted from God. He lost track with their occasional moves. The longing ached mostly in a place he couldn't pinpoint. He grew accustomed to stomach aches until they seemed to fade to a general malaise. He knew now that he took for granted the time he had spent with God, but it was all he had known back then. He loved it. God loved it, so why would it end? The thought that it *could* end never entered Adam's mind. Now God's warning not to eat from that tree, *or you will surely die,* replayed over and over in his mind. *Now.* What was he thinking *back then?* Why hadn't he thought more about it *then?* When God said, "You will surely die," it was not an immediate physical death. His fellowship with God suffered that death. It meant *"in dying you will surely die,"* or their state of perfection, the man himself would slowly slide down the gradient to mortality. Being so close to perfection still, it seemed not immediately evident to him. The only white elephant in the cave was the loss of fellowship. It took some hundreds of years but the man degraded and man has ever since. Adam's mind was acute, busy troubleshooting crises, challenge and opportunity arising from every angle. Every evening, he retired exhausted. Some morn-ings, he arose only because he had to, and move forward they must. On some days, fear, confusion, frustration, or exhaustion drove his anger to an explosive apex. At these times, Adam might burst out in a verbose squall. In the early days, it frightened Eve, but with time, she simply closed her eyes and allowed his storm to pass. She still carried the guilt for their expulsion and current circumstance as she would to her grave. It was never specifically addressed; what for? They were both there, and she carried it as all her fault. It drove her to despair whenever she saw Adam reduced to a crumpled mess of tears on the ground. To be sure, Adam attributed all of the blame to Eve as well.

Once, trying to comfort him, Eve said, "He'll fix it... He...said. He would fix it..."

To this Adam could not find a way around his temper. He threw an armful of tools to the ground. "Did He say when? Did He tell you *when?* Since you listened *so well, when?* Oh, I feel as if I could just *kill* you!" Adam stormed off toward the fields. His outbursts sent Eve off in another direction, thrashing about in a sea of guilt and tears, waves slapping over her head. In all her days, the guilt never abated. After some years, their physical state of gradual degradation set her auburn locks to whiten. Even so close to perfection, their decline was gradual but sure. On good days, a tree became a pole, became a joist became a lean-to, a frame, a shelter. On lesser days, everything was cannon fodder. Failed experiments became projectiles of various dimensions, thrown long, down, trampled, pushed, or burned. These were complimented by grunts, verbal squalls of anger emerging violently from Adam's deep sorrow. All of this expression was observed daily by little Cayin, their firstborn son.

Eve's guilt from *that day* lived as a constant companion like two beings sharing one body. The latter, an uninvited, unpleasant intruder. Eve lived as a continual source of self-doubt, nervousness, and insecurity with an obsessive need to please her spouse, as if to somehow compensate, to make things right in some way. Eve knew this could never be, but there it was, a permanent resident within her psyche. She had always been married, so she had always wanted to be his helpmate. Ever since *that day*, it was everything. Some days manifesting as desperation, sometimes as sorrow. Eve was largely silent until Cayin was born. She flourished in motherhood, lavishing attention on her child. This provided a daily diversion from the white elephant in their lives, which every day forced them to move forward.

While Adam was out working the fields, baby Cayin was Eve's audience. Even as she explained to the little one how things were perfect until *that day*, he did not have the emotional responses as Adam did—no cutting looks of anger, remorse, no terse remarks, no painful silence. Cayin gave her nonjudgmental curiosity, laughter, and levity. They became fast companions. Cayin had surely inherited the gentle curl of his hair from his father. With his mother's intense need to compensate, he learned her poor habit of haste, bringing with it inferior consequences. As Cayin grew, Adam brought him out to the fields to help work the soil. Cayin later revealed a gift and love of farming. In it, he far surpassed his father, much to the relief of Adam who turned his attention to his multiplicity of fledgling inventions, his mind still functioning highly albeit overly strained. Eve found further comfort in her second-born son, Abel. Younger Abel, later a herder, gentle and gracious in manner, made a softer touch on life as his mother did. He spent much time talking with her, understanding her grief and guilt, optimistic about every new day. His nature was different from that of his older brother. Abel deeply pondered the stories that his parents told him about God.

"Well, if this is true, won't God forgive you? Won't God make all of this right again? He created everything, so won't He fix all that has gone wrong? Surely he will, Mother. We must ask Him how."

Abel's inexorable faith in God fought hard against the obsessive-compulsive guilt that had taken up residence in Eve. He was her healing balm and solace, a palliative gentle child who became the gentle pastor of flocks. Abel was Eve's ray of sun, validating her self-worth, helping her work through what she knew. She knew only today not how to get back to the beginning and not what lay ahead.

Adam softened the edge of a large flat of stone. With some manipulation, it became the mealtime table. With some time, it became the evening focal point. The days were still long, hard, and unforgiving, each seemingly boundless with lessons to unpack or archive—what to do, what never to do again, what to try next. The dinner table began the evening's review of each day, where all thoughts, experiences, and concerns were laid out. As teens, the boys were admittedly disappointed at the turn of events, understanding that Adam once had only to care for the garden and now fought a relentless struggle against the stony, acidic soil to access a meager harvest. Abel grew calm and contemplative, tender in caring for livestock. Cayin adopted his father's frustrative explosions and his mother's obsessive, shortsighted, nervous need to please. He worked the soil next to his father. Forward progression was slow. Cayin saw it systemically rend the once perfect man—the sorrow of something lost from above, which Cayin had never experienced, combined with the struggle to get something to grow up from the ground. These things scratched and picked at the first man, scrubbed him until the joy and light in his eyes shone dim, and dimmer still, with the years. As a young man, Cayin had once gone to the place, that first place, where his father said they began. Adam had said there was a beautiful garden and a river that split off into four branches. Cayin found the place of the river branches, but he found no garden—no idyllic paradise, only a few trees. The very large trees in the midst of a wild dance of its branches; they were not there but only marshy land threatening to wash away its secrets. It was difficult for Cayin to reconcile the story, but for the detail and continual corroboration of his parents, questioned together or separately. If it was true, surely God could be entreated, and all of the misunderstanding could be remedied.

It came time to offer sacrifice to the Lord as Adam had always led his family to do. The young man, Abel, chose fine, fattened calves from among his flocks. He presented this gift to the Lord, which was received well. Cayin had chosen from his harvest of crops. The Lord did not receive this sacrifice, and Cayin's countenance fell. He felt such a rush of anger that the Lord spoke directly to him. The Lord exhorted Cayin to make the good choice, as choice was indeed what he had. The Lord always gave guidance, but it often required contemplation. Cayin had the opportunity to dialogue with the Lord. His father would have relished that opportunity, but the realization slipped past Cayin under the flood of jealousy and anger fording across his heart. Perhaps God would have entertained the questions Cayin had stored up during his young life. Would God have explained in more detail why Cayin's harvest offering failed so that he could have done better? Cayin turned angrily away from God. His focus was not on improving himself but on ruining another. So a short time later, Cayin lured his brother Abel into a field saying that he'd found a fine patch for livestock grazing. Unsuspecting, Abel allowed himself to be led away and slaughtered by his own brother, Cayin. Over the years, Eve's shortsightedness worked hard on Cayin's heart. Now he had a failed offering and a dead brother. The unchecked wrecklessness of his heart prompted the Lord once again to speak directly to Cayin.

Doesn't the Lord see everything? Could not the Lord hear the blood of slain Abel? Cayin must no longer till the soil but wander vagrant. Cayin did not utter remorse for his action but petitioned sympathy for his new circumstances, and still the Lord showed mercy. He put a mark upon Cayin to ward off any who would think to kill him in revenge or as trespasser. Cayin lived out his life as a wanderer, married, and produced progeny far from home.

Eve—in much anguish over the death of her beloved comfort, Abel—gave birth to a son. He became Seth, *the replacement.* Over the years, the family had floated east, west, and now south with their numbers growing, branched off and growing, still. Adam built sleds to pull their possessions, mostly preserved food, tools, and some garments, blankets, a few animals. Finding a suitable cave-domicile near a fresh spring, Adam set about first with a lean-to for the chickens and later a series of quonset huts to cover his inventions and provide limited shade for domestic animals from a blazing sun. Eve, still flourishing in motherhood, lavished attention on her children. It helped her think of other things.

Their many children grew. Members matured and broke off to spread their posterity across the regions. Still close to perfection, they were able to intermarry, increase, spread out creating a neighborhood, then communities, villages, cities. The two had turned into multitudes. Even as Eve bore more children and enjoyed grandchildren, it was Abel—the light of her eyes, lifter of her countenance, comfort of her heart—whom she ached for. With the dispensation of time, the first two met the warning—*in dying you will surely die*—the Word of the Lord God, which she had once doubted and he had ignored. God returned them to the soil from which they were taken, tired and relieved.

The succeeding generations of Seth, Cayin, and the other offspring of Adam and Eve grew wreckless under the instigation of evil, overcome by their own pride and self-indulgent mission to become that which they cannot—the lie of the serpent back in the garden. Man grew belligerent, shaking a fist at the face of God. The Lord felt remorse for having created man.

The Walk
(Gen. 4:8)

"I'm wrong because I love both of my sons?" She didn't look up from her kettle.

The boy shot back, "No! No… I'm *not* saying that you're wrong for loving both of your sons—"

"One's tall, burly, gentle. Kind of a quiet soul…the other, he's sharp! Medium tall—"

"Mother… I'm… I'm not tall."

"Medium tall, ruggedly handsome. A strong constitution—"

"What's that supposed to mean?"

"It means you're a stubborn boy. Here, come stir the stew. It's nearly ready." Eve's slender frame stood erect as she extended the thick, roughly hewn stirrer toward the exasperated young man. He turned the great spoon as if the pot's contents did not really need to be stirred, which in fact, it did not. Lying aside the spoon, Cayin surveyed a good landing zone. With a thickly folded pads of corn husk in either hand, he grabbed the heavy kettle, moving it from the fire to its cooling place, to his mother's approval. Cayin gazed a long moment at her slender, strong, young but somehow worn-looking posture. His mother looked as if she had many more hard, long years than she actually had. Her hazel eyes always had a sparkle as if there was some delightful secret they wanted to tell, but she forbade them. And Cayin always felt this was true—that his mother was holding something back. Some information, some tidbit, undoubtedly the key to understanding life as he knew it—the explanation of what really happened back then before he was born. Those two, his parents, had some secret between them, and what happened back then had to be what the secret was about. Had to be.

He exhaled a deep sigh and began again, "Well, I'm just saying that everything *Abe* does is great. Everything *Abe* does is perfect, but when I drag in after working in the heat all day—"

"We appreciate you just as much. You are the same! We love our sons—"

"No, Mother, no, you don't. You never have and don't even try to speak for...*him*! He hardly speaks at all!"

Of all of Cayin's poorly aimed arrows, this one hit its mark—always did. Eve heard herself thinking quietly, *"Oh, here we go..."* Knowing that they were about to go down a familiar path. *"The boy just couldn't understand. All these years, telling the story over and over. Him watching his own parents struggle in all things. And now, this boy is struggling himself, somewhere between boy and young man. But he still doesn't get it—or won't get it. We've told him everything, plain as day, a thousand times. He won't get it—because he doesn't like what the story means for him. His inheritance is thorns instead of beauty. Wouldn't I change that if I could? Wouldn't we have gone back home if we could? It's over! It's gone! I don't know how to get it back!"* Eve found herself shouting inside her head. She buried her forehead in the palms of her hands, rubbing in small circles. It did nothing. It was just something to do while she collected her next words. Eve let out a sigh of exasperation, reached for the stirrer and laid it across the kettle's wide top. A few droplets of the thick broth took a free fall from the end of the ladle, crashing to the stone hearth's floor, spreading a bit of greasy shimmer down the sides of the stones. For a moment, Eve seemed to be studying the stew pot's contents—bubbles, agitating and rolling, some finally bursting. Along the inside edges of the pot some of the boiled contents tried to climb high up along the sides, only to slide back down, turning carrots, beans, bits of squash, basil, cumin, and turmeric onto itself. Bubbles of heat deflated as the stew cooled. The magnificent aroma should have filled the air with a sense of warmth and comfort. Instead, warmth and comfort were pushed aside by the strife of a troubled home. The hot stew sent waves of heat curling up from the cooking pot. It made a thick clump of long dark hair stick to Eve's forehead. She used the back of her left hand in a great sweep,—pushing her head back, catching up beaded sweat and sticky hair, landing it all in a disheveled pile atop her head. The salty wetness of the sweat irritated her left eye, and it began to tear. The other eye teared too but from sorrow of the past darkness that Eve was certain would never leave her. Assuming her familiar somber posture, she looked hard at her boy. "Cayin, don't talk ill about your father. He has a lot of grief that he's trying to deal with." Her tone softened, "He's just not a talkative person. That's what I loved about you two little baby boys, my first little ones. You came around jabbering and chattering all the time! You were such happy children—"

Cayin threw his weight backward onto a softly pillowed seat. Letting out a tiresome bawl, he lowered his tone. Cayin respected his father, sort of remembered their father-son connection—times of joy in his boyhood, but they seemed long ago. The man had been a sullen heap of silence for the most part of Cayin's adult life, and he tired of hearing Eve intercede with excuses for the man's mental absence. When the man did talk, it was almost like he was talking to himself, neither Cayin nor his brother Abe really knew what he was talking about. He seemed to be always living in the past mumbling about what wasn't fair and what he could've had to give to them and who knew what else. Cayin suspected that Abe understood more about it than he let on to. Abe could reach them, really connect with them, whereas Cayin felt some…thing, between himself and his parents but he felt it growing colder with time. Abe once suggested it was because Cayin demanded that everything and everyone conform to his terms. Cayin dismissed that as nonsensical. Easy for Abe to judge; Abe and their mother were always huddled up somewhere chatting, or they'd be in the kitchen having more fun than is truly possible just peeling carrots, *his* carrots. His endless toil warring against the dirt, turning it into soil, persuading something edible to emerge. Cayin agonized over his failed crops while the others seemed to just shrug them off. Neither did they appreciate the endless vigilance required to defend his fields from birds and an endless host of beasts that came to feed. How could those two just sit and giggle while they picked beans and chopped carrots? Life was not that delightful! Every moment was a struggle, yet according to *the man*, it wasn't always like this. Cayin demanded to know how to get back to the way it was, when food grew without a struggle. That was, of course, if any of what *the man* mumbled about was true. He never called his father a liar outright. That would hurt his mother too much. In fact, Cayin didn't believe his father was lying. *But in that case, let's just go back!* Their lack of resolute action made him angry. His demands always drew blank looks and silence from everyone else. He was sure his parents were holding something back, and he had to know. He was tired; he had to know. Cayin worked hard in his fields and, year after year, pulled up all manner of vegetables from the recalcitrant soil. Did they think it was easy? They'd just cook and eat and cook and eat as if the stuff just appeared from out of nowhere, with no effort and as if more was surely forthcoming. They seemed to appreciate neither his skills nor his sweat. Cayin hunched over, put his face in his callused hands, and let out a hot breath. He massaged his bushy brows as if it was helping him to think. It wasn't.

Eve was always delighted in the young men whom her boys had become, and she languished over both of them. Cayin had this gift of gardening, and what a good thing because his father needed the time to become an inventor of everything—how to construct a home, how to construct a cart, tools of every sort. Everything needed inventing and took a great deal of thought. Even so, there was always still time to contemplate *that day*. Over so many years, Adam went over and over and over it all in his mind again. It seemed but a moment, yet he spent his lifetime reconsidering that brief time. It became the mile marker for everything and every event in life. He thought how he could have raised a family *on the inside*. If a baby had been born, born *on the inside*, how could he have lived, how this weight he now bore on his shoulders would not be if only if they had stayed inside the garden. Adam flowed from confusion to anger to pathos, to desperation; and when he'd wake up every morning, eyes red from salt tears and from being still *on the outside*, he'd force himself to swing back into determinate mode. There was nothing but forwardness, so that's where the man's feet took him daily. His heart, however, was lost in yesterday.

Cayin would have none of his father's struggle. As close as he was to the man's loss, he didn't see it. He didn't see it physically nor could he make sense of "their story." Having gone back to the point of origin, Cayin didn't even see a garden. He would have simply written the man off as some dreamer if his mother had not been in corroboration with his story down to the detail. Thus he cast a doubt on her but she was kind, doting, and tolerant of it all the same. Cayin just wished the stories would show themselves somehow or be gone altogether so he thought best not to dwell on them. He grew short when either or both of his parents would go into reminiscence. *If all of what they say happened and happened not all that long ago, surely the wrong could be undone as simply as it was done.* Cayin's supposition always earned the same blank stares and head shakes.

"Well, what was it *exactly* that I didn't understand?" The parents would look at each other sorrowfully and return a long gaze to Cayin as if to say, *Let's start from the beginning. Again.* No, Cayin had heard the, "In the beginning" story since the beginning of his life. No, Cayin wanted something he could touch and feel for an answer. Maybe "in the beginning" was good enough for his younger brother, Abe. But then, *Abe.* Cayin didn't really remember much about life before his younger brother was born, but he did enjoy being an only child—that much he knew. Still, as young children, they were close and closer to each other than the other siblings. Eve poured her every moment into those first two babies who saved her from living with herself. In return, she wanted to protect them from what, she had no idea but Eve knew that things in life could go very, very wrong. She'd told them *the story* so many times.

Cayin loved his brother, of course. But he felt a little bit of jealousy ever since he was old enough to realize that as a sibling, life would be different than it had been as an only child. The problem was that Abe was not unlikeable. He was altogether pleasant, fun, actually or *fun-ny*, as there was little time for fun in everyday life. He had warmth and compassion; he was a great talker but a better listener. He listened to all the parents' stories. Maybe that's why he and the parents could lose hours on end in conversation. Eve tried to share the same way with Cayin, but he was a man of the material—had to see it, feel it, taste it for himself. Eve wondered how Cayin had gone from calling her Mom to Mother. It seemed distant to her. With the younger son, it was all love. Cayin saw the love but didn't see his own disconnect. He focused instead on the connection between the three of them. Even when the sullen man needed quiet time, there was still the two of them and the love. He saw love when Eve shared a thought, a conversation, with her younger son. They loved cooking; they loved shearing livestock. They loved cleaning up the stalls. Chitter, chitter, chitter! Did they love the task or the time? Cayin couldn't think with that much clarity; he lived in the now.

"Well, we're not children now, Mother, and I'm just saying that everything Abe does is just, 'the best,' beyond the best to you! I mean, how hard can it be to sit around in the pastures and watch a bunch of animals eat. After all, what does it really take to be shepherd? Really, Jolo does all the hard work. That poor dog runs in circles around the flocks all day long moving them from here to there. He's the real talent there! And I dig and dig and dig and chop and haul. I work till dark till I can barely drag myself in from the yards. I bring baskets of potatoes, beets, carrots, berries, melons, everything that I can pull out of the dirt, and it just never seems to be enough. My fingernails are black from the dirt, but it never seems enough. You never show me the same love like you do Abe. He slaughters some poor little animal that he just stood around and watched eat until the wretched thing got big enough to kill. You guys prepare the slaughter for sacrifice and just *delight* over it. You guys giggle while you scrub potatoes, pick beans clean, laugh while you collect eggs, chat-chat-chat while you bundle thatch… I mean, you *love* him."

Eve's heart had been heavier than she could hold on many occasions, but this was one of those "oh so very heavy" moments. Whatever it was that held back tears, broke. They poured forth, eddying, swirling about, pulling Eve down so that she sobbed choking on tears, gasping for air and haplessly confused. How could one son receive her adoration and another not? She favored not one over the other. She showered both of them with attention. They were, in fact, her escape from the shadow that lingered just over her shoulder ever since *that day*, since the day she and Adam were driven out of *the garden.* Having the babies gave her a distraction, something else to think about besides the wrong that she couldn't ever undo. They gave her conversation, a thing that seemed to dry up in Adam as he shrank into himself, leaving her alone. Eve, the woman created and immediately married, had lost the light and life in her marriage that dark day. With the boys, Eve was able to take that darkness and push it behind her. Although she always knew it was there, right over her shoulder, as long as she stayed busy, too busy to look…, she could find some joy in her everyday life. The busy ness was partly why she loved the office of motherhood. But why could her son not receiver her love? What was his trouble? Why was his mind and heart unyielded? Where is this bitterness from? How to make it go away?

Cayin buried himself in the pillow seat as if he was trying to disappear. Eve gazed at her grown son but saw the boy the sullen child who would not be consoled. He got the sullenness from his father, not that Eve could blame Adam, but look what it was doing to their son.

"Well, I don't know what to tell you that I haven't said so many times before, son. We love everything that both of our boys do. Abe's an optimist and a funny guy. You're a practical, nose-to-the grindstone, see-it-to-believe-it, get-things-done guy. You're different, and that's fine. Why do you resent that you're different? I love both of my sons. I'm not wrong for loving both my sons. I love all of my other children as well, but you two, you were extra special because you were my first, and you brought me relief from my suffering."

"Aaaauuughhh…" Cayin's fist sank into the mud/thatch wall. "You don't understand. You don't get it!"

Eve watched a bit of wall crumble, cascade along down to the floor, and blend in. Although the floor was swept clean, if one knew where to look, one might find numerous like crumbles. If one knew where to look, one might find other like impressions in the walls, documenting evidence of the rage Cayin refused to confront. Eve knew where to look. She studied the walls around her cookpot and said, "Well then, *help* me to get it!"

Where did she go wrong with this one? Not that he's like his father but the anger! *So much sorrow like Adam.* Eve remembered when Adam was kind, gentle, pensive, and always ready with a smile. Once she asked him if he always smiled. He gave her an odd look, remembered that he was created before she was. "I remember sort of waking up. Not as if I was asleep but first coming to consciousness, I guess. My eyes, blurry a moment, then saw the beautiful light. It was Him. He smiled at me, and I've been smiling ever since!" All that had since changed, and Eve longed for the impossible—to go back to that time in the garden when they took so much for granted, just thinking that what was would always be. Now her husband had become irritable, worrisome, and sullen, often bearing long periods of silence. Eve supposed he was still trying to imagine some way back in the garden. They hadn't lived within several days journey of the garden in a very long time, but the last time they had happened back that way, the area was virtually indistinguishable. Anyone who hadn't been there could hardly have imagined the paradise it was. In fact, her other children showed little interest in the site for exactly this reason. That is, except for the second eldest, Abel. Eve was grateful for the distraction each child she bore provided her, but Abe, he was just sunshine! Where Cayin was reserved, Abe was outgoing. Cayin had always been jealous of the attention baby Abel demanded from their mother; he seemed to harbor resentment always. Eve threw her life into her children, but this firstborn, it was as if he wanted to be an only child forever. Eve knew that was not God's will. She didn't know why this stubborn child would not embrace the happiness children find in everyday living. As Cayin grew old enough to notice the taciturn furrows in his father's forehead; the overly sunned skin peeling from the biceps; the recurring sessions of his father lost in the silence of deep, remorseful thought, Cayin became more like no one Eve knew. Her son took all of the darkness of Adam's sorrow but none of his humor, pleasantry, or the joy he took in fatherhood. Cayin was all glum, and the more you tried to pull him out of it, the more he dug into his resolve.

Eve—having had more sorrow that one ought to have in a lifetime, pretty much all upfront—showered her children with everyday love and joy. Cayin seemed like he just wouldn't come "round the bend" for some reason. It was like he wanted some pat solution to life because it was not like the life his parents described. He'd been demanding the answer, *exactly*, that needed to be done to get back to that idyllic life because what they were all living right this moment was not grand. Cayin never got the straight answer, the specific steps, the recipe he sought; and in fact, it made him quite angry. He imagined there was indeed a way to turn the clock back. Information was being withheld and so, there he was, beating the dust until something edible crept forth. Did they think this was easy or in some way entertaining? Yes, he had the gift, but it demanded a great deal of sweat. His father had all but given over the tilling and cultivating to Cayin, in order to devote time to developing ideas into workable tools. But the answers to Cayin's questions evaded him, and how many times had he just flat out told God exactly what he thought of the rotten situation only to hear silence, silence, and more silence! How often as a youth Cayin had shouted to get God's attention—shouting his disappointments, telling his fears to the passing clouds with never a break in one of them. God never from the other side pushed a cloud aside and said, "It's like this, son…this is what has to happen…" As a youth, Cayin often agonized, "Where is God anyway, and why won't he walk and talk with *me?*" Cayin didn't so much as want to fellowship and learn more about God as he wanted God to fix things the way he wanted to understand them. If Eve could have perceived this, she might have taken a different approach with her somber son. Instead, her heart released him as one unties a ship bound to its mooring. Her mother's heart hurt as she watched her son slowly drift away from her.

"Oh, Mother, I'm going to work the northwest field." Cayin got up from his seat to go out toward his tents where his tools were stored. In passing, Cayin brushed shoulders with his younger brother Abel.

Abe always had a way about him—easygoing, personable. He was like a hub in a wheel that connects with all points. Abe listened well to his parents. He reasoned with his elder brother and guided the younger siblings as a loving brother. Abe was the fellow everyone loved. He walked while he talked, listened for God in the wind; that's why he loved herding. Able saw God's stars when he slept out in the fields at night. Hills, flats, rocks, oases—Abe pondered the Maker and shepherding gave him that time and peace to do it. So often when his elder brother sought him, Abe would say, "Let's walk..." and the brothers would walk, talk, and wonder about the world. Abe worked out the wrinkles of life in *the walk.*

The walk soothed Cayin, although he scarcely noticed it himself. He did notice that Abe seemed to make more sense than their parents. Even if they couldn't solve the puzzles of life between the two of them, Cayin knew that his brother understood him, and that Abel got the significance of whatever happened back then in the garden. When anger bested Cayin, his mother would balk just enough to make him check himself. His father just stared at him as if to say, *I have told you this a thousand times, why are you not getting it?* That, of course, would only make Cayin angrier because he didn't get answers the way he wanted them, certainly not the answers *that* he wanted; and no matter how he tried to talk to the Creator, Cayin seemed to get no answer at all. Abel would say something about talking to God and not at Him. No matter, Cayin needed answers and yesterday at that. He had his methods, but surely, God could see that he had his reasons. Surely, He had seen how hard Cayin worked tilling the miserable soil. Surely, He could see how hard the cold nights were and how hot and dry these plains were by day. All the bickering of siblings added to the melancholic tone of their lives. *Why does He not answer me?* When Cayin walked with Abe, Cayin could vent some anger and try to work out the incongruities. It was all part of the *walk.* Whatever was fair, unfair, incomprehensible, unimaginable, or simply divine—it was all reduced down to simpler terms in *the walk.*

On this day, brushing past his brother, Cayin supposed he was angrier than he had ever been. Admittedly, he held much jealously for his brother Abel, who always seemed to get it all right. On this day, the Creator had spoken to him. "*Finally,*', Cayin thought "—*and it's a rebuke?!* Well, "I've got something for that perfect altar boy of His, today!" In pondering alone, Cayin found more frustration, no answers, and the end of his rope. "Abe," Cayin called to his brother, "Let's walk!"

Song of the Oceans
(Gen. 6:9–9:28)

"I know, I know, *I'm a simple man!*" The duet echoed together, for Mrs. Noah had heard this many, many times before. So often so that she could anticipate the declaration and join in with her husband. They shared a long smile between them and a sigh of relief. What price for a friend, a most trusted confidant, in this day when men and women seemed evil, only self serving? In this age when men had charged headlong and dangerously far off the mark from where they started only a few generations before—a man, a woman, and God. In this day, the people worshiped anything, mostly objects they made with their own hands, or they worshipped themselves. Theft and murder were the normal incidence. The rampant bloodshed ached the very heart of God, the Creator. Mrs. Noah appreciated her husband, the son of Lamech, son of Methuselah, the long lived one. Her companion, conspirator, friend, mate, the one who understood her heart and she, his. He was a simple man who stuck to the intrinsic good laid in the fiber of mankind by the Creator.

Not even for a day did their neighbors ever share in the spirit of revival. Every effort of the Noahs to suggest a return to the essential basics was supplanted with resistance: "Who are you to tell us what to do?" To this, Noah would reply, "I'm a simple man, but I know that God would have us turn back from our sin and seek His face. He would that we search for His heart, and He will let Himself be found by us. He did not create us to revel awash in sin. Brothers, let us turn from evil and return to the God of our beginnings." Noah meant to persuade all men to return to God and make offering to Him as the first man, Adam, had led his family to do. Mankind had grown unrepentantly violent, caring only for self indulgence, wholly neglecting to seek the wisdom of God. For all of Noah's ministering, there was not one man who would heed the admonition of a righteous man.

Instead, the Noahs were ridiculed. Their three young sons—Shem, Ham, and Japheth—earned the general public's contempt by way of association. They became "the odd family."

"Why can't you just be like the rest of us and just enjoy today? Have whatever you want! Do whatever pleases you! Tomorrow's coming, you know!"

"Indeed, it is," the simple man would reply. "And He will judge us. Let us be found in Him."

The day that God said *enough*, He gave Noah specifications to build a very large structure—an ark. God told Noah to pitch it because it was going to rain. The simple man said yes.

Noah and his three boys set packs on their donkeys, provisions for three days travel, and a tent cover. The foursome set out early, leading their pack animals southwest to explore a wooded patch. Upon reaching the grove, the boys diverted to find berries. Noah observed the field ahead of the wood, its grass green with vitality, intermitted by a strong flowing stream of lucent water framed by floral puschkinia and anastatica. It was perfect for a homesite, and the wood behind it hosted a more than ample supply of timber for the commission. The place was yet unoccupied. Making camp gave them time to explore the low-hanging tangled branches of very tall gopher trees, largely flat terrain, date, and almond trees. Around a small evening fire, they enjoyed the dates and modified a stone mortar and pestle to crack nuts to accompany their packed rations. The scout party struck camp in the morning and returned home, the boys having gathered enough dates and nuts to please their mother. Back at home, the Noahs discussed relocating their homestead next to the wood source and immediately set about it. Initially living in tents, the Noahs eventually constructed a small home at the new location. Mrs. Noah chose the shade of a thick oak to site their hearth. Mud and straw bricks, stone firepit, and a thatch roof—it was a more than sufficient dwelling for their commission, the ark. During all the years that Noah and his growing sons cut timber, honed planks straight, and fitted lumber to the Lord's specifications, the Noahs also maintained their home, tended fields, and raised flocks. Noah preached to the communities. It was usually convenient as the people came from miles to see the spectacle developing out of the wood.

*****

Ebrenez was a foolish fellow and rather proud of it. He felt that he was not obliged to work hard, as everyone else in the city did, his father being the local lord. Of course, Ebrenez's father didn't feel this way, but knowing that he had overindulged his first son, he spoke little of it. He'd spoiled Ebrenez ruinously in fact, and now, as a young man, there was nothing to be done with him. The world would have to live around him. There was comfort in the thought that Ebrenez was no leader. He would be so ineffectual that the villages would never allow him to step into his father's footsteps. Should Ebrenez try, there would surely be a challenge and a shifting of power. Not that any father wished his own son's death, so indeed Ebren took comfort in his strong suspicion that Ebrenez was not completely stupid and that he too could see this probable outcome. Perhaps that is why Ebrenez spent his days in complete sloth and gaiety, accomplishing nothing with every passing sunset. At this point in his son's life, Ebren was powerless to change its course. After his civic duties, Ebren went about repairing the damage inflicted by his reckless son. Usually it meant paying for property ruined in drunken stupor, whispering a word of correction in the ear of a youth lest he find a role model in Ebrenez, Ebren sought refuge from his life in his work. He made money. He made a lot of money, and being of title and generosity kept him his position and kept his foolish son alive.

Ebrenez knew that other people had to work, and he was just fine with that. But still, a body had to find time for entertainment at some point. He roused several youths to accompany him out to the Noahs homestead to see them chopping down large trees, stripping branches and bark, fitting planks and soaking them in pitch. Most days, Ebrenez made a foray out to the Noahs with a few new spectators to watch the events until word spread sufficiently and people came on their own. Ebrenez led them in a riotous good-time laughing as the Noahs felled trees.

"What do you need a boat for, Noah? You live by a little creek! The river is days away from here! Ha ha ha ha!"

Noah, a simple man, kept his focus on the Word of God. In so doing, he felt compassion for the crowds led by a fool. His three sons, however, now at an age desiring social interaction and daring to entertain thoughts of marriage, received every thrust of the hecklers' dagger. It stung, but they continued to work with their heads hung low. Every day the simple father poured his faith and history into his sons. The young men naturally balked at being the objects of jeering crowds, but as they continued to hew and fit planks, they saw the difference in their father, Noah. His communion with the Creator made him different—peaceful, loving, but fiercely defendant of his God. Ebren saw it too. He occasioned a trip to see the phenomenon developing in the Noah's backyard. Though it was spectacular in itself, Ebren dismissed it as nonsense. Everyone had gods, usually sitting on the hearth, as Ebren had in his own home. Why would a god live out in the open air as this Noah preached? And if Noah needed some gods, Ebren would see to that. He would have the local metal worker make a few for Noah *this day*! It might help quiet things down and get back to normal. This nonsensical construction and talk should stop. Such a lot of work, and for what? But through all of his thoughts and through all of the jeering, Ebren watched the Noah boys closer than anything else. Over some time, he saw the boys held their heads up—no embarrassment, no immodesty. And what bearing they appeared to have. Ebren felt that they held their heads higher than he himself could. And this Noah, every day taking time to talk his nonsense to the public, but otherwise, what a sound man he was. Ebren often invited Noah to sit with him at the gates as the elders of the cities and villages did. Noah always refused but turned the conversation to his outdoor God, too big to be put on a mantelpiece. Ebren hadn't time for this nonsense. He had to oversee his holdings, consult with leading citizens over every matter—crime, trade, markets, religion. He hadn't the time, although it seemed a harmless enough distraction for the people. Indeed *all* the people, for it seemed that they had come from everywhere to see the Noah's construction—what was it now? Some sort of great boat because it was going to…to rain. *Rain. Now there's the mark of an impaired mind, yet see how well he comes about with his sons. I give my foolish child everything and what a failure he is to me. To everyone. Rain, and from a god too great to be a statue of gold and live indoors on a mantelpiece. Won't he get wet, this big god?*

Ebren committed soundly to putting Noah's message out of his mind, although in truth, he could not put Noah out of his mind. Ebren would admit it to no one, but Noah was a fine role model and would have made an excellent governor of any of his cities. There were several officers whom Ebren meant to remove had he anyone to replace them with. Noah wouldn't have it, and so Ebren, leaving his foolish son behind to lead the heckling crowds, returned to his home. Ebren could never get the impression out of his mind, this simple man. How different he was among men, but this Noah could not be pried away from his outdoor God. It had been years since Ebren had known anyone who seriously believed in the outdoor God in that way. In fact, Ebren had not known anyone himself. People were too busy, so logically, they made gods to fit their convenience. It's still a god, right? Everyone needs a god, and everyone has a god. One of his early fortunes was made in smelting small figurines. No home went without several. And they had dual purposes; some of them were of precious metals and could be traded as coin. Indeed, these were the most versatile and useful of gods. Others, more utilitarian were license for certain behaviors and not to be exchanged. As for Noah's ideas of modesty, the masses have to be contained, controlled, and entertained. They need an outlet, which is bound to be evil and a justification to pacify the conscience. So, no, Noah's ideas of goodness and peace were an ill fit with the great numbers of people to be managed. That's just the way it was. There was nothing more to that.

The descendants of Tubal-Cain, the toolmakers, outfitted Noah with saws, mallets, and sturdy rivets to bolt the frame together. Noah paid fairly, so the toolmakers fashioned exactly what was commissioned of them. The toolmakers delivered the items themselves so that they could see if further profit could be made from the backyard project. The very large structure in the backyard at the Noah's was the focal point of its day.

Ebrenez, who never had anything better to do, visited frequently but no longer had to lead a crowd there. People continued to come from far to observe but mostly to gawk in laughter at "the fool who says it's going to 'rain,' whatever that is!" Laughter or no, it made Noah's evangelical mission easier as it brought the people to him. He could speak as he worked and whenever he occasioned a break. But the heckling seemed endless:

"Where are you going anyway, Noah?"

"You can build a special cabin for me and panel it with fine woodwork!"

"How fast does your giant boat go, Noah? I'll wager me and my horse can outrun it!"

"Sure you can, you fool, you'll all be on dry land! That boat's not going anywhere!"

"Ha ha ha! Ha ha ha!"

Daily chores took everything the Noahs had with fields to till, animals to tend, hearth to maintain, and then the "backyard project." And who wanted to associate with anyone in that crazy family, anyway? At marrying age, the matter of finding wives was easily remedied. While Ebren didn't condone Noah's unique life-style, there was not one man in whom he could have conferred more trust—enough trust to place his daughter under the household of Noah. She was all Ebren had left that he truly cared about. At least she would be safe out there, even if Noah did make her move into the great box. She was safe. Ebren felt the end of himself coming. His foolish son would marry, of course, because he had Ebren's money and influence. Ebren had no doubt that his foolish son would choose a foolish girl for a wife and produce foolish progeny. He would have to look elsewhere for a successor. He found that he was not the only father who considered Noah a worthy father-in-law despite the great oddity taking shape in his backyard, and so the sons eventually took wives.

The Noah family swelled to eight adults who labored in all a hundred years on the construction of the large backyard structure. Noah explained to the metalworker that he had no need of any of the selection of idols the smithy presented in his cart. The smithy shrugged; he had been well-compensated by Lord Ebren to visit this man and offer him as many idols as would please him at no charge. Ebren wondered if his daughter would make a plea for the familiarity of her youth. The young women appeared content to leave behind the mantelpiece figurines and embrace the Great God who created the heavens and earth, who dwelled in the heavens. The metal worker returned to the city with his cart of idols.

Ebrenez had never sailed a day in his life. Such an undertaking would resemble work, an idea he held in diffidence. It wasn't altogether the idea of work but that men worked hard, long, and it often caused one to sweat. To this, Ebrenez took offense. And not so much that it must be done, for someone had to work, just not him. It was somewhat like the idea of smoking—some chose to, some simply chose not to. Sailing was definitely out, but he certainly knew what a ship ought to look like for the most part—bow, stern, deck, et cetera. What Ebrenez had mastered was the art of foolery, so with the help of a few others, he worked his craft.

"Stern?"

"Check!"

"Bow?"

"Check!"

"Mast…what? No? Oh well then, wheel!… Oh? No? Then perhaps oars?"

"Ha, ha ha!"

"Hey, Noah, you forgot the sails. How are you going to steer that thing?"

"Ha ha ha!"

Ebrenez studied the very large structure. Numerous large compartments filled out the structure's roughly 65 × 400 foot space. It was, for the most part, a large wood-planked rectangle, its perimeter entirely pitched with bitumen for water fastness. It had one very massive door way, currently acting as entrance ramp. The internal stairwell served several floors, and the uppermost level had windows. The younger son, Ham, outfitted them with pitched shutters, which could be opened as needed for fresh air or fast shut. As the younger generation got their father's vision, they worked more keenly—a living area for themselves and numerous living and storage areas for animals, food, and other supplies.

"Hey, Noah, who's going to be the captain of this fine boat? What about your boy here? You look like you could handle the rough seas, I mean, a little creek! Ha ha ha!"

The jeering of onlookers was tiresome but no longer stung nor did it dissuade any of the Noahs from the veracity of their father's mission to obey God. To be sure, they were a close-knit family; who else would befriend them in their hundred years of odd behavior?

When harvest time came, the family stocked the structure with foodstuff. Adding kindling wood for cooking fires, Japheth packed sacks of grain in the cells beside the hay. One early morning, he went out while it was still dark and little more than shadows could be seen. Dawn slowly broke over Japheth's bent back, gathering what had been bundled a day earlier. He loaded the donkey's cart not too heavily. There were many more trips to be made. As darkness exchanged for light, Japheth made out queues of slow-moving silhouettes all silently heading toward home! In panic, he abandoned the cart to race home in a moment returning for it, steering the donkey as quickly as possible for home. Were the jeerers up to mischief? They'd never done more than stand about laughing at the odd family. Who had time for pranks during the harvest? His heart accelerated with his pace through the field. To the house, all seemed normal. Out back at "the project," the morning was as silent as a natural wood could be with all manner of organisms cooing, squawking, and singing in the early hours. Running around to the back of the project, Japheth stopped the donkey to stare, not in disbelief but plainly in surprise and awe as the animals had begun assembling, quietly queued, orderly as disciplined soldiers. Shem had already been moving about in the midst of them, feeling invincible! His hand grabbed the length of a lion's mane, which stood acquiescent as the sheep.

With Shem's other hand raised high in a fist, he shouted, "Yeeesssss! Ooohhh, yessss! Where are they now? Where are all the fools now, Father? Japheth, get *over* here! Look at this, man!"

Ham said, "Who could be doing this work but God!"

The simple man gave orders directing the trio as to which the animals were to be placed in what stalls. They moved with pride now, fully ready for the gawkers to come and see this spectacle. All these animals had come seemingly on their own and stood patiently in line as Noah had the giraffes put in a low-level stall with abundant head-room, raccoons tucked away on a higher level. All of these creatures? How could the gawkers explain *this*. Surely, this supernatural feat would trump all ill reason. Surely, this would be the tent peg, which dismantled the nonbeliever's camp.

Of course, the scoffers came, but sadly, the sons found that this miracle seemed to pass right by their eyes.

The blind continued to jeer, "Hey, Noah, is your wife going to cook for all of these beasts?"

"Oh no, she's going to cook them!"

"Ha ha ha!"

The sons argued emphatically alongside their father to convince onlookers to turn their lives back to God.

"Hey, Noah, you ready for your big send-off?"

"Ha ha ha!"

"Hey, Noah, make sure you're back from your voyage in time to sow…"

"Or he won't have anything to feed all his pets!"

"Ha ha ha!"

A man asked if he could have Noah's house and field since Noah was "about to sail away." The simple man gave him a long, doleful study. Filled with great sorrow, he simply nodded.

Mrs. Noah hurried about as one does with last-minute pack-ing. Loathe to abandon anything of use, she continued to stock the already-filled store spaces. After all, forty days and forty nights in confinement is one thing enough, but with four boys (therein she includes her husband), three daughters in-law, and this unusual collection of animals to feed, that's *how much* food, exactly? Forty days in this giant structure, which seemed much smaller once all the tenants were installed, but then what? Surely, her garden would be gone, washed away. How long after this "rain" would she have to wait before she could till her garden bed? Will it be there? Would *they* be there? Thus perusing in her scuttle, Mrs. Noah grabbed the edge of her apron to pat dry her head. All of the packing, loading, storing, having been accomplished; next came a final check for anything that could be utilized on the ark. Their little house had been reduced to a skeletal state; the backyard commission had been completed! Assembled in front of the ark with last-minute thoughts, all the Noahs found themselves patting heads. Now no words but cautious glances at each other and then upward. The eight sets of eyes met droplets of water in free fall settling on lashes, in gentle collision with eyeballs, coursing down their cheeks. "Ahh...so this is 'rain'...yes, of course, from the sky!" Noah's neck, still craned upward, wondered at the armies of billowy white clouds amassing. They were dark on the bottom side. He'd never thought about clouds before.

"So many. Perhaps a storehouse from which He will pour out onto the earth..." Noah mused softly, "God, you are uniquely creative!" True, God had warned them. Even though they had been working on the project for the last hundred years, the idea, rain, was still somehow unsettling now that the day had finally arrived. The three sons let their faces wash with vindication in the slight rain. They anxiously looked for their mockers who would surely *now* change their attitudes. Noah sighed as if he was about to rest from a great labor. In all of these hundred years, he had not seen even one wretched heart seek repentance. Not one soul beyond his own house sought to turn to the Creator, but Noah had done his best to warn the people. He felt certain that everyone knew because he had travelled out to them, but even more so over time, the people had come to him and seen the backyard project, the ark, in construction. Ultimately, Noah left it up to the Creator, who would read all hearts. Noah took a cloth and wiped the steadying precipitation from his head. He gathered the hands of his small family. Together they offered a prayer of thanks to the Creator. They gave thanks for His mercy, patience, help with the construction, and the salvation of the family and the creatures already onboard.

No visitors on this gray day. No more hammering, cutting, gathering either. Stillness was broken by a lengthy and deliberate rod of light and heat that ripped across the skyscape. A rumbling crescendo followed it. Watching the lightning slice through thickly massing clouds, Noah thought it might perhaps resemble a finger of God. The finger of electricity exploded onto a patch of earth and raced across fields to the old thick oak tree, which shaded the Noah's little mud thatch house. Effortlessly, it cut the trunk of the oak away from its roots. The old oak remained standing for a moment but then slowly leaned over, its mass resting on the thatch roof, pushing it to the floor. The tops of the walls popped outward, strewing mud brick about the yard. The eight turned around toward the ark and walked up the ramp, standing just inside the structure. God raised the ramp—shutting off the only entrance—and sealed it tightly.

The previous few days had been cool, gray, and breezy, so the hecklers had not come out to the Noah homestead. As the sparse precipitation slowly grew into a steady rain, a few came out, Ebrenez amongst them, no longer in cruel derision; Ebrenez was past that. In truth, he had long been afraid. He had visited the Noahs so much that Noah's words and warning became constant companions inside his head. But sloth has no company if it is not laziness, pride, and stupidity; so in all, these many years, the rich young man did nothing. On that day, no one had to tell Ebrenez what "rain" was. Leave all your excuses about the curious weather to someone who doesn't know. Leave it to one person who has not heard Noah say it. There was no one. There was not one man, woman, or child who could say that they didn't know because they'd all heard Noah tell them this was going to happen. Yes, yes, all true, but in good nature, of course, Ebrenez would visit just to see what new developments had taken place. Perhaps to negotiate an extended tour of the structure's inside and just long enough to see the peculiar weather pass. And who doesn't need money? Ebrenez had brought along a sackful of coin to help his argument.

Now sealed inside the great structure, Noah's family sat together quietly through that long afternoon. Raindrops slapped heavily against the dirt. There were now so many that they could not be heard individually but as a steady rhythm. Winds drove the rhythm with a sound the woodland had never heard before. A solemn intensity that sent a chill through each of the members gathered around a small fire. For a while, the Noahs could hear the jeerers outside calling politely. As fear mounted in their voices, they began to shout and beat on the structure, demanding to be let in. Some tried to scale the structure's height, to no avail. There was only one way in; and only God, who had shut the door, could open it. Hearts inside and outside the ark beat briskly. Outside, the rain accumulated, covering soaked sandals. Ebrenez and some of the outsiders walked home through the mud to wait out the phenomena. He held his money sack with both hands. The fabric was now so wet the weight of the coins might tear through the bottom. At home Ebren and his wife stared at their son. There was fear in their faces, mud on their sandals, raindrops rolling into the house from underneath the door. Ebren knew now, as did everyone, but he knew it was too late for him. He grieved inside for having raised his son with such a worthless nature. He gave his son privilege and gold. No wisdom, no moorings, no restraint, no great God of the outdoors. Ebren put an arm around his wife, walked over to the mantelpiece, and fixed a gaze on the variety of metal carvings—gods of curious shapes (part animal, part human), all animal. A couple he couldn't identify what they were meant to be, but having been smithed of pure silver, they were valued. Ebren didn't know all of their names, titles, or functions; but one by one, he began to push them off the mantle with his right forefinger. His wife's tears fell onto the tiled floor damp from seeping rain. His son was still at the door, staring wide eyed at him. Ebren's palm swept the mantle, sending the remaining figurines flying to meet the tile, a few bouncing with what energy remained in them. One rolled to a stop at Ebrenez's wet feet. He'd never seen his father cry before. Late the next night, Ebren sat down, his wife sat beside him, and they wept.

The following afternoon, some tried to make it back to the great "boat." The road was gone. They waded through the waist-high water, everyone now clearly afraid and remorseful of their disbelief. They moved along all sides of the structure, beating, cursing, begging to be let in. Ebrenez, carrying more gold than the first time, was not above advertising it. He had to get in. He always got his way. He had money and prestige. He was the son of prestige. He had a sister on the inside. "Let me in!" He promised all of his wealth—that of his father—his future holdings, for as long as Noah wanted. He beat on the sides of the waterproofed boat. It was as beating hand against stone. Ebrenez did not know that inside, he could no longer be heard. As for the Noahs, these sounds were muffled by the great storm growing outside and the soft cacophony inside of the stall residents. Birds, lions, bears, giraffes, deer, sheep, monkeys, and raccoon all settled into their places into their bits of hay in comfort, into the hands of the Creator. Ebrenez waded home.

Outside, the rain surpassed thatched rooftops, swirled and eddied, pushing over the stone blocks, which had made the city gates. Strong metal hinges let go of their doors, some of which floated, some tried to sink. The aggression of so much water pushed and pushed. It pushed some things up, some down. A man grabbed a gate in effort to make a raft of it, but the water stood up and pushed him down. Ebrenez, intent on going in the opposite direction this time, bundled a few belongings, some coin in one hand and a carved image of some household god under his left arm. He caught hold of a basket floating past and tossed his few possessions into it which caused the basket to begin to sink. Ebrenez would not let go of the idol under his left arm although he could not swim with it. He fished for his basket of items in the muddied water with his right hand until he caught hold of it again. Paddling with his feet, Ebrenez used the items in his arms—basket in one, idol in the other—as he paddled, trying to stay abreast of the water. Refusing to release his possessions, he sank with them.

In similar fashion, the entire population on the outside of the ark met their end, cursing the very things they refused to let go of.

Muddy water pushed the tiles loose from the floor and worked the stone blocks loose from each other until everything the lord of cities knew was buried or floated away. Gradually, the storm turned soil and worked tree roots loose of their moorings and sent them about as great battering rams. As if manned by an invisible army, the rams crashed through temples of worship, creating gaping caverns into which water poured followed by more battering rams. Their branches grabbed everything, knocking over images of gold, mixed metals, silver, and altars—some of which floated, the rest sank, first circling round, round then down into the smallest of cyclonic swirls, lost trying to find bottom; the pushing water would not yet allow it.

Water rolled, and wind pushed it, knocking everything, which man had contrived from its place. Water pushed hard by wind churned to cut canyons. Swells of water lifted the great boat, the ark, not made to navigate but merely to float and rocked all of its residents to quiescent sleep.

There were no more hecklers. The water was too deep. Water was everywhere. There was no dry land. The ferocious wind was on the hunt for anything of man that had been. It was to be removed by command of Him on High.

For days and nights, the ark floated on the oceans, which had been earth. The whole world became water—unimaginable oceans that clashed at times, converging into powerful drifts, which cut rock, tunneled through high places to find low. Swirling torques of pressure reshaped mountains, pushed hilltops into valley places, moved the dry land corpses to deep-sea bed graves, settling familiar and unfamiliar together in mysteries destined to confound the future unbelievers, the progeny of this family of eight who sat together many quiet nights as their cabin rolled high and pitched low. In these early days, the aloft windows were fast shut against the terrible crash of pounding waves. Noah didn't try to guess where they were. He knew all that he needed to know: in all the earth, he was in the safest place—in the palm of God's hand. Wind howled its frightful whistle. Thunder reverberated through the waters, even shaking the makeshift table Mrs. Noah used to cut vegetables as she prepared supper for her little family. Every meal seemed solemn, mostly quiet except for the thunder answering thick charges of electricity that bolted in any direction cutting swaths of light through the night's darkness. The world had become an ocean, a storm raging rampant, upending everything that had gone wrong these last generations. Water washed all the bloodshed, all the idolatry, greed, hatred, and selfishness. Does not the Potter have the right to place His vessel back on the wheel?

On the inside of the pitch, Noah recited the history of creation and genealogy—from the first human pair, Adam and Eve, down to himself. He offered praise to the Creator for His wisdom, creation of a beautiful Earth, for His mercy and desire that all be saved. Of course, Noah gave thanks for the preservation of the eight.

"Mother."

"Yes, daughter."

"Mother, listen. Listen. Do you hear it?"

"Hear? My child, I hear the wind calling. The water is washing the earth. The storm is vindicating God. That is what I hear."

"Listen, listen closely." Shem's wife rose and moved toward the stalls. "Listen."

Shem rose to follow her, quizzically, trying to open his ears and mind to whatever she was experiencing beyond the storm.

"I... I hear it too! Something! I hear something, sshhh...do you, oh, come! Listen!"

The other two young couples arose and moved toward the stalls. Thunder cracked through the dark skies, vibrating the tempestuous ocean, rocking their cradle.

"Huh? Uh-huh...ooh. Ohh! Its... Mother, Father, it's a song! Come and see, come and hear it. They're singing."

Noah and his wife finally got up, overcome by curiosity. It wasn't so much what they saw: all the stall residents were comfortably settled, content in their spaces, all sleeping. But Noah heard it as a hum, a melody, like a low, soft, gentle song.

"And, Mother, come see. It's like they're all singing the same song! The lion, the raccoon, all of them! It's like they understand. They know that God is protecting them!"

Noah thought aloud, "Does He not use the simple things to confound the wise? So simple a raccoon could see and sing a song of the redeemed. It is the song of the oceans. Praise be to God, Creator of heaven and earth! Glory be to Him forever and ever. Amen."

The song of comforted sleep, the storm, the gentle rock of the ark put the eight to a restful sleep their many nights aboard the ark.

Noah cut a hash on the wall, to mark the time, as best he could keep the days straight. Even in tight confinement, there was rudimentary work—feeding, cleaning out stalls and such to be done so that time seemed to slip as sand through the fingers. And the storm. He forgot when the tempest subsided down to a rainstorm again. But he spent hours daily in the top windows marveling over the power of the almighty. Noah thought himself the smallest spec, yet God had seen him. God knew him. That, and called him out, held him in His great hands. It seemed as if it was dark outside always, like it was dark on both sides of the clouds. Lightning made frequent forays through the dark, but for the most part, they floated about in a storm in the dark. In the midst of the storm, they were in the safest place on earth. Noah knew it, and he slept soundly every single night.

Eventually the rains stopped, but the eight knew that they were still floating. With many more hash marks, the great structure settled. Under more hash marks, Noah went up to the top windows with a dove and let it fly. After some minutes, the bird returned. With more hash marks passing days, Noah again let the dove fly. After languishing for some time, the bird returned with an olive branch in its beak! Another chance Noah let fly the creature, and it never returned. Noah knew then that it was safe to disembark, the waters having receded.

Noah and all the residents of the life-preserving ark moved out onto dry land in what has since been called the Valley of Eight. It was there that God made a covenant with Noah, a covenant between God and the earth for all generations: never again would He bring a flood to destroy the entire earth. Whenever God brought clouds and rain, a rainbow would appear afterward as reminder of the everlasting covenant. *"The sign of the covenant I have established between Me and all life on the earth."* There, Noah built an altar and made an offering to the everlasting God. It was there that man started out new, once again, to populate the earth there at the foot of the Ararats in the Valley of Eight.

Abraham
Genesis 12

The patriarch Abraham is being interviewed by a local media station regarding recent events at his camp. We pick up midway in the interview.

INTERVIEWER. So what happened next, Mr. Abraham?

ABRAHAM. What happened next? Well, you know how you do something but first you think about it for what seems a reasonable amount of time and then you do it? Well, anyway, my little wife, Sarai—and who knows what goes on in the mind of a woman—they are a special gift from God. Special indeed! Anyway, she thinks we should adopt the local custom of a barren woman bearing a child at the knee of another, a surrogate. What does that mean? I can tell you now: it means *t-r-o-u-b-l-e!* Well…ahem, anyway, it means the man impregnates the surrogate in place of his wife. Oh, who thought of that one? Can a man really have *two* wives? Of course, it is understood that the child is that of the wife from the beginning, not that of the surrogate. That is the rule of man out here. And, yes, arguably a tenuous situation, at best, but out here, who tells this people we're living among what is right or wrong? They do what is right in their own eyes. These are not our people, these masses. So (*sighs*) anyway, Sarai tells me this is her wish. My little wife. Her wish is my wish, so I acquiesce. Ahem, hem.

INTERVIEWER. So what happened next?

ABRAHAM. What happened next? Well, it's mostly a blur since then. But things got loud. Well, it brought *you* out here, right? My

peaceful domicile disintegrated, well, more like "exploded"…
heh, heh, heh…aahhh. I've no doubt that great events across
this earth will be pushed into motion because of a woman—
don't even say it! Yes, it's already true. We all know that, don't
we! Heh, heh, heh…aaahhh. Aaahhh…my quiet home…out
here under the stars…you would think…

INTERVIEWER. Well, Mr. Abram, what happened, *exactly*?

ABRAHAM. Exactly eh? Well, the surrogate, a handmaid of my wife,
Sarai, began to despise Sarai once she knew that she was pregnant by my seed. I mean, make any law you like, but God made
a woman bringing a new life into the world a thing of beauty
and pride. And who is to share that pride when the woman is
not married—why, the man who impregnated her, of course! So
where now does that leave *said* man's wife but out in the cold.
Oooohh, make any law you like, but none can supersede that
natural law given to us by God. So…*naturally*, in turn, Sarai
hated the surrogate, the surrogate hated her back, feeling she had
the upper hand. In short, a war churned to ravage my tents! The
farther along the girl grew with child, the greater the rage-slash-
jealousy between the two of them, each wanting part of what the
other had. What a foolish law! Who is this child going to look
like and take after but the two who conceived it! Meanwhile,
the wife, who truly is just a third party, lives with this glaring
in her face for the rest of their lives. Sarai's maid, she was only a
poor slave given to me when we had sojourned through Egypt.
Oh, what was I even doing in *Egypt* in the first place? That was
my first blunder! Nearly got myself killed there, by the way. But
that's where we picked up this slave girl, altogether bad idea, but
who was thinking then? Just trying to stay alive. So…once she's
pregnant, and don't even say it… What's this all about? I'll just
tell you. My wife, my one and only little wife, Sarai, has been
barren, never once pregnant in all of our years. And now, well, I
look a good forty-five, but I'm nearly a hundred—

INTERVIEWER. Oh, my, well…you don't look—

ABRAHAM. Stay in prayer and keep moving. Don't let everyone do
everything for you! Move about! That's my secret to health.

When you stop moving, things start to pile up on you and wreck! Now, ladies like to keep you guessing, but I'll tell you, if you promise not to print this part—

INTERVIEWER. Oh, I *prom*—

ABRAHAM. She's, well, I'd better not say. Enough uproar going on here as it but anyway, in that respect—we're long past finished! And not one child, not even a girl, of course, who wouldn't want a son, but we had no children and that's just how it was for us. Until one day, these visitors came. I'll tell you about them in a minute, but they just sort of came on to the scene, and, my friend, I don't know what you know, but there are times that you *just know* something. And I *knew* that these were not ordinary men. Like, flesh and blood, ordinary, I mean. And they said we'd have a child. Well, that was a long time ago, and Sarai didn't really believe it in the first place, but you know, it put this thought in her mind, and she kind of held on to it all that time. Since nothing seemed to change for us, she decided to take things into her own hands, thus the surrogate idea and that's how we ended up here. And thus, the war amidst my tents, the end of my peaceful domicile. So…true, it was Sarai's doing. If I had said no, what would she have said? Well, whatever it would have been, it would have been preferable to the war I'm living in now. Now, I know. My wife made the daily life of this pregnant servant girl nightmarish until the poor waif ran away. She took nothing with her, and that's dangerous. Out here, in such open spaces, that's a death sentence. Out here, only sand for as far as the eye can see in any direction. It's hard to follow the sun for direction. It's so harsh, and it seems like it's all around you. You must follow the moon as well, but you must *plan* to be out in the elements. The little waif was an emotional wreck of a pregnant girl. She had no need to follow sun, moon, or stars. She just wanted "out' of her life of no autonomy. I'm sure she just wanted to die, but she intended to do it with her own child. You see, make any law you like, but none will supersede the natural rule of law. A woman knows her child is hers. And so, the girl ran off into the desert to die, and so, we thought she *had*. And now, what with Sarai telling me that it was all *my* fault! What? I mean, there I was, sitting outside my tent, on my stool *in peace* when Sarai first came to me with this "custom"... anyway, the deed done, there we were with enough ruckus that the entire camp knew what was going on, hah! Everyone did I guess, because here *you* are...and then the girl runs off, and we take her for dead. Who's responsible for that? Me, of course! I mean, no one even knew which direction to start looking for her or how long she'd been gone. Maybe she found a caravan or... something. And so, yes, things quieted down! But a *bad* quiet. How was I to feel anything less than guilty? Anyway, after a few days, the little waif comes back! How? Yes, exactly! *How?* We all -took her for dead, but here she comes riding the heatwaves off in the distance, just walking back in amongst the living. While she stood afar off, I sent a servant to receive her. It was only right. She stood there as if she didn't really want to come back, who could blame her. But she was my responsibility. Now, how did she come to be...well, alive? She said she met "the God who sees." She said no more. Never a talkative child, the little waif. But the infant conceived was my responsibility to bring along. That's where the maelstrom really began...

INTERVIEWER. What do you mean? Things got worse?

ABRAHAM. What do I mean? Where do you live? Where *could* you live that you could possibly not have heard heaven and earth shake? The lad moves in a swirl of controversy since he learned to blink. Fighting, arguing, talking back to elders. Everyone— my servants, their families. Now I admit that I may have started out showing the boy favor, after all, he was the only child I had, but he always seemed to enjoy challenging authority. He even vexed *me* beyond my limits, and he was still a youth, so I took a more steady hand with the lad. No matter what, there was war from every corner: the boy lived and breathed controversy. His birth mother began to demand rights for her child. Did I say "her child"? Yes, for you see, no matter what this people calls it, a child is his mother's son. Never mind this birthing at the knees of someone else. All a bad idea. Make any law you like. Anyway, all of this that leaves Sarai, *out on the hot sand,* as we say. Disenfranchised, with nothing to show for her plan but trouble and resentment for her handmaid and now for the child, who is growing into his own tempestuous person daily. So, all the tents were at war about this thing. Some having the opinion that the act meant that I had taken the handmaid as another wife, and oh, what a poorly conceived thought that is. No need to deliberate on that! The one wife is enough in a lifetime's work, thanks kindly. The older this child grew, the more reckless, violent, and contrary he became.

INTERVIEWER. So did things quiet down?

ABRAHAM. Did things quiet down? Ah, my friend—have we just met? Everything went *wild!* All this in my old age. I was eighty-six when this child was born. Although I still looked a good forty-five. A difficult child from the start. Contrary, wild, always fighting. Every breath was spent in rebellion, except perhaps in his quiet sleep. Indeed, it may have been the only quiet we had since he was born! You think about something for what seems a reasonable time, and then you do it. If I had thought a little more…this would have been the something to *not* do. Aaahhh, a man cannot truly have two wives and live to tell about it! Sooo…thirteen years later, He appears, the visitor that I told you I just knew was not any ordinary man. He came back and changed our names: I have been Abra*ham* since and my wife Sar*ah.* And tells me that He's going to make a great nation from me—me and *my wife, Sarah.* So many people that they will be like sand! Who can count sand, eh? And how can a ninety-one-year-old woman have a child? But He said it, so I believed it. But you didn't hear the *ninety-one* part from me.

INTERVIEWER. So your wife had a baby?

ABRAHAM. Did my wife have a baby? Not that simple! As it happened, one day, I was sitting on my stool outside my tents. Just sitting, not looking at anything in particular. There isn't much to see out in the open spaces. At that moment I was watching the heat wave up from the dusty ground. The waves look as if you would burn your palms trying to shoo them away from sizzling at your sandals. More closely, I'm sure I could see each grain of sand pop as the oil does on the pan. They pop up and wind down…anyway, then He just seemed to appear on the horizon, two others with Him—three men walking toward our compound.

INTERVIEWER. What did you do?

ABRAHAM. What did I do? I jumped up from my stool and hurried out to greet them! You don't exactly see a lot of travelers out here in the open spaces like that, just three souls, all alone, just walking—walking as with purpose, but still so far from well, there's not much to be far from, but there's nothing out here for certain. Anyway, here alongside the tents, under a great, great big tree with lots of shade. My servants attended them and washed their feet while others set to prepare a meal on the quick! A freshly slaughtered roasted lamb, vegetables, bread and wine, of course. My wife makes a little dipping dish of herbs and oil for the bread. I don't know what she calls it, but it's delicious…anyway. Cheeses, figs, and some dates. It's our custom to welcome strangers warmly. And these were most agreeable gentlemen but unusual. One did most of the talking. But I wasn't fooled. I knew they were not ordinary men. I knew, *my soul knew*, it was *Him*. Our people have always known about Him and worshipped Him. We are of the line of Shem, the middle son of the patriarch Noah, whom He preserved in the midst of the Great Deluge. Anyway, the why here? Why now? Why me? So I listened. Years ago, He told me to move, so that's what we did. That's why we are here now. He told me where to go, so I had everything—goods, flocks, servants, tents—everything. Heh, heh, heh, aaahhhh…packed up and we moved to the place He told us. Right here! Side Story about that, though, later. My unfortunate nephew Lot. He went yonder, and things went badly for him. But anyway, then our guest tells me He's going to make a great nation out of me. All very agreeable to me. Now, my wife, well, she's a trifling thing, precious, but she doesn't understand the matters of men. She was behind the veil in the tent, listening intently to every word. When He said to me, "Look at the stars in the sky, I'm going to make so great a nation of you, like the stars of the sky, that you can't even number" my paraphrase, of course. My wife, Sarah, did not take His words to be true. Then He said we would have a child. well, that did it for her. From behind the tent lining, her laugh broke out low but heard by all of us. It was a laugh but a scoff at the same time. Like something you say without thinking, like it just fell out of her mouth. You see, Sarah, my blessed and only wife,—we have never had children. She has never carried a child. So those words kind of hit her right where she lives, you understand. And of course, all the trouble of the surrogate's son and all. Anyway, my guests had finished their meal. He rose up, went over to the tent veil, and pushed it aside. It caught Sarah off guard. She just stood there exposed, frozen like a statue. Remind me to tell you about my nephew. My, you should have seen how reddened her whole face was! Against her dark hair, she looked like, well, anyway, He looked directly at her and said, "Why do you laugh when I said you would have a child?" Poor Sarah didn't know what to do, so she tried to back out of it. She lied, "I-I didn't laugh," she said. He said," Oh but you did laugh." He never took His eyes off of her. Hers were on the ground. When He looks at you, it's like He's looking right through you. Through the stories, the front, past, who or what you purport to be, to the core of your heart, it can be quite disconcerting, but anyway, here's the best part: He said, "Is anything too hard for the Lord?" Well…all the servants and me, not that any of us was talking, but you could have heard a raindrop hit the dust! Our eyes raced from one to another because with that, *everyone* knew who He was. Except my trifle of a wife, Sarah, still embarrassed for being caught in a lie red faced. She didn't believe Him because I was round about ninety-nine, though I still looked a strong forty-eight. Sarai was eighty-nine…ish, but you didn't hear that from me. And she never had been able to bear children. And possibly, because of the failure of her attempt at surrogate motherhood. Childlessness was her sorrow all of her years, and I suppose that by eighty-nine, she was settled into the way it was, and then here comes some stranger who upends it all somehow. "This time next year," He said, "Sarah will have a son." Anyway, we spoke more about my nephew, Lot. Remind me to tell you about that, and shortly afterward, they left. Walked out of the tents and disappeared into the horizon just the way they had come. Unusual, *very* unusual.

The next year, as He had said, Sarah gave birth to our son, Isaac. The surrogate child, about thirteen by then, was always wild, controversial, generally disagreeable, and a continual source of contention and mockery. This, such that Sarah grew cold, cold*er* toward the surrogate and the wild boy. She insisted that I put them out. Me? Why me, and how could I do such a thing. Difficult as he and the whole scenario was, he was still my son. But God quieted my soul about the matter and reassured me. So as my wife would have me throw out a mother and child, I set them out at least with some provisions out into the desert. The mother went seeing nothing to do but die. There they went into the brutal open desert space. It was unthinkable. I mean, this was still my child. Will a man not love his own child however it comes to be? However contrary his spirit is? Oh, to meet whoever thought of this surrogate plan! How can a man be full of regrets and yet love a child? This is me. Sarah had me throw them both out, mother and child. Who knows what goes on in the head of a woman…

INTERVIEWER. So what became of the woman and child?

ABRAHAM. What became of the woman and child? God interceded to provide for them. They lived in the desert, in Paran. He grew up to be an archer. When he became ready to marry, his mother got him a wife from Egypt. That is his life, completely separate from our own.

Once they left, my tents quieted. We enjoyed watching our son grow, *our* son, Isaac. This is the son God gave to us. We were old, but Isaac was an agreeable child, always a pleasure. Grew into a fine young man.

INTERVIEWER. Didn't you try to kill your own son? I mean, really, that's why we're here because of this rumor.

ABRAHAM. Didn't I try to kill my own son? Well, not that simple, but simply yes and no. God told me to go to a certain place and sacrifice him. So I made ready for a trip of several days, and I brought along firewood, just in case. We set out with a few servants, and then my son and I travelled a little further yet by ourselves, to where God directed me. We set up an altar, I bound Isaac—

INTERVIEWER. You did *what* now?

ABRAHAM. I did what? I tied Isaac's hands behind his back. He was a young strong lad. I was getting up in age by then, but I had poured everything I knew and lived about God into my son. He was going to be the next step in the great nation to come, so he needed to know all about God.

INTERVIEWER. So, *one*, you were going to sacrifice your own son, and *two*, he was cooperating?

ABRAHAM. In a word, yes! It's simple and complicated: Complicated is, he is my flesh, my love, and I took strong cord and tied his hands tightly behind his back. But here's the simple: *He* told me. Remember, God said my nation would become like the stars in the sky and the sands. Who can count either? Right? Well, If He said it, He's going to do it. So I just figured that He was going to bring Isaac right back to life. I didn't know why He wanted me to make the sacrifice, but I *did* know that He promised to make me father of a nation, and it was to be through Isaac. Isaac couldn't do that if he remained dead, right? So simple! I sacrifice the boy, God brings him back to life, we saddle the donkeys and go home. Simple.

INTERVIEWER. Wow… Uh, I mean, so is that what happened?

ABRAHAM. Is that what happened? *No!* My friend, that's *not* what happened, although it would have been simple. At that time, even Isaac wasn't sure what was happening. He said, "Father, I see the wood, the fire, and the altar. Where's the sacrifice?" I told him that God would provide the lamb, and then that's when I began to tie his hands. His face flushed. He was clearly afraid, but he stood quiescent as I tied his feet as well, and remember, I'm an old man. I was not without his assistance as I hoisted him on the altar. He was afraid but quiet. He knew God well enough to know that he should trust Him. Isaac knew I had always tried to live that as an example to him.

INTERVIEWER. So lemme get all of this. You've built an altar complete with firewood to light it up, tied up your only son who is really a *full*-grown man physically capable of stopping you, but he possibly helps you or at least, does not hinder you from setting himself up as the sacrifice...

ABRAHAM. In a word, yes.

INTERVIEWER. Man alive! I have the exclusive on this interview, so please proceed and tell the recorder what you did after that!

ABRAHAM. What did I do after that? I'm glad you asked this, friend! I raised my harvest knife, ready to make the strike—

INTERVIEWER. Aye, yai...

ABRAHAM. And someone calls my name!

INTERVIEWER. Wait, *what?*

ABRAHAM. Out there in the open spaces, *someone calls my name!* But I knew it wasn't a man. My *soul* knew. I knew it was a spirit. He told me not to harm the boy. He points, I look, and there was a ram just nearby with its horns caught in a bush! So I cut the ropes off Isaac, much to his relief, and we took the ram and sacrificed it to the LORD. We returned to the other servants and walked back home. Simple.

INTERVIEWER. Amazing...

ABRAHAM. Simple. *He* is amazing!

Cooperation
(Gen. 22)

"In the beginning God created the heavens and the earth. And the earth was without form and void and darkness was upon the face of the deep. And the Spirit of God was hovering over the waters…

…And God said, *'Let there be light,'* and there was light. God saw that the light was good, and He separated the light from the darkness. God called the light 'day,' and the darkness he called 'night.' And there was evening, and there was morning, the first day… God saw all that He had made, and it was very good. And there was evening, and there was morning, the sixth day… Then the man and his wife heard the sound of the LORD God as He was walking in the garden in the cool of the day, and they hid from the LORD God among the trees of the garden… Now Cayin said to his brother Abel, 'Let's go out to the field.'…

…This is the account of Noah. Noah was a righteous man, blameless among the people of his time, and he walked with God. Noah had three sons—Shem, Ham, and Japheth… This is the account of Shem… Arphaxad… Shelah… Eber… Peleg… Reu… Serug… Nahor… Terah—"

"Grandpa…"

"Grandpa… Terah became the father of myself, Nahor, and Haran. Haran became the father of Lot… I married Sarai. Nahor married Milcah. Father uprooted us to go to Canaan, but we stopped in Haran and ended up staying there…then the LORD said to me, 'Leave your country, your people and your father's household and go to the land I will show you…'"

"Why?"

"What?"

"Why?"

"What, *why*? What do you mean by *why*? I've told you this story hundreds of times. What are you asking 'why?' for? What kind of question is that, why?"

Abraham was more than a little upset that his son chose to interrupt his rhetoric. Oral histories are not a simple matter. Everything has to be included at just the right interval, or it could be lost forever. Why would the boy start asking questions now? He maintained his step but looked at Issac wishing that he could really see inside that boy's head. *Kids do the darndest things. What could he be thinking asking me why?*

"Because, why?" Isaac kept looking ahead as they walked. He bent down to pick up a few small stones to skip as they walked. He saw nothing wrong with the question, except maybe that he should have asked it a long time ago.

"What?" Really, Abraham was a man of few words. He could tell this was going to require more.

"I'm just sayin'. You've told me this story hundreds of times but you never told me why. Why did God make you move? Why didn't He just do things where you were? Why?" Isaac pitched a small stone of his arsenal out, striking another stone. The hit stone shattered, sending bits flying in every direction. Isaac looked up at his father with a smile awaiting approval for his marksmanship and a response to his hanging question. He saw the question as sound, again, only lacking in punctuality.

Abraham stopped walking. He'd come out as he frequently did to observe the livestock grazing pasture. He'd have one of his men move the flock further over to the west. There'd be more space between flocks, and the pasture was well rested. The next point he wanted to check was a good walk away, but he enjoyed the air and the walk. He wanted to empress upon Isaac the importance of knowing, really knowing the condition of his assets, not blindly relying on some third-party report indefinitely. The walks gave him alone time with his son who sometimes asked probing questions, and today was one of them. This was tough, and Abraham wasn't sure where to begin. "Well…well. Well,… I suppose… Well, haven't you ever wanted to do something special for someone you love? Like, remember when you were eight and you wanted to surprise your mother for her birthday so you hunted all those rabbits?"

"Yeah, I skinned them and prepared them for the roast, only that didn't go so well. I killed one of Mama's pet rabbits too. When she found out, I didn't know if she was gonna hug me or squeeze my head off!" Isaac winced at the recollection he'd tried to put behind him.

"Well, yes, well, admittedly, *that* didn't go so well. *But* what if *God* saw something special in this land—the resources, the flora, whatever. Whatever His reason was, He's God, so I obeyed. Anyway, I don't know. I only know this: He loves us, always has our goodwill in mind, and that's enough for me. If God says, 'Do it,' I do it. End of discussion. So, anyway, we got to the great trees of Mam… Oh, son, look ahead of us. What do you see?"

"Kasha chasing his tail, a butterfly! Now he's after a butterfly!"

"No, no, ahead, out there…what do you see?"

Isaac stopped walking and looked his hardest. Nothing stood out as unusual in the pasture, mountains beyond or azure above. It was a regular perfect day. "Nothin," Isaac gave up. "Some grass, sky, a mountain. It always looks like there's a line between the grass and the sky…"

"Right! But when you get there—"

"When you get there, there's nothing! Just more grass. More sky." Isaac was beginning to wonder if he simply had never travelled far enough. Was there something else that he was supposed to see? Were they going there today?

"Horizon. It's the horizon. What's beyond it?"

"Ummm…nothing?" Isaac guessed without confidence.

"Oh, no. Not nothing. Something. In fact, *everything*."

"What'd you mean?"

"Son, you see nothing. A few birds, grass, and sky but no more. I see the same. But I know what's there."

"Well? What? What could be there?"

"The future… Look again. What do you see?"

97

"Ummm…the same nothing."

"Exactly!" Abraham said. "But God sees. He knows and creates. He is all-knowing, all-seeing. Isn't it wise to trust the one who can see what we cannot?"

"Ooohh, right… Right. Right!" Isaac resumed his stone skipping. "So, when God tells you something, you just do it because you figure that He knows something you don't."

"Do it because you love and respect Him, but understand that He knows *everything*, and we know so very little. We are all little children in the hands of the great God. But we know that He loves us. He's told us that. And He shows us how to conduct ourselves in order to live well every day. That's love. It's like, when you were little and your mother made sandals for you. That was love. And when you got older, you learned a trade. I taught you everything I know about livestock so that someday you can succeed with your own business and household affairs. Even so, when you were smaller, didn't I discipline you with a rod?"

"Oh, yeah, that you did!"

"But it was necessary to help you walk your life with Him. In this way, God also gives us good things and sometimes chastens us. So anyway, we got to the great trees at Mam… Isaac, take those two donkeys and leave the others with Relez and Ober. Tell them to camp here. You and I will go further to that yonder mountain and set up the altar there."

Arriving at the mountain's base, Abraham selected a choice location. Father and son erected an altar using the stones around them and loaded the kindling. "So anyway, when we got to the great trees at Mam—"

"Father?" Isaac looked around him. He slowly turned in a full circle. He could see the servants who accompanied them on this walk. Back at the campsite, they appeared to be small dots. The way they had come from was smaller. There was nothing on the panorama—a few small trees, an occasional high flying bird. It was terribly quiet. If it was this quiet come nightfall, Isaac thought, he might feel afraid. Now, in midmorning sun, he felt disconcerted. There was really nothing about, more than the meager supplies which they had carried with them. Isaac began to wonder about this particular trip out of the hundreds he had taken with his father over the years of his life. Wherever Abraham went, Isaac followed. That's the way it had always been. Isaac was his father's son and had never felt a day of lack, insecurity, or fear until now.

"Father…"

"Yes, son?" Abraham responded matter-of-factly.

"God, He's your God. Right?"

"Well, yeah, but not mine only. Remember that boy you used to play with when you were around twelve?"

"Oh, yeah, Ashur!"

"Whatever became of that boy?"

"Uhh, you don't wanna know."

"Really?" Abraham knew. At that time, he wondered if his son understood the impact of what had happened with the family who came to stay with them for a short while. He was about to find out.

"Yup." Isaac continued his recollection. "His dad made some bad investments and couldn't pay them…"

"Oh dear, indentured servitude?"

"Umm…no, Dad. More like permanent servitude. I don't think he'll ever see home again."

"How sorry. You two were thick as thieves back then. But a father must act in the best interests of his son or such entrapments may befall them."

"What were you going to say about him anyway?" Isaac fixed a gaze upon his father.

"Well, remember when you first met? You didn't talk much at first, but then once you reached out in friendship, you boys became great friends. It's like that with God. He reaches out to you. If you reach out to Him, you will find a relationship that will last no matter what. So, yes, God is my God, but He's not mine alone. He's Mama's, Relez's, Ober's, and anyone's who will reach out and get to know Him. He'll change your life for the better, which doesn't mean you'll never have problems, but I promise you, you'll never be the same old person again. But you know, son, everyone doesn't want that. Some people want trappings."

"Huh?"

"Trappings, the material fineries in life. That's how Ashur's father got in debt over his head and lost everything. So don't let the things you want make you forget the things you have. The most valuable thing you can ever have is this great God. He makes my soul right."

"What do you mean by that?"

"I can't say that I can explain all about Him. I cannot. But there is some inward connection, and I know that He speaks life and blessings to me. I know that I can trust Him, and having that, nothing else matters. Remind me to tell you about my nephew, Lot—"

"I know, Dad, you've told me about that story plenty of times."

"Oh, it's not just a story, Isaac. Take a field trip out that way some day. You'll know when you get close by the smell. The brimstone. If I think about it, that had to be the scariest day in my life."

"Well, what happened, anyway? I mean, why?"

Abraham laughed to himself for a moment. This time because he welcomed the *why?* "You know the story?"

"I mean I do, but maybe not really…"

Abraham sat down on a long rectangle of flat rock a few feet from the altar. He looked out toward the dots of Relez and Ober and panned the area, not really searching for anything, then he looked down at his sandals, picking at them with his staff. "God blessed my herds. The cattle got big, the sheep were everywhere. Goats, donkeys—Lot's flocks were blooming, too. It got so we couldn't keep track of whose was what. Even the hired hands were fighting about who's sheep drifted onto whose grazing areas. So, I thought we ought to split up—world's a big place, right? So, I gave Lot first pick—any direction, and whatever he chose, I'd do the opposite. That way, we wouldn't have to worry about bumping into each other for a long time to come. *That's* when we came to the great trees of Mamre."

"So what did Uncle Lot do?" Isaac dusted off a spot of ground and sat at the feet of his father.

"Well, that's when things went south—"

"I thought he went—"

"He did. Lot went east. It's just an express…never mind. But, Uncle Lot went east, he did. He liked the plain of Jordan and the big cities along the coast. Parked pretty near to one of them, set his tents up not far from the city gates."

"Sodom, right?"

"Yup. Bad move."

"Why?"

"It was a bad move because Lot was drawn by the trappings. He liked the lights, the activity, and all the goings-on of those cities. They were like big dots on the coast brimming with action, and he let them draw him in. Oh, now I'm not saying that Lot *participated* in the evil going on, but he overlooked it to enjoy the parts he did like. He could have stayed away from there. There were other fertile plains. We've done all right, haven't we? Lot went all the way through the plain and settled on the edge of it, next to them. I'd imagine he might have made acquaintances—he's an engaging guy, became friends, after some point. I'm sure they found him as intriguing as he might have found them. After all, Lot was a new face among them, with his own stories to tell. I'd imaging your uncle Lot may have found for himself a seat at the gate with the city elders after some time. Thing is, when you make friends, you generally have to spend time with them, and their habits rub off on you. And sometimes good habits don't rub as easily as bad, so Lot may have been seeing a whole lot more bad than good. And there musta been a lotta bad because God decided to destroy the lot of them, no pun intended, all five cities."

"And that's when Uncle Lot tried to save an entire city full of people, right?"

"Well, yah, right, but he didn't, and he nearly got himself killed." Abraham rose and returned to the altar. "His wife died before it was over too. But I'll say one thing for old Lot."

"What's that, and what're you doing? Why are you tying my wrists?"

"After that ordeal, he never again fell for the glitter and glamour of the superficial. He's been out on the plains far from urban life making God his everyday priority ever since. This is as we must do, remain obedient to His word…"

"Whaaa? Wait! Wait! What's... Father! I thought you always said that those who don't listen to God perish..."

"Yes..."

"Well, why is it that I'm cooperating and things don't look good for me. I'm looking up at the harvesting knife...oh, I can't look...oh no, oh, ahhh..."

"Isaac! Isaac? Isaac! Come on, son. Come on, now. Here's some water."

"Oh, ah! Ahh!" Isaac gulped the water then quickly checked himself for injury. "What happened? I'm alive? There's no wound! There's no blood!"

"You passed out for a minute, son. You're untied. Aren't you going to get up?"

Isaac jumped up. "What happened? Why did you do that?!"

Abraham replied with his usual calm disposition. "Goodness, you *were* out! Didn't you hear anything?"

"Hear what?" Isaac asked nervously.

"Son, four days ago, the Lord told me to come to this place to sacrifice you—"

"Me? Me? Why *me*?"

"The 'why' is HIS," Abraham answered. "But we are here. And you were at the point of the knife when the Lord spoke out and told me not to harm you. He said, 'Now I know.'"

"Know what?"

"That I would obey HIM and give him even what means the world to me."

"So...all of this was a test?" Isaac asked flatly.

"I guess. But look, He said that if we look, we'll find a suitable sacrifice so—"

"Over there! There's a ram with its horns caught in a thicket!"

"That's it! Let's get it!"

"*Gladly*, but why, I mean, how is it that you would have so easily sacrificed *me*? I mean, without a tear. A flinch?"

"Son, how many times have I told you the story! I was—"

"I know, I know," Isaac interrupted the bound to be long story. "You were like, a thousand years old when you had me."

"No, wise guy, I was a thousand when the Lord *told* me I was going to have you. I was a thousand *and ten*, when you finally arrived. You were a divine gift. He even named you. *I* would have named you *Wise guy*, not Isaac. But anyway, HE is the reason you're here. He said that He would make me the father of many nations. Now, how can He do that if you're dead? So—"

"So you figured that even if you killed me, He'd bring me back to life—"

"And we'd pick up and go home, yes! I told Ober and Relez we'd be right back. *We*—"

"Oh, well that makes sense!"

"Yes, it does. But I am glad God provided a ram in the bush instead."

"Well, *so* am I, Father! But I see another lesson here—that bad things can happen to good people too."

"That's very true, son, but trust in the Lord God, and sooner or later, you'll end up on your feet and the better for the experience! Are you ready to head back?"

"Thought I'd never hear you say that!"

Much and Twice as Much
(Gen. 27)

You can't always get what you want, right? Everyone knows that. You think I'm not asking for a *bad* thing. I'm asking for a *good* thing. I'm asking for what any normal person would want. And truth? Would I ask for more? 'Course! But I'll take one! Who knows, God can do great things. Maybe after He sees how much we love the one, He'll give us another. Life is good. God is good. But I sure would like the one.

So we asked, and we waited. And you can't imagine what it's been like for my wife not being able to have a baby. Now I know what my mother must have felt. I mean, not exactly, of course, but you know what I mean. It's like your life is going along and then something happens. Could be anything—could be your fall, could be you get bitten, could be a bone gets broken. Around here, could be all three! I know a guy who lived not far from here. His boy wandered up a cliff, nothing too steep, after one of their livestock. The boy tripped on a stone, carrying the animal. Broken bones everywhere, poor thing. Never walked again. Whatever that thing is, it punctuates the storyline that is your life. People come around for a while. They bring you food, kind wishes, gifts, a lot more food. Then they stop coming after a while and go back to their own stories. And you, you are left to navigate this, your new routine. Maybe by yourself, to some extent, by yourself, as you reconsider your new storyline: how it's gonna be from here on out.

So I was figuring this is *how it's gonna be from here on out,* and not that it's bad! I married the light of my life, and she's an absolute joy every day. But, oh, to have children… I mean, it's just a natural want.—marriage, children, someone to teach, someone to give your best—whatever it is, to. You know, my father was a whittler. Well, he was a lot of great things, but as a boy, I valued his skill with a small knife and a piece of wood. He'd cut little animal figures for me, and I'd play with them for hours. I'd pretend to ride my camel until I could find where the sun set! Silly things, you know how children can be. To be honest, I'm sure I still have a couple of those little things packed away somewhere. My father also taught a servant and then myself to train our dogs. The dogs help us drive the herds. I loved the work as a young man, and I took it seriously, knowing that I would inherit my father's possessions someday. I would love to teach a young son. Did I say son? A daughter! Daughters are good too! I would love to teach a child to inherit the business. It was a longing inside me, inside both of us, naturally.

We prayed, waited, prayed, you know, God has a timetable that doesn't seem to be anything like mine; but then one day, my wife said, "We're gonna be parents!" After that, every day was sunny, for me at least. That nine months was hard on her. She had so much pain, so much that she prayed. I guess 'cause it wasn't what we were expecting. I guess we thought everything'd be happy and nice, but she was sick, throwing, and kind of miserable most of the pregnancy. She even asked God, "What's goin' on? This isn't what we were expecting. What's all the pain and sickness about?" D'you know what God said to her? *"Surprise, you're having twins!"* He said. That's even better than finally having one, I mean, I thought so. *"Two nations."* He said. Something about them striving, older serving younger. I may have gotten that wrong cause that's not how it is; everyone knows that. The eldest son gets the preference, but anyway. But the part about striving, oh my lands!

Has there been a day of peace since these boys were born? They've been bickering since before they could even talk! Barely able to walk, my wife's servants were breaking up fights between them. I took them with me out to the fields. They were a little young, but I figured it'd keep them busy, get them interested in something besides wringing each other's necks. Teach 'em the business. Neither of them really took to it. This isn't what I expected to happen, not that I'd complain! Just not what a father expects. But at least my elder son took to the outdoors—doesn't care to herd but he loves to hunt, wheh...that's a relief. At least he loves to hunt. Now my younger... ahhh...what does a father do when his child isn't...well...quite what he was hoping. He was a lean boy, sharp-minded, though. The wife took to that one. He stayed back with the women mostly. It was not that we took sides but more like we were trying to manage the tempest that had grown in our laps. And at least the boy's clever enough. I taught him to read, so maybe he can handle the business end... maybe God will give me another child who will be somewhere in the middle of these two...'like normal,' I thought. Ha, ha! But then, what if God gives us another and this one fights worse than the first two?

Esau, my brawny one, is always moving, always on the hunt. What man doesn't appreciate his son coming in every night with a fresh kill slung around his shoulders? I love to sit and listen to his stories, how he tracks down his prey. I mean, this isn't anything I've taught him, and he's very good at it. It's a good thing. It makes a man proud.

*****

He's weak! He's a weak-bellied manipulator, always trying to get something from someone. He's a hanger-on, just ask my father! That guy's been hanging onto me trying to get what's mine since the day we were born. I hate a weak man, always hangin' back with the women. What kind of a man is that? We're out working all day in the hot sun. He's some clever talker back here all comfy in the tents. Always talking, always negotiating his way. I'd really like to just fight him. I'd show him how I talk with my fists...but I know it would hurt my mother. Aaughhh, that guy just *burns* me! At least, my father understands, and he'll do right by me. *I'm* the one who works hard every day. *I'm* the firstborn, so *I* have the rights. I don't care what that weasel says or does. D'you know what he did? Here I am working to provide, and I come in after a long day. I'm tired! I'm so exhausted that I don't know how much longer I could go without a meal. I come back to my father's tents, and there's that low-bellied weasel pretending he can cook. Well, no one beats my mother's stew, but when you're hungry enough, I suppose a bowl of peppered dirt would taste good. I follow my nose to the tent with the cooking pots, drop my gear outside, and I step inside. I'm home, I'm tired, I want peace and comfort for a while. I just asked him for something to eat. I mean, between the *two* of us, *one* of us *does* work...so...a bowl of stew; it's the least he could do. But what *does* he do? What he does! Negotiate! *What? Man, just shut up and give me some stew! My eyes are half shut from exhaustion, but don't think I'm not watching you!* I see him eyeing me, sizing me up, criticizing me up! That's what he does. He's a jealous sort. What nerve! He'd never measure up to me! From here to the stars, that's how different we are. No chance there's anything he could do for me, the weak coward! What a mama's boy. Then comes the talk. The more he talks, I can feel my hand balling up into a fist. Really, don't wanna hear whatever he's talking about. I'm tired, I'm hungry. I want to eat and then I want to rest. I feel myself getting angry at everything about him all over again. *Oh, for all that is good! Just shut up and give me some stew!* I look around, but he appears to be in control over the only readily available meal. I'm about to just shove him out of the way, but Mother sits nearby, watching. I wonder how it is that she favors that coward over me. Well, of course, she denies her favoritism but anyone even an outsider with eyes could easily see how she caters to him. I've heard her and father arguing about us. I'm glad Father's on my side. Father's a real solid man. And, no, I'm not saying he has to hate his other son, but well, I'm just saying he understands *me.* He appreciates me. I know I can trust him and he can trust me to take care of all he's built here. But *him,* oh! Still talking! And finally now...the bottom line, what he wants...*Oh sure, you fool you can have anything! I'm so hungry, just give me a bowl of food!* He wants my birthright! I knew that thin coward was scheming something. I'll tell the fool what he wants to hear! You can't *take* someone's birthright. It doesn't work like that; everyone knows that! Firstborn is firstborn. Period. I'm firstborn; he can't talk his way around that! What a fool. Oh bother you, I'm about to die! You can have anything you want. Just give some of that red stew already! Fool...

*****

Look, I just want what anyone would want—children. What any mother would want—I want peace in my home. I'd like not to feel divided about the boys. But...my husband is so keen on the one boy because he's a good hunter. True, it's a natural gift, and he's a strong young man. Our younger son is my worry, and I admit that I've been overprotective...maybe gone to extremes a time or two, but I'm a mother. I do what any mother would do, right? *Right?*

Like when? Well...like just before Isaac died, I really pulled the wool over him. Really, like, literally. Oh, it's a long story, but now look, you can't just hear what God says and then go off and do whatever *you* want! God said the younger would lead; the older would serve. I knew Issac was gonna stick with the tradition and give everything to the firstborn. I just felt like time was running out, Isaac was coming to his end and...was just trying to protect my son...and... maybe help God out just a little bit. Look...it all turned out, didn't it? Oh the boys are a little heated now, but it'll all blow over, and they'll forget all about it in a day or two. Everything'll be fine.

*****

You know, if you really consider it, resolving conflict with physical force is just unproductive retrograde. I mean, you still end up with bad feelings; the other person still has bad feelings; and nothings resolved in the end. So I just think that compromise is a more satisfactory approach: I have something you want; you have something I want. I might *not* have something you want, but I might just help you realize that you want to give me the something that *you have*...it could happen... Could happen.

So, the way I see it, it's is a matter of utilitarianism. You may have something useful that you will never, ever use. The best case for the situation is to give it to someone who can use it to its potential. For instance, let's say that I somehow come into these, ahem, those few spears lying over there. They're large, with heavy shafts. It would take a strong man to use them to their maximum utility. So, me myself, not being a spear handling type of an individual, I would be inclined to arrange some sort of beneficial exchange. Perhaps live-stock, a musical instrument, a measure of cloth…some exchange which would benefit both parties. That's what I do—negotiate, for the benefit of all. *Intelligent* people can see, that it is for the benefit of the community as a whole…others just struggle with balled fists. You, for example, wouldn't you value parchment, ink, and quill to take notes on all of your investigating? Well, I happen to have a trove stored away that I acquired from a traveler at a fair trade. I'm sure you'll be impressed by the quality, and I'd be delighted to show it to you. Oh, I trust you have coin…

Dearest One

Dearest One,

When I was a boy, I would lie outside on the soft grass and stare up at the sky.

Sooner or later, I thought, *you'll peek around the clouds. I'll see your face. I know its kind. You'll smile at me, your child, your friend.*

I didn't have a lot of friends back then, but somehow, I always knew I had you.

Life was hard, I guess, from my young point of view, but somehow I always knew I had you.

I was loved and hated at the same time. Ten to three on the bad side. Your parents are supposed to love you, pretty much their job. The other ten wouldn't give me a chance. If they had, they'd know that I'm as good as the next guy and a great brother, but they chose hate. Day in and day out, they whispered hate to one another. How they tired of me. My own brothers longed me away as a constant joke until that day. *That day.* The one that turned my life in another direction, starting with *down.* Betrayal by those who can do the most hurt, not strangers but your own. I guess there's no point in asking why. If you wanted me to know, you'd have told me.

I guess with all this hate, the only thing left to do is love. I guess I'm supposed to learn a greater love. There are easier lessons to learn in life. Wouldn't mind anyone of them right here instead, but I guess there's no point in asking. If you wanted me to be learning something else, you'd have shown me.

That first day away from home was hard. Because I told them about the moon and the stars. My anguish and tears were lost on deaf ears. Unthinkable that those boys could be enjoying my culinary fare while they threw me in a hole without a care. I don't mind admitting that I was scared back then, and I might even be a little scared now. And I know they're family 'n all, but while they decided over lunch how to make me go away, I let go of them slightly. I'm holding on to you more tightly, so I'm having some trouble with my task. Somehow I know that I'm supposed to love them through this. I guess there's no point in asking.

Do they think that I don't know how they hate me? None of their anger escapes me. But I ask you, what is my crime? Being born alive? I've often thought of an alternative, but I would miss all the things here that I love. All of your inventions, like water. I can tell you ninety-nine ways to use it! How about trees, another thousand! All the animals you've made—big, small, and miniscule.

The armies of tiny creatures I can barely see. I know they're all working, but to figure it out, it's up to me! I can tell you're a fun person by the things you've made. Music and dance and some stuff Mama mixes called lemonade. Goes down smooth and sweet. Really, it's a delightful treat. I could explore your inventions forever. All kinds of things to do, and that I could be taught, but for the longest, I sat there in that hole for hours and thought things might be all right after they got tired of their game and we'd all just go on home. Now that I look back, I feel badly because I'd fallen off my track. I know I'm supposed to be loving them through this. I sure don't know why their struggle has to hurt me so much, but I guess there's no point in asking.

The hole was cold, dank, and dark. I was coming to the end of my rope waiting for them to let one down. Then we all heard an unusual sound, the far away jingle of a caravan had come 'round. I'd never seen a caravan for myself. But that day, I did and much too close. I was hoisted up out of the hole only to be bound and sold. I became a soulless thing. Dragged away with a string of other souls forlorn, lost and tried who'd seen no day more dismal than that when their hands were tied. The day they ceased being human, at least the sort that mattered. At the vendor's gavel, monies exchanged, and away we went to become someone else's gain. Not the destiny you desired for any man. Subservience, hard work, and misery were to spell out their days and mine. Every day I wondered again, *now, what was my crime?* I thought, how hard was it really, in my early days as a child? Now to have it all back, even the bad ones. But I knew there was no point in asking. I didn't walk that camel's mile for nothing.

What you must think of me, sometimes I shudder to think. How I've wasted or ruined yet another day which should have been spent in some other way. You gave me thoughts. I dared to dream—to the sky and beyond but right here things have gone well out of my control. I can't figure out what you're doing up there any more than I understand the armies of tiny creatures under my feet. It seems that my boldest challenge was the ten boys in my own backyard. I guess I've always known their fear. I hate to call it "hate," but it's definitely not an act of love, the way things have turned, of late. I knew they just didn't know me, and if they'd given me a chance, they'd have been proud to call me their own. They never allowed me even one good day. Their minds were set against me every step of the way. I know I've fallen off track. I'm supposed to love them through this. Sometimes I wish I knew what you were doing up there. If I were there, I'd be building mountains, making snowballs and counting raindrops. Maybe you'll invite me to your home sometime. We could talk about the difficulty of staying on track. And you could tell me what ants really do.

Sitting here in this dark cell, I see a window high up on the wall. It's filled with a ribbon of your blue sky. I guess this isn't really the best time to toss out the question, *why*? Why all the pain, grief, and sorrow? One finds a morsel of joy today, but it'll all be the same misery again tomorrow. What could be the purpose for all this hurt? One day, I'm seeing stars bow down, and now I'm sitting in the dirt.

Can I tell you then what it feels like to be sold? I can't put that low into any words. It's almost as bad as knowing your own brothers don't love you. But sitting here with nothing but time, I realize that you do know about pain like mine. The heartbreak of betrayal and loved ones gone wrong. Your home was violated too. Pardon me, then, for my selfish indulgence. Let's stick together and get through this, shall we? You have the power, the plan, and the vision. I have the trust. It's enough for the mission.

Me, in the meanwhile, I'll have to change my style. Every time I wear an overcoat, it sets me back awhile. It lands me in a hole, and I'm forgotten yet again. Seems like I just can't ever win. I try my best to be honest, true, and right. The unthinkable came against me, and I put up a good fight. I thought the best thing to do was to make flight. To leave the scene, and quickly, before sin found a way to trip me up and grip me. But I'm innocent, sitting here in this cell while the guilty are out there finding life just swell. It's not fair, but I know I won't find all of the answers here. I'm just saying don't forget me. It's been yet another year. It's one thing being wronged but another having your daylight stolen. While I'm down here in this cell, while my years are slipping from me, I will do my best to stay on track. I know I'm supposed to love them through this. There's no point in asking why. If you wanted me to know you'd have told me by now. I'll still tell them about you and the gracious God that you are. I don't think they hear me when I tell them how kind you are so, I guess I'll have to show them how your love is by far the best way to live in this crooked world. If they want to know more, they'll have to meet you themselves. You give every man the power of choice no matter what life hands each of us. That's what I have locked up here in this cell; the power to choose you. How can I explain that? How can some people miss it? Too many questions. In these moments, I only want to tell you that it's okay. It is all right. Whatever happens, I know that everything belongs to you, even this day, so I am all right. You've allowed me some time on this earth, and I've gotten to see a few of the beautiful things that you made, so, thank you for that privilege. That's pretty much what I wanted to say 'cause I'm not sure I'm gonna make it out of this dark cell. I wanted to make sure that I tell you that I love you and I've loved life—at least the part I spent with you, and thanks for all of it.

Your friend,
Joseph

Everybody Loves Ben!
(Gen. 45:24)

Reuben raised an eyebrow, the one he always raised when he got in one of his *matter-of-fact* modes. "We're supposed to argue. That's what brothers do!"

"At least," interrupted Gad. He leaned across two brothers sitting next to him, extending his right arm in front of both to point at Reuben. "That's what *he* thinks because *he* thinks *he's* always right!"

"Well, I wouldn't *think* it if—"

"Okay, okay..." Simeon stood up in between the two as if to stop a fistfight before it began. "Break's over. Get back to work. Besides, we've all heard how this conversation goes, so let's skip it this time!" Asher rose and quietly approached their attendant, Amir—tasked with making sure the eleven brothers received their gifts, grain—packed animals and made ready to return home. It seemed like a simple enough task, but the eruption of shouting and chaos moved Amir from director to bystander.

Why is this so complicated? Why do half of them think they are in charge and the other half push back? Is this normal activity for this family? How does this family ever get anything accomplished? Why are they still not finished packing?

In the midst of the commotion, Asher sought to offer enlightenment to his director, "The argument wasn't an argument, exactly, Amir. It was a continuation of conversation that had started earlier—"

"Sixteen years earlier! I mean, more or less." Naphtali didn't even look up as he spoke, "Ever since the boy was born, he was special, special, special. We may as well have packed up and left, for all that any of us would have been missed."

"So as you can guess," Asher tried to continue, "it was a family issue for a long time. You could say we were all jealous, but from our perspective, we were loved much less. No child should feel less loved by his parents because of another child. What could anyone expect? Joseph was always sure to get an extra helping of food, an extra garment, the easier chore—anything to make him see that he was preferred."

"To make all of us see that the rest of us were not!" Naphtali added, still not looking up from his organizing activity.

Amir studied Asher's face and the rest of the storytellers. On the one hand, this simple packing task was a marvelously joyful event, but their recent fear was not forgotten. Although not fluent in their language, Amir knew that just a few days ago, these men feared for their lives, and now they were in sheer happiness, preparing to go home for a short while, then return as guests of Egypt for the duration of the famine. *Unloved by their parents?*

"Well," Naphtali pulled a final tug on the rope, which bound his packs together. "I'm not saying that we were unloved. But *clearly* not loved as much, for sure."

"Neither were we," Judah interceded, "above reprehension. We were not the best that we could have been."

Judah had grown into a solemn man ever since *that day.* The weight of his sin dragged heavily on his heart, but the years of hidden bitterness were detectable. "We were not loved as much, but there was always work to be done, and that was where we all came in. We weren't good for nothing, you know. Just *not as good as.* Would you want to grow up knowing that you're perhaps not unloved—just not loved as much as another particular sibling?" Judah reasoned with the attendant as he carefully packed his back sack. He was very particular about what went bumping around on his shoulders and back on long walks. Judah got it that he didn't handle the situation in the best possible spirit. He should've been more accepting of whatever God was doing. He was too busy thinking about his small world. He got it.

The attendant, saw continuity in that they all agreed on what the problem was and that they were truly remorseful about every aspect of the event. He sat attentively, head and eyes bouncing from one brother to another as each added his critical piece of the story. Judah rolled his garments carefully, as tightly as possible. They would have to fit in on the bottom and then some of the grain would have to pack on top, and he always kept a skin of water fixed to the outside of the pack for easier access.

"So, we'd been angry and envious for years and for no particular reason, you know. Can a man choose his parents? So are we to blame that our father loved our mothers less than his mother?"

Levi sat cross-legged on a fine layer of straw, leaning on his already packed items as if they were a huge pillow. "All of our lives we were treated like second hand offspring. If we got one, Joseph got two. If we got nothing, you could be sure that whatever there was to be had was given to Joseph. We furnished the labor and carried the blame. How much of that can anyone take from childhood on?" He spread his arms to each side, palms down and facing backward, legs stretched ahead. "He was always spying on us. Everything we did, he ran and told our father. We didn't know that father had sent him to report on us. We just saw a spy. A nosy spoiled brat of a spy. And then the dreams. That was the last straw!"

"Definitely the last of many last straws!" Naphtali added, still struggling with his pack.

"Tal, we are gifted with pack animals to help with the load. Don't put so much on your own back." Dan came from across the room to help his brother.

Naphtali's gray eyes met the attendant's, Amir, dark eyes. "The dreams. It was as if Joseph rubbed his fanciful, *I'm better than you*, in our faces with these dreams, and it just made me *so angry!*"

"We thought," Dan interjected, momentarily shifting his attention from the task of packing, to the listening attendant. "We *thought*, he was rubbing a 'better than you' attitude in our faces. And we had already had sixteen years of that from our father. And it wasn't just that because, even before Joseph was born, we all seemed to detect disappointment from our father. I mean, he didn't abuse us, but a child knows when he isn't loved and valued for all that he is. Ten of us all felt like we weren't exactly what Father wanted. But we were useful around the property, as Judah said. We *thought* our favored brother was rubbing his preferred status in our faces, but he wasn't. Now, granted, he could have been more discreet—"

"Yeah, like keeping his wild dreams to himself!" Simeon piped from his spot.

Dan continued, "Yeah, but see how wrong we were. We all were, to accuse Joseph. The dreams were from God, as we can all plainly see now, and they've all come true." His voice betrayed the exhaustion in his soul. The staged secret "death" of their younger brother took a toll on all the brothers these many years. Dan knew the early gray in his beard was caused by the stress of the sin that the brothers tried to cover over. He wasn't the only one. Rueben had been bitter and joyless ever since *that day*. The day that Judah talked them down from outright killing Joseph. As they pondered *What now, then?* the caravan's bells came around seeming to answer their question. So, they sold the boy. Reuben planned to go back to the pit and pull little brother out and have a good, long talk with him about being such an overbearing goodie-goodie. But when Reuben returned to the pit, the boy wasn't there. Impossible to get out un assisted, he later learned that the brothers had sold him to a passing caravan. A terrible, impossible twist of events. It had gone horribly wrong and completely out of his hands. The years of angry talk that turned into a plot, the plan that turned into a heinous crime. The deed that had to be covered up, and on and on the trouble went for years afterward. A crime against God, a brokenhearted father, and for what? Reuben always felt that he should have been in charge of things, being eldest. Nothing should have escalated to this point. This thing chased his sleep away, kept his joy at bay, and he became the insufferable critic. But who could respect him knowing the secret? He became critical of everything anyone did partly because no one took his advice, but none of the other nine brothers respected his efforts at leadership. He tried to stop the crisis with their sister Dinah. But Simeon and Levi would hear nothing of it. After that incident, the family lived in fear of tribal reprisal, which would have completely wiped them out. Rueben was a bitter man forged out of his own lies. Each of the brothers could claim some calamity from the coverup. Now, all these years later, everything coming out in the open and being forgiven by

Joseph was the burden of a lifetime lifted from their shoulders. God had restored them to each other and provided for them so that they could survive the famine.

Zebulon preferred his new self-declared title as optimist. "Because now we have grain to carry us and we're going to get our father and then come back to Egypt. And that's how the story ends. Besides, I was the only one who recognized Joseph before he revealed himself."

Issachar dropped his back sack and grabbed at his chest, pretending as if he was suffering a fatal attack. "What? *You* stood closer to him than any of us and never saw that it was him. We hadn't seen him in nearly sixteen years. None of us recognized him…"

"Well, I could have," Judah injected, "but I was so occupied with negotiating for the sake of Ben.

"*You? You?*" Reuben shot back. "*I* was the one who—"

Simeon spun around, pointed a long finger at his elder brother, "If it hadn't been for you, none of this would have happened!"

"At least the bad part!" Naphtali added to soften the blow.

These boys had been mad so long that no one person could really claim the 'plan gone wrong'. They had all been wishing that Joseph would go away, disappear, or just die, for so long, that somehow…somehow, they found themselves at that point.

That's it, I'm in!
In for what?
You know what. Count me in!
It's got to be done. That dreamer's gone too far.
I wish he were just…
Him and that pretty, pretty coat.
Fall in a river!
A lion!
A bear!
Or at least, just GONE!
Fake the river!
Can't fake a river, you idiot!
But…

That day, it was as if they all saw themselves wildly running toward a cliff and they dared to do it. They *jumped* and found it was only a ridge and they landed on their feet. That was when they'd thrown Joseph in the hole. It was daring, bad, and no one had really hurt the little wretch, only taught him a lesson about spying. But Reuben was right; their cruelty at that point should have been more than enough. When they were bitter enough to throw their little brother in a hole, sully his coat, hear him crying for help and still sit down and enjoy their lunch—shouldn't that have been the point where the score was finally even and all the frustration released? That deep, empty pit should have filled them with guilt. But somehow they found themselves daring to *run another cliff* and consider murder. It was Judah, not Reuben, who mitigated the crime. A paltry effort to protect his younger brother, but at least he steered away from the *crime of Cayin*. So that day, ten dined on lunch, then nine sold their young brother as a slave to a passing caravan. What could they have been thinking seeing his face, his agony, hearing his cries? What stones had they for hearts in those moments? When the caravan's sounds faded in the distance, they must have set about to devise a story to tell their father. *A lion! See the blood on his coat!* His father must have rolled the tattered coat up and hidden it among his things. *A lion? And not one brother came to his aid? The wretched lot of them.* Perhaps he slept with the shredded coat under his pillow in many years of silent mourning for the beloved son of his beloved wife. How so very bitter life is.

But God.

Reuben, done packing, walked through the handiwork of the brothers, inspecting their work. "And God took the evil that we did to that boy. We good as killed him but God not only turned it to amazing blessing for Joseph, but also He turned it into life for us! My head has turned gray from the guilt of that day, but at least now I know that God has forgiven me."

And Joseph—after all of this?, queried the director.

"The same!' Naphtali added. "After all these years and the crimes he's endured, he's still kind, gentle, and still has a sense of humor!"

Reuben injected, "Yeah, Joseph said he never wears an overcoat. Every time he does, it lands him in confinement! You know, I was the one who nurtured his sense of humor…sure did. I started telling him jokes when he was just five years old…"

Amir's eyes rolled around in their sockets. *Is he serious?*, he thought to himself.

"Yep," Issachar answered Amir's facial expression. "He sure is…"

"Hold it! HOLD ITTTT!" Amir was exhausted just trying to keep up with the storytellers. He understood why they were always arguing; there were just too many of them not to. He noticed that Benjamin worked quietly and steadily throughout the entire morning. "What about him?"

"*Well, everybody loves Ben!*" The brothers chimed in unison and then continued their hectic dialogue.

Amir asked Benjamin what he thought of the events leading up to this day. Benjamin replied, "I am content. I am loved by all of my family. My brothers love each other. This is their way. I am content. It *is* going to be a long trip home though, but this ruckus is all I know! Didn't you notice that Joseph said, 'Don't quarrel on the way'?"

The Sky Is Falling
(*Job 1–2*)

"**F**ire! I am on fire!" Elian fixed his eyes on the cloud above him hoping for some measure of the peace it seemed to possess. He clenched his eyes shut from the piercing pain radiating down his leg, once slightly squinting as if to check that the peace cloud was still there. It wasn't working for him. Would the madness of this day ever end? After everything, now this unspeakable pain! "What are you doing there? What's that you're pouring in there?" Elian asked, thinking that right now, fainting would be considered wholly acceptable in his case. He sat up with some effort, trying his best to glare at his friend through the sweat and clumps of dirt hanging onto his eyelashes. He rubbed his eyes with roughed, sooty hands but that only spread more dirt, making it harder to see.

Raim continued working on Elian's damaged leg. The gash was deep and nearly the length of the thigh. After he picked out large bits of wood, he poured water over the wound and then some substance that just felt like fire. "This will kill the poisons in your blood. I hope. And anyway, I'll have to stich it closed." Elian's back found the hard ground again in a hurry. Looking straight up toward his peaceful cloud, he mumbled, "He said, *I hope…* and *then* he said *stitch*, and all in the same moment." Elian closed his eyes. It was going to be a long moment.

"What happened anyway?" Raim asked studiously, as if not a detail of this story would be lost to disinterest as he wandered around the yard picking up very small twigs, enough to ignite a fire. Having done so, he heated a thin pin with a tiny head on it and set the needle aside. A thin length of dried animal sinew tied to the top of the needle would have to be woven through the broken skin across the wound to close it up.

"What happened, indeed!" recanted Elian, his eyes still shut. For sure, he couldn't really know. He tried to go into a corner of his mind to get the story, but just then, every corner was screaming about a needle and thread running through the already swelled skin on his injured leg. He couldn't find the story or a corner that sheltered him from the pain. Either of which would have been well received.

Unable to escape his physical torment, Elian resigned himself to his immediate fate but thought conversation might be some buffer. He decided to start with the facts and see where that led him. And there was one curious fact. "Well, first of all, it was a beautiful day. It was a gorgeous and a regular day, and that's a fact! Just the right sun, just the right shade, just the right warmth. A lot of business about the house because of the birthday party—food kept coming out of the kitchen, lots and lots of groups of people dropping in and out." Elian's voice drifted off.

"And then..." Raim encouraged as he threaded another length of sinew.

"And then... I don't know...it was crazy, like the world just went mad for a while. I mean, everyone was having a good time. Oh, the place was packed for the birthday celebrations! Food, food, food! Drink, music, kids, uncles, aunts, cousins, neighbors—everyone laughing, eating, playing, dancing, and then the bottom just dropped out of the sky..."

Raim missed nothing, both engrossed in his surgery and in Elian's story, but that stopped his makeshift needle just at a halfway point through a bit of flayed skin. "What's that supposed to mean? And hold on, this might hurt!" A tug pulled the finely drawn dried intestine "thread," through the layer of swelled skin. Raim ran the needle from one side, across to the opposite, and back again. He worked all the way down the length of the injury as quickly as he could trying not to aggravate the throbbing mess but realizing that he had to finish the sealing job or he'd have to wash the wound all over again. He graciously ignored his friend's choice words, and kept him engaged in conversation, optimistic that it would all be over in a moment—a long moment. Hopefully, this would heal well, and in a few months, no one would ever know this injury had ever occurred, save the scar, but those make the best stories. It's best to be thorough with these things, and Raim was nearly done. Anyway, it was a good opportunity to try figuring out what was going on on this otherwise factually perfect day. "Whaddya mean, 'the bottom dropped'?" he asked again.

Elian's face, already paled from his impromptu surgery, seemed to empty of all color. His eyes, still closed, seemed crowded in the midst of his facial grimace. Raim glanced up from his sewing, quite pleased with the outcome of his handiwork, and waited expectantly for some hearty gratitude. He looked again at Elian and could not figure where he was by the distant look on his face, but it was a frightful place. He gently shook Elian's shoulder both to bring back his presence of mind and let him know the sewing was finished. Elian opened his eyes, studied the peace cloud, and then struggled to sit up to inspect his newly repaired leg. He continued quietly, "All the sudden, a dust storm right there! The beautiful day turned to black darkness, and a violent wind whipped everything about with a horrible noise. I couldn't see much. There was dirt kicked up all about. The wind was so loud that I could barely hear the screams of the guests. The wind pulled the roof off the house. The thatch and dried mud flew around and around in a howling circle. People were running through the house trying to hide while the wind, ripping around in a circle pushed against the house. The main beams swayed until they gave in. The house collapsed on everyone inside. The wind picked up everything and slung it about, and I mean *everything*. The livestock flew about the property in the great circle. Once the roof was gone, the barn rooves too, everything inside the houses and barns were caught up into the circle, and everything outside was thrown in it. The courtyard's stonewalls were knocked down, adding bits of rock to the rotating airborne mess. I ran to the back courtyard and through the rear gate. There's an old dry well. We don't use it anymore. I slid down in there quick! The howling wind was terrifying, but from the low point in the ground, I couldn't believe what I was seeing.

"In front of me was the madness of a sudden and vicious storm. People were screaming and running to find safety, struck by stones or timbers or caught in the swirl and flung to the ground. Carts, wagons, stones were flying round and round like they were caught in an invisible funnel. But behind me was a perfectly blue, tranquil sky. This dust storm didn't come from the east or west. It didn't seem to come from *anywhere*. It was just *here*! Like some band of enemy attacking us, but there was no one—no one but the wind, and the vicious wind stopped as quickly as it started. It just *stopped*. Everyone was dead, even the poor animals died. There wasn't a sound—no fear, no screams, no crying, no wind. The silence was as frightening as the noise was, but I climbed out of the well. Slowly, I walked back to the courtyard. It was no more. The house and courtyards were heaps of stones, timber, dead animals, and, worse, dead men. All the women and children too. I searched as I could through the rubble, but most of it was too heavy to move by myself. I came back to the master's home to tell him what happened and to get help. But they're all dead. All…dead! Augh, my leg!"

"I think it's going to heal just fine," Raim consoled.

"I had to run back. All of the livestock and animals died. There was no one living, man or beast, save myself and I had to come back and tell the man that every last one of his children is dead. How horrible a day for me to bear such a burden! But, what happened to you? What are you doing here anyway?"

Raim finished cleaning his tools with eyes fixed on them as he spoke. "Well… I was among the farmhands working the fields when raiders came and killed the men who were working with me. They stole all of the livestock, except what they couldn't catch. They drove off in the opposite direction. Me? I'd gone back after one little straggler lamb, which was still at the creek. I heard a stampede and saw a cloud of dust, and the hooves of frightened livestock below it, charging in my direction. Trying not to get trampled, I rolled aside and was taken for dead. The thieves rode off and left the fields scorched, the men dead—all but me. I'm the only one who survived. Like you, I came back to the master's house to report what happened and get help, but when I got back, I found him in a heap of emotion out front, and you here a bloodied mess, out back." Raim lifted his gaze toward another. "So you there, Nessin, why are you here?"

Nessin, still visibly shaken by his ordeal, couldn't stop his eyes from darting from one man to another to surveying the courtyard then checking the house as if everything and everyone was really real. As if whatever just happened to him was confirmed by the looks and stories of the first two men. Survivors they all were, but of what? "I don't know. I just know that fire came down from the sky and killed the sheep and the herders. I came back for…well, you know the rest."

"For help," Elian finished his sentence softly. "There's no help. The sky is falling! We're being decimated, but by whom? Or what? Tell your story. Maybe we can put it with ours to make some sense of all of this."

Nessin fixed his eyes on Elian, as if leaning on him for strength. He continued on in fear to tell what he saw. "Well, I was drawing water for the camels and the other men I work with. One minute I was watching the bucket going down into the well, and the next minute, I heard wild shouting. I looked around and saw bandits running everywhere. We were surrounded—the Chaldeans! They split into three bands to surround us and got us from nearly every direction. They rounded up all of the camels and tried to kill all the men. They died except for me. I grabbed the rope which held the water bucket and shimmied down into the well. I hid there until the raid was over and then somehow I made it back here. I was coming for help, too, but now I see there is something more happening here today. How could so much calamity fall upon one man in one day. May the LORD of our master be merciful in our time of weakness." Nessin's head sank as if his neck could no longer carry its weight. "My two elder brothers, killed!" he cried. There was no shame in his crying, so Nessin cried, and the other two survivors shared his grief with tears that crept around the bulwarks of men's strength meant to hold them back.

*****

The woman wasn't old, neither was she young, but this newly birthed sorrow put a heavy grief on her. It bent her neck, stooped her shoulders, and pulled down on her cheeks and the outer edges of her eyes. She was an unkind person but so new to this sort of misery that she did not negotiate it, but let it swallow her entirely.

Her incessant wailing! The men couldn't wish her silent because who among them had ever endured such grief to say it was too much? And what man really understood women anyway? The only thing to be certain of was that it was of no comfort. None that the three of them

could see anyway. Elian, trailing behind the other two, noted them staring at the woman as if they had trapped a bear in their barn. What to
do with her? Undecided, all three made a wide girth around her to the
curious form out beyond the house. Still walking, the two slowed down
to allow Elian's limp to catch up. A safe proximity to each other and
cautious distance from the objective, they approached its shifting form
slowly. Relief, surprise, sorrow. Raim saw him first, the master! It was
him—tall, strong, handsome Job. He'd torn his clothes, throw ashes all
about, mostly on himself from the head down and sat in a slump. He
wept inconsolably, and the three men heard the names of each of his children now and again in the midst his sorrow. Job, north of the house—
and the woman out back wailing to the south. The woman seemed to
bear her pain with an anger the three men found inapproachable. The
master was a gentle soul. Even in his sorrow and look, not only his soul
was in agony, but also his flesh rose in red pustules from head to toe! So
there was their master, man of wealth, family, servants, and life as good as
anyone could want it. Now he was reduced to a lump of flesh sitting in
a heap of ashes offended by the putrefaction of blisters that bubbled up
from beneath his own skin. He sat near a tree whose few branches offered
occasional shade, the only consolation anyone could give. Job looked out
staring at—what? The future? The past? The present indicated nothing
more than the eruption of boils that occasionally burst percolating thick
fluid that leached around the fragile shell of their adjacent domes. The
woman of misery, his wife, had left Job a pot of water and a cup with
which to drink. He smashed the cup against a stone and used a small
piece of the broken pottery to scrape away the crusting, cracked film of
the pustules. The fluid leaked slowly across skin, this way or that. He
scraped it up and slapped the edge of the pottery against a stone, flinging
the substance away. The pustules yielded more and more still. Only dust
caking over an open sore abated the puss. The sores covered every part of
his skin—the soles of his feet, legs, arms, and face. Sometimes he would
stop his scraping to stare or weep, but Job remained out in the open air,
out in front of his home, in an ash heap and a world of questions.

*****

128

The three men sat on a ridge overlooking a plain that left the house, barns, and ash heap of a man seeming like a few small dots on the horizon. Elian sat on a smooth boulder, grateful to stretch out his leg. The injury had begun to heal, to his relief, but the scar remained as predicted. He was grateful to be walking. He felt compassion for Job's plight. "See how he remains! How fragile our lives are! Still an ash heap, still in sorrow with flesh beleaguered. His friends come to comfort him, yet he becomes more broken. The woman grows more sullen and angry in her wreck of a home. She is bitter and hard. He is humble and broken."

Next to him, Nessin collected a handful of pebbles and skipped them down the hill, single file. When he ran out, he stretched his arms out and grabbed more handfuls of pebbles. "But she's right! She had every right to be angry. She's not deserving of the hard hand which she has been dealt!"

Raim borrowed pebbles from Nessin's collection, also skipping them down the hill. "Well, didn't Job, too, suffer the same loss? Why is it that he mourns but she curses? And hear what she says? She talks like a crazed woman. Can a man raise a hand or tongue against God? She grows angry and more broken. He, in his brokenness, cries out to God. Job is trusting God. He seems to know that God will work everything out in the end and that He is just. So, everyone knows bad things can happen to good people. Does this woman think herself exempt? Look; the harder life gets, the tighter Job clings to his God. You know, Job always says, "'*The* LORD *gives and the* LORD *takes away.*' Maybe God will answer his hurt. Maybe God will answer him."

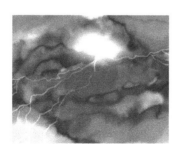

The Locust Years
(Gen. 37–50)

I am a stonecutter. My father was a stonecutter. My father's father, well, actually, *he* was a sheep herder. And of much sheep, indeed! Well, I can't count that high, but I can count to a hundred; and if I could count more, I would have to because my grandfather had many, many sheep. And goats, which he kept for milk and sold for skins. Camels and the like. Here in Goshen, camels are essential for travel in and about Egypt—the long dry distances between reservoirs. Not that I know from personal expertise, of course, but the trade caravans come through routinely with those lanky workhorses, heavily laden. Me myself, I've never left Goshen. I was born here. Not Egyptian, but we here are Jews. Well, it's a long story how I came to be a Jew born in Egypt, a slave.

It's such a long story, in fact, that I'll start somewhere that's not the beginning. I'll start with my great-grandfather, Israel. His name used to be Jacob, but I said I'm starting not at the beginning, so here's a good spot:

Israel, my great-grandfather, had a son named Levi. This was his third son. Well, hang on, then, I'd better back up just a bit! Suffice to say that Israel had two wives, which ought to be a story to be told in itself! That's not the way *Israel* wanted things but rather how they turned out. And the wives, being women, were incessant rivals; and even worse, they were sisters! The elder of the two was rather plain, but God blessed her with a fruitful womb. The younger sister was very beautiful, and the apple of my great-grandfather's eye, his true love, but she was barren in the womb. The elder wife bore sons, always hoping that this would make her husband love her, knowing as she did that she was wedded to him by trickery and not by his choice. As she gave birth, the younger wife who was barren, gave the husband her handmaid in order to start a family. (Shouldn't that be yet another story in itself?) In jealousy, the elder sister gave *her* handmaid to the husband in order to give her even more children. Finally, the younger wife bore a son whom she called Joseph, and so on went the birthing by wife or handmaid for the sum of eleven sons, most on the part or behest of the elder wife.

Now here's the sticky part: the beloved younger wife finally became pregnant with her second child, but it was a treacherous carriage that killed her. The child survived—a son, a most beloved son, of the beloved wife. So great-grandfather Israel had eleven sons and then the last child, number twelve, so entwined with the mortality of his beloved deceased wife. These two sons of the beloved wife were his consolation, his balm, his joy. The older son of the beloved wife was lavished with the best of everything great-grandfather had. Well, now you tell me: how would you feel if you were the bready crust and not the plump pudding of the pie? Exactly…so after years of watching the elder beloved boy, Joseph, being overly doted upon, the ten sons—who were not of the beloved wife—grew to hate him. They excluded Joseph from their games, their secrets, their clubs—everything in the lives of boys that made it special to be a boy, they excluded him. All ten unanimously turned a hard shoulder, cold heart, or a coarse tongue to Joseph. Now, believe me, this boy Joseph didn't make it any better for himself! He would tag along uninvited, which made the ten even more angry! Worse, Joseph would report their every mischief to their father! No one likes a rat, eh? Sposeph, they'd call him, pegging him as *the spy*. *Spy* plus *Joseph* equals *Sposeph*. See? Eh, well, anyway, he kept tagging along uninvited in most of their activities, or he'd at least show up at some point to check up on them. The other boys didn't want a "monitor," even though it had often been their father who had sent Joseph out to check on the ten; they didn't care. They blamed Sposeph. Now, did young Joseph choose who his mother was? Do any of us? Here we are as God calls us, and we do what we can with what He equips us. Now, just as an aside, let me tell you that this can be a lot, if you walk with the God who created you. But God equips you for every good work so you don't have to be afraid to face whatever task He gives you. If He tells you to do it, He'll make sure you're able! The ten boys of the elder wife were too busy being jealous and mischievous to walk in love. They set a trap for failure and then walked right into it themselves. Here's what happened:

Remember I told you they called him a spy. Well, they had other names for Joseph. One of them was *the dreamer*. Well, one day, Joseph—*Sposeph*—eh, well, anyway, he tagged along to report on the ten's activities. While he was amongst his ten brothers, he told them about a dream he had.

We all had sheaves of grain, and your sheaves bowed down to mine... Well, *that* fell over like a drunken camel! Rueben rolled his eyes at Simeon who rolled his eyes at Levi to Judah and on down the line. But Joseph Sposeph wasn't finished; He told another dream: *and there were ten stars, the sun and the moon, and they bowed down to one star...* oh, the unmitigated gall of that boy. Naphtali told their father, and even their father reprimanded Joseph for his lack of decorum. How disrespectful to suggest that even Father and Mother would bow down to Joseph! Why didn't he just keep his wild dreams and visions to himself anyway? And what was he doing there anyway? Spying on them again? As usual? The brothers stoked already hot flames of anger, but Joseph didn't seem to notice. He continued to be the unassuming, ever-friendly, ever-loving, and ever-spying brother. Shortly after, the ten were off with their flocks in a field, tossing the ball of hot anger around.

I'm so tired of Joseph this and Joseph that.
He gets the best of everything, always has.
It's like we don't even matter to Father.
Reuben's the oldest, and Joseph is treated better than him!
The nerve of that...boy!
Oh, brothers, your sheaves bowed down to mine.
He even angered Father with his dreamer stories.
We ought to kill him for that.

Sudden dead silence. Reuben looked at Simeon who looked at Levi who looked at Judah who looked at Dan. Everyone looked at Naphtali. Naph looked at Gad, who looked at Asher, Issachar, and Zebulon.

No.

Come on, boys!

Wha, wha, what're, what're we gonna do?

You know what needs to be done. We all know.

Are we all in agreement then to be rid of this dreamer boy once and for all?

Let's…do it!

Young Joseph, largely undisuaded by the mechant nature of his brothers, continued to share with them and attempt to be part of them. He was of very sharp mind, very creative, and loved to tell stories. Usually he told them to no one because the others would simply walk away whenever he began to expound. Joseph would stand before his departed audience and continue to orate. His full-blood little brother Ben was Joseph's only devoted audience. Indeed, Joseph's only devoted friend. To little brother, Joseph told stories about being a caravan leader driving a dozen camels loaded with gold, spices from far places, finely loomed cloths, and precious metalsmithings across the sands. He wove stories of taming lions and bears, leading them with only a nose ring!

What a dreamer!

Where does that boy get this stuff?

And more importantly, who cares?

"Why does he always have to follow us around. Why can't he get it when we say, 'Get lost!'?"

"Let's ditch him. We can out run him! Let's split up and meet at our secret hiding place."

"We'll have to make a new one. The snitch found that one."

"Now the little spy will tell father everything we say and do."

"What a loser, oh, here he comes again."

"Everyone, just be quiet."

Silence never daunted Joseph because he was his own sunshine! He made his own music. Every day he was as chipper as a yellowbird tugging on a worm! For Joseph's part, it wasn't that he didn't know their hearts; indeed he did and always hoped to see a change of love. But he decided in his heart to be an example of love, which the ten never caught on to. That was a heavy burden for so young a lad to take on against the current, eh?

Well, the ten hatched their scoundrel's plot, lured their half-brother Joseph to a remote area far from their father's tents and tied the poor fellow up quite tightly! The eldest of the ten, Reuben, had second thoughts about the plot to kill his little half-brother, even as annoying as he was. So he suggested they lower Joseph down into an old dry well, which they did, and had a fine lunch while the boy was down in the nasty hole. Rueben went off having planned to come back and rescue the boy afterward and have a good talk with him about being so annoying. Unfortunately, things changed, and Reuben's secret plan was no longer viable. While Judah successfully convinced the other brothers not to kill Joseph, just then a caravan rode through and the brothers on a whim decided to sell Joseph to the caravan to be rid of him. Reuben didn't know about this. When he went back to the well to rescue Joseph, he couldn't find the boy! Imagine how horribly Reuben felt to have failed! And worse to later find out that the others sold their own brother as a slave. He had no way of finding the boy, or if he had, how could he get him back now? How horribly the whole plan had turned out!

Joseph, after a cheerless slave's trek to Egypt, stood bound in an auction until he was purchased and delivered to the house of an Egyptian official, Potiphar. This official saw that the living God was with Joseph, blessing everything he did. Potiphar soon put Joseph in charge of all of his affairs. All of that went well until Mrs. Potiphar falsely accused Joseph of attempted adultery, which promptly landed Joseph in prison. No matter, the living God was with my grandfather Joseph, even in the depths of prison. The prison warden soon put Joseph in charge of his affairs there! A few years later, God made the pharaoh bring Joseph out of the low place of prison and made him sit in a high place, the second highest authority in all the land of Egypt! Pharaoh had a dream wherein God warned of a coming famine. Joseph explained the meaning of the dream to the pharaoh. The Pharaoh put Joseph in charge of everything to ensure that the nation would have enough supplies to make it through the famine.

Well, now, this famine reached Joseph's family back in Canaan, and the father, Israel, sent the boys to Egypt to buy grain. Joseph was about thirty years old by the time the brothers arrived in his court. He did not speak to them in Hebrew or call attention to himself, so the brothers did not even recognize him. Joseph was the second highest official in the land, so when the brothers came before him to state the nature of their business, guess what; they bowed down, just like those sheaves of grain did years before in Joseph's dream! Joseph eventually got the entire family to Egypt, and guess what, Father and Mother and all the brothers bowed down, just like the sun, moon, and stars did so long ago in Joseph's dream! Once Joseph revealed himself to his family and had forgiven all, he said, "You meant it for evil, but God turned it to good!"

God, the Living God, was with great-grandfather Israel's clan. The seventy or so persons whom Joseph brought to Egypt settled here in Goshen and boomed! In this way, the line of Israel was preserved alive. The Living God blessed their hands. Over time, their wealth grew, so much so that they prospered more than most of the Egyptians here. God blessed them with many children. They swelled into a great populous, so many foreigners doing so well in someone else's land. After some time, the Egyptian pharaoh, died, the one who knew Joseph. A new pharaoh came on the scene. This one didn't know the Living God. Well, now, I don't mean that he didn't know *about* the Living God because Egyptians are fine recordkeepers. He knew about the years of plenty and how Joseph had stored up all the grain so that the entire nation had food for the following seven years of famine and enough extra to sell as well! The whole world knew about that! But this new pharaoh chose to follow his culture's gods, not giving deference to the Living God. As the years passed and we prospered, the pharaoh and his advisors became afraid of us; we were so many and had so much. They were afraid that we would take over their country and perhaps enslave them. That's when the pogroms began. Egyptian laws took away our wealth, our livelihood, our right to govern ourselves—everything, all virtually overnight. One decree came swiftly after another, each stripping us of more of our rights of personhood and self-determination. If you are not a person, then your God-given rights cannot be violated, can they? They don't exist. We began not to exist as persons but as property of the government. We became property of the private citizens of Egypt, the Egyptian ones, that is. The ruling power turned their army on us, holding us at bay by the tip of the spear. We became prisoners, then in short order, slaves. Since that time of the pogroms, we have worked with Egyptian whips on our backs and guards surrounding our district. We cannot leave, not alive. At first we worked for the smallest of subsistence, then. Now, we just worked for our lives, just to stay alive one more day. We have no rights;—we are worth less than the cattle, but for the labor our hands are capable of. But now, remember the Living God, He rescued my great-grandfather Joseph from the hands of his own brothers, pulled him from a low place and set him on a high place. These generations later, we have been brought to a low place. I am now imprisoned in a cast system of slavery, which is all that my children have to inherit. That and the dreams of Joseph, my grandfather.

I cannot see ahead. I begin work while it is still dark and return to our hovel late in the day. Tomorrow I will do the same thing. My wife goes to the dispensary for our rations of food and water. We try to keep a small garden for food. It seems as if those who were most intimidated by our prosperity are now our most devoted persecutors. They lavish the whip and put more and more unreasonable loads upon us. I have seen many of my family tire out and die. My children are of marrying age, but the only future they see is bondage. I remember the dreams of Joseph. I remember the pit. I remember the prison and the butler he helped out who forgot him yet another two years. God restored Joseph in His time. God will restore these years to me in His time. God will redeem His people. He did not preserve us through all of that famine for nothing. He hears us. He hears our cry, and He will redeem us. We are covenanted with Him; He with us. Our forefather, Abraham, is the grandfather of Israel. He heard God, listened to God, and obeyed

God! Abraham said *yes* to God. Things may look grim now, but we are His own. The LORD will rescue us! He will!

The Student
(*Exod. 2–3*)

W ell, here's the thing; it wasn't like that. You don't understand. Everyone thinks it's so easy, but it isn't. Well, no, I didn't have to do tha—no, no. But *everyone* is watching you *all* the time, and everything that you *do* must be done perfectly the first time, every time! Can't ever make a mistake or your reward is scorn. Scorn searches for weakness, and weakness lives for a plot. So in order to stay alive, one has to be the best at everything, and who is? Athleticism was not my thing. Never was. And I was average, at best, at the fight. Better at numbers. So, eventually, I was given administrative duties. But it was more than just all of that. I was *the open secret*. At least if you knew, you weren't supposed to talk about it, but who does that? And of course, everyone *knew!* I didn't even look like anyone else in the family! So, the adopted child hits it big! May as well been the six o'clock headline! Not just adopted but scooped out of the slave class and into the royal house! Who does *that* happen to? And bet me that there were plenty, especially in the royalty, who didn't want it to have happened at all! Well, at least no one could say that I manipulated my way to the top; I was only a baby! Even so, as soon as I was old enough to figure out what was going on, I always slept with one eye open, so to speak. I mean, as soon as I was old enough to understand the ramifications of who and where I was. I mean, that's a lot for a young person to handle, but I did all right. I worked extra hard as if I needed to prove that I could earn my lot in life. I tried hard to be the king's son. That's a hard thing to do, especially when I knew there were others, lots of others, who would do anything to have my spot.

Anything. All the while, the humble family who started me out never left my heart, not one day.

Anyway, since business was more of my thing, I got to be the logistics guy, eventually, over nearly everything—how cumbersome that was. I had a couple of full-time copiers just copying everything—notes, receipts, invoices, orders, trade transactions, caravan schedules, trade routes, profits, losses. Records for this, records for that. And then I had another bunch of guys down the hall who archived the stuff—purchases, sales, projections, construction estimates, plans, permits. Those were the least interesting tasks, so for me, they were perhaps, the staff that I appreciated the most. Then the human resources—labor lists, pay rates, immigrant workers, child workers, indentured workers, slave workers. Overwhelming but droll. Are you seeing an exciting life? But this is what everyone wishes they had—*that guy's life!* My life. Not so glamorous then, is it? Well, I'm not even done yet… I haven't mentioned the incident report detail. I usually saved that pile of scrolls for the end of the day. Sort of an "end of the day" news blurbs. Most were serious. Some were actually amusing to hear and correlate for official records like Guy A trades some junk to Guy B, who discovers that it's not junk but treasure, sells it to Fella C, making handsome profit, and then Guy A wants it back. Fistfight ensues. Or: Three boys put croc eggs in tutor's lunch bucket…eggs hatched at noon… Or: Woman defrauds customer by putting stones in soup kettle thereby increasing the volume. Or: Snake found in village bakery, patrons found outside. Amusing. Something at least to remind me that there was some pleasure in my dull but pampered existence.

Sometimes I went out to the work sites. It was unpleasant business, usually delegated down to field agents whom report back to…*someone*…handles that kind of thing…in my office. I wasn't required or desired to go, but I did. Sometimes it seemed there was a death a day at the construction sites. The work is grueling and low. The heights are dizzying and the hours, long. Too many people have to be held accountable, and who checks them all? Well, no one, and that was the point. Workers are written off as "acceptable losses." The idea's okay if you're talking about shifting a few numbers around on parchment. But talking about a person, a some-one—old or young. That someone is somebody's son, daughter, husband, or wife. *A person.* It is…odious, to just blot out a number when behind it was a *person.* Slave workers are people. It is enough that they cannot even govern their daily lives, but imagine now, a slave woman goes home at the end of a grueling day wherein she has toiled to no profit of her own, as have her husband and children. Their scanty hovel is scarcely suitable for livestock, but they must call it home. She gathers a few wilting vegetables to boil in a broth, but her husband does not come home. After some time, the elders of the community come to her home to bring her the news that her husband will not be coming home because he was killed at the work site. They spare her the details because it was a needless death caused by a frayed rope that failed to hold the stone that crushed him. Her crushed life is further ground under the pestle of slavery. Have you not a heart? How can any warm-blooded soul not feel a burden, yet I saw so many turned heads, overseers who took no diligence to maintain optimum working facilities. So I would go to the work sites occasionally to oversee the overseers. They in turn resented my imposition; and my copiers had yet more to copy as I ordered rest breaks, fresh drinking water, new tools, and documentation of equipment inspections. I know it didn't all happen, but in good conscience, I had to do my best. To be honest with you, it was like scooping up a handful of sand. How could I ever keep it all together? It only made more reading—manufacturing requisition orders; export production levels of the forced labor groups; orders to decrease rations and increase output, which I routinely denied. I demanded documentation showing improved conditions behind specific work-related accidents. Correspondence contesting magistrates filing concerns over increase of labor populations…forced labor groups. There I'd be, back at this same junction again and again. "Forced labor" is such a clean title for a bad situation. Those were the slaves. Those were the people always in the news, but no one read it with compassion. It was read, though, because there was a lot of middle management whisper about the "problem"—their ever growing population—despite the work-related losses. Egypt's population was not bounding or leaping, but the slaves! It baffled because, well, face it: it's not like they were living well. So how could they find joy in life? How could they want to start families in the midst of their slavery? I was living the best of "the good life," and I was miserable! So how could it be so different for them? I decided to go see.

The slave sector was a place I had never been to before. And I wasn't supposed to call it the slave sector, but what else were they? They were kept prisoners here and forced to work for nothing but subsistence rations. May as well call it what it was. The royal house had nothing to do with them directly; that was left to lesser levels of management, but this district drew me to it. Some kind of pull. Maybe because I knew the language. I learned it as a child. It was more than that. I was one of them, and everyone knew it although the royal family didn't talk about it openly, at least. For years I lived the masquerade living as high royalty in cleanliness and quiet, but I looked beyond that. As a child, I had been nursed by *them* and taught *their* history. It pulled at me from inside. I knew their story— Abraham, Isaac, Jacob, twelve sons, famine brought seventy. Now millions strong but out of favor. Seventy came welcomed. Three million cannot leave.

I suppose you'd think me insane; I ought to have run as far and fast in the other direction from what so nearly could have been my fate. But knowing a little, drew me closer. There was some invisible net pulling me in like a sea catch. Their lives appeared to be one giant travesty. It seemed like every day we recorded deaths due to construction, deaths due to illness, and deaths due to the absence of law with respect to this population. The fact is that they could have soon outnumbered the natives and, although living here as guests, could have easily turned the tables on the indigenous population and taken the government just by sheer numbers. Everything they did here turned a profit. Everything they did turned to gold. So I guess, before the tables could be turned on Egyptian population, the Egyptians turned them first. With the press of the king's signet ring, the guests went from working aliens to occupying enemies. Accordingly, they were stripped of the nice homes they built and the possessions and monies they earned and herded into specific sectors for the sake of logistics, where they ceased to be fully human. They had little more rights than any livestock or wild beast. But they had one thing better: skilled labor.

So began generations of institutionalized inhumanity. A faceless, nameless labor pool, forgotten by everyone, as if they were absorbed into the land and just vanished. No one asked about them; no one inquired. Meanwhile, the dominant nation developed an unparalleled construction industry, designing and building structures of unprecedented proportions. And this (sigh) is where I found myself. Counting sacks of barley, wheat, corn, ships of bitumen, cedars, silks, and bodies. Bodies of these slaves. Worked to death bodies. Bodies fallen from ship decks. Bodies crushed under boulders. Bodies crushed under the whip. I was supposed to turn my head when I heard their cry. Surely this cry went up to the heavens. The God they clung to *had* to hear. Then one day, the day that I saw one too many acts of violence, I decided that *I* was going to do something. No, I don't know that I decided; I just did. I knew that what I saw was wrong, and I wanted to make something right in their lives. So right then and there, why was I even there in the first place? I don't remember. But I remember the empty husk of a slave that fell into the dirt when a work overseer struck him from behind. He was just a shell of a man who seemed to turn into the dusty ground he hit and vanish. And that pipe he was struck with—I wouldn't use on a stubborn ox! I was so fed up with this reckless pack of overseers, running amok as if they have no accountability. They berate this labor pool, starve, overwork them and then beat them to complete or near death for any or no reason. When I saw that overseer strike that gutted-out frame again and again, rage for his powerlessness rose up in me, and I grabbed the pipe. He beat this slave with no remorse, and none rose up in me. I felt like I had to fight for that broken man. Maybe it was for me, for my own conscience. I could have easily been one of the faceless among them. At any rate, I struck the assailant, but it wasn't enough! I hit him again and again for the years of the injustice. A second passed, maybe a few, and next thing I knew he was, well, I'd killed him. I didn't plan it. I didn't want him to die exactly. I wanted him to feel what he had done to that poor, broken man, what all of them had done to this people. Surely. I wanted the hate to stop. I wanted the beatings, forced labor, squalid living—all of that—to stop. And, yes, I wanted him to stop beating that poor broken man. Things blurred for a moment. I heard voices coming to help the broken one, and they quickly faded. I felt eyes heavy on me for a long moment before they all vanished with the broken one into the darkness of the evening. I remember the stillness of the assailant's corpse at my feet and the panic that raced all over my body as I quickly realized what I had done—the unthinkable! Seems like this world doesn't care if a slave dies. I mean, there might be some rudimentary investigation but only for the sake of logistics. They really weren't valued much more than the cattle because there were so many of them. And if you killed someone else's slave, you only had to pay about twenty pieces of silver—just enough to buy another—and the matter was done. But you can't just go and kill a *citizen*, even a lousy one. That's an act that is answerable and punishable. Death—the punishment is death! So what was I going to say? *While in a district that I shouldn't have been in, I stopped an overseer from beating a slave by beating him to death.* That wouldn't work—a slave's life over a citizen? Not a chance! So now, in panic, I tried to hide the body of the man I had killed. It was late, and there weren't many people about, but I did notice that no one helped me. I mean, I tried to help *them* and got into this mess, but no one would help me. I know people saw, but somehow the place seemed deserted, so I dragged the body out of plain sight. I didn't know what to do, so I dragged this heavy corpse down several dark streets until I came to a remote area at the edge of the housing quarter. I had no tools. I used what I could find around me, but as fast as I could, I buried the body.

It seemed as if my life, every moment that I'd ever known of it, had replayed in my mind as if I was evaluating its worth. What had I done? It could not be undone. It could not be told. It was not unseen. It would not be excused. From that day forward, I was nervous, always. I was obsessed with the activities of the slave sector more than before. Not to do it again, oh no! Just to know to have reassurance that no one else would know or at least would tell. I was seen by a few, but surely, it would be in their best interests to keep silent. Look, *no one* keeps silent. People talk; it's what they do. And my dreaded conclusion came to meet me. Again, I found myself in the quarter one evening at the end of my duties and I saw a fight. Past all the noise of the construction, traffic and animals, I heard a fight. One fight! So I went to break it up. I couldn't believe it: with all the wrong in the world, why are two slaves fighting each other? I pushed my way through to the center attraction with my authority. *Isn't the whole world against you already?* "Why are you fighting your own brother?" I demanded, making a hard pull to get one very strong man off another. A bully. He could have just as well worked for the other side as an overseer, the side I was on. Instead of reason or shame, he looked at me—no fear, no respect for my position. He said something like, 'So whatdryou gonna do, kill me like you killed that guy the other day?" He was mocking me! His life didn't even matter to him, speaking to me like that I could have had him killed, but just then, everything blurred! I remember his face but I don't. It was worn and leathery like he was wearing the face of a man much older than himself—a scar on his chin, a missing tooth. Couldn't tell you what color his eyes were, height, build. Don't know. I don't remember letting the man go but I must have. I don't remember the crowd dispersing, but it must have. I don't remember how many heard, but they must have. I don't know who saw in the first place, but someone had to have. I was in trouble, deep and quick! At that moment, I knew that others who knew my crime would talk. My life would be forfeit because it was no secret that I was really one of them anyway. This is just what the royal house needed for a reason to get rid of me. I suppose, the *one mistake too many* was bound to happen. Now it *was* happening, and the only thing I could do was run for my life. I did.

Surely you've never been in that kind of trouble, but I was. At that instant, I devolved from royalty to outlaw, and everyone—both sides—were against me! I knew that I didn't have much time if I meant to escape. I'd like to tell you that I got smarter when I needed to most; that I devised a plan, plotted a route, ha! Went back to my home and got supplies and money or even packed a lunch! None of that. It was evening, as I said, and I pushed my way through the crowd as if I had some official matter to tend to, shed my fine clothing, and slipped into obscurity. I knew that as soon as news of what I had done reached the royal house, I would be finished. After all, I'm the guy who shouldn't have been there all those years. I should have been part of the labor pool, not the royal house. Someone else could have had my place of privilege all those years. That was always in the air at the royal house thick enough to cut it. Now I was effectively cut off. I begged a few food scraps from bewildered homeowners on the way out of the quarter. I headed east in a hurry and kept going. You think the desert looks the same? Try it at night! I kept going till I saw river, then plains, mountains, another river, and I knew I was out of their reach. I knew I was somewhere in Midian territory. That in itself presented its own dangers, but where exactly and which way next? There was no "back" to go to. I moved forward, slower and slower. I was hot and tired. I had such a deep thirst, which overwhelmed my hunger. My fear was the worst of all. My heart said goodbye to the mother who tried to make me like her and goodbye to the mother whom I was like. I wondered about the people I worked with. Many were kind in a genuine sense. What would they be thinking when they got the news. Big-shot Moses, a nobody now. They'd all be mocking me, in a short while if not already. I wondered what good all of my years of studying was for if this was my end—to become a pile of desiccated bones in some remote place. No one would even know whose bones they were. That's good though, I thought, so that no one would think of catching me to return me for a price.

That's how I fled with those thoughts wandering in my head as my feet wandered the land. And of course, I came to a point of exhaustion where I couldn't take another step; my eyes couldn't even focus. When I thought I couldn't take another step, I realized that I was practically standing in front of a well, a well with a bunch of people. And not just people, bullies! Seems to be my specialty—a few rogues picking on women. Those fight technique lessons from so many years ago stuck with me better than I thought. I ran the thugs off. You know, I was never as good a fighter as the other soldiers and princes back at the palace, but out here, I must have seemed pretty fierce, at least, until I passed out! I fell down into a heap of bone and rested into a sleep that would have taken me to the comfort of death, but, then I was drowning! So I thought, I was drowning! My eyes opened to find that it was water drizzling on my face to wake me, and it brought me back to consciousness. Your daughters poured water on my face and brought me back to myself.

You know the rest, Jethro; you have made me your son-in-law. I have been wandering with the sheep and goats, for all these years, ever since your daughters found me wandering. It is so peaceful here, out in nowhere. I left big cities behind! All the construction projects, trade deals, people moving to and from everywhere. Here there's nothing. Not nothing in a bad way but so different. Midian is flocks and pasture, quiet and honest simplicity. I often wonder what all of that 'other life', was for. I tried to do a little good in a world of bad, and everything turned upside down on me. I wonder what happened to my mother, my *real* mother. And my father. That life back there kills. What is this life for? It's dirty and hard and sad. Oh, I know all about the God, the Great God and Abraham, Isaac, and Jacob. I know all about the promise, but I don't see any promise. I don't see any big powerful God. Why do they hang everything on this God while they spend their lives enslaved? How could they believe all of these things like its true? God's going to make them great? They are anything but great now as I see it. What is worse than slavery? Even that poor soul with the weathered face and missing tooth believed in the greatness of this God. I just wonder what it's all been for—my parents, all the babies who died when they hid me, the words God said to Abraham—I wonder what it's all for. Why was *I* spared that early death? Then later, I was a good student. I became a good administrator, the number one numbers guy in the most powerful nation, and now all I count are sheep out in the scrub. I wonder, am I supposed to be learning something from this life I've lead? Oh, Jethro, you say it was all for something. What kind of something could *that* be? Maybe I could ask Him? *Every day* I wonder about Him, the real God. I wonder about my life, and I count sheep. Do you think God would explain something to me, Jethro? I'm dreaming! Like God's gonna talk to a wandering sheep herder on the lam! Yep, Jethro, He's gonna just sit right down here in the middle of Eastern Nowhere

Pastures and chat with an old has-been fugitive. I'm crazy… I've been out in the sun too long! This big God who talked to the patriarch Abraham is gonna talk to me? Suuurre… He's gonna say, *"You big has-been admin guy, so you want to know what all that was for, do you?"* I mean, seriously, though. I would ask Him questions if I could. Could you imagine *actually talking* to God? Well, what would *you* say, Jethro? Me? I might say something like, "Excuse me, Sir, but so many people die and so many people suffer and then why would you pluck me out of the grip of death, educate me, make me administrator of many functions and people, and then let me wind up administrating over sheep?" Well, okay, sure you're right; I'd be too afraid to say all of that, but that's what I'd be thinking. If I could talk to God, if I could actually talk to God…can you imagine actually talking to God? I guess I must be out of my mind. I'm getting too much sun out here with the sheep. *Ha, ha, ha!* Hey, Jethro, do you see that out there! I see smoke. No…looks like a brush fire. Looks pretty big from here. This could be a lot of trouble if the shrubland catches fire. You stay here with the flocks; I'd better go have a look.

The Wall
(Exod. 12:31–16)

"**G**ettt Outtt!"

That's what he said, only bigger. Oh, then he said, "And bless me," on the way out! That's what the old pharaoh said. And then Moses told the elders to call to everybody: "We're leaving! We're leaving now! Get your things, move, move, move!" Mama said some people didn't think we were really going, but I did. I had all my things packed. I had a cot all rolled up, my other tunic, my doll baby, a little satchel I carry snacks in, and my own flask of water. I knew that old pharaoh was gonna get God good and mad and that God would make him let us go. And guess what, that's what happened! Papa had most of our things packed and loaded on the donkey cart. I guess he knew God was gonna let us go too. Mama rolled up their mats, blankets, a few cooking utensils; and we were one of the first families pulling out—out of four hundred years of slavery! I had eight years of it, and that was enough for me! Papa said after all that old pharaoh had been through, he learned a lesson about God, so we were free to go. We walked pretty fast, leaving out of there! There was a lot of noise—shouting, creaky overloaded carts, and lots of animals. There were a lot of excited people asking way too many questions, if you ask me. I say, "Just go! Moses will tell us what to do next. He talks to God and God talks back to him. Just do what he says and go!" Sometimes grownups make things way too complicated.

We walked a good while, still too much noise. I saw a lot of ladies crying. I thought they were happy; that's what Mama does sometimes anyways—cries and smiles together. I don't know. The men were pushing everyone and everything to go faster and faster.

All of our poor sheep were all mixed up! They weren't going to their usual place. All the noise scared them and me too, a little. Plus, it was a really cloudy dark day, and the wind! The wind was strong like the coldest of days. It seemed like the more we walked, the louder the wind got. After a while, I didn't really have to listen to all the shouting 'cause I couldn't really hear it anyway until I heard screaming coming from the back of our caravan. Some of the elders were running lengths passing along messages to the next elder who then ran the length of his section and passed the message to the next elder in another section of our caravan. So a message reached Moses up front: the army was coming after us! It looked like that old pharaoh forgot his lesson and changed his mind to come after us. A lot of people got scared and started screaming, and that just made everything worse. People started panicking and tried to run. We were walking very fast already, and I couldn't go any faster. We all had a lot of stuff to carry. When we left, the people we worked for gave everyone a lot of things, so on top of our things, we had a lot of gifts to carry, and I had to hold my little brother's hand. The problem was, when we got so far, there was the Reedy Sea—big as the world—straight ahead of us and the army coming from behind. I didn't really know what to do myself, but Papa always said to trust God especially when you think you know what to do and even more especially when you don't. I figured this was a good time for all of that, and besides, this was the way God told Moses to go, so I figured God would send a boat or something and we could all just sail across the water. The grownups started to yell angry things, and that made me nervous so I started to cry; but if they would just listen to Moses, he would tell us what to do because God talked straight to him, and like I said, God was the one who told Moses to take us out this way. I figure God knows His way around pretty good. The grownups kept screaming, so I just stopped listening and listened more to the wind. It was so close, like when my little brother talks right into my ear when he tries to annoy me. It was blowing around and around my head. Papa tried hard to keep our animals together, but I think they did pretty better than some people. They kept their heads down and just kept walking. Moses was telling everyone something, but I didn't understand what was happening.

Some of the elders stepped into the water and Moses held up his staff. The sea started changing real quick. It was so windy I thought we might all just fly away. The wind blew the water so hard that it pushed the water up like a wall to the left and the right while down in the middle, the ground was dry as a bone. So we walked! We walked right into the sea like God rolled out a carpet of dry ground in front of us! Imagine that! That's a better idea than a boat; it would'a taken too long. At first it was kind of steep going down into the seabed, but then once we got to the bottom, it was pretty much even to walk on. We all marched right across the Reedy Sea bed. It was completely dry; it was completely awesome! God put a gigantic pillar of fire and cloud in between us and the Egyptians to keep us safe while we all crossed over the sea and out of their country. We all moved as fast as we could, but we had a lot of stuff and a lot of animals. Since Papa had our goats and sheep to drive, Mama had to lead the donkey, which carried a lot of our things in a cart. I made sure I held my little brother, Levi's, hand. There was so much shouting, but all I could really hear was wind and water. I'd never seen so much water! It was so loud and kept crashing against an invisible wall on our left side and also on our right. The men were shouting to each other to help everyone in their groups keep moving, but we could barely hear each other! I know I was supposed to hurry, but when I was walking, I saw so many things on the ground. And the shells! Such pretty colors! I let go of Levi's hand but only for a moment! I ran over to collect some of the shells that were right next to the invisible wall! The wall was so unbelievably loud being right next to it. I could see right through the wall, but it was dark, like muddy. The water was swirling around in the sea and slamming hard against the wall. It was frightening! I turned my head and saw my mama, scared and screaming. My Papa was telling a big man something and pointing at me. It seemed like everything went silent and in slow motion for a little while. I turned back to face the wall again. I don't know why, but I wanted to touch the wall that held the water back. I put my hand there on the wall, but I couldn't feel anything, so slowly, I stuck my finger through it. *Wet!* I turned around to look, and I couldn't see my family anymore, but all the people seemed far away, and everything was so quiet. I looked back at the wall and pushed my hand through and kept going way past my elbow! There was so much water, and it was swirling so hard it was bending my arm! It scared me, so I yanked my arm back out through the wall. My hand, my arm, and my tunic sleeve were all soaking wet! I pushed my arm into the wall again, nearly up to my shoulder. I had to stand with my legs apart so the water didn't knock me over. I looked behind me and people were still hurrying by in slow motion and perfect quiet, so I just took a moment. I put my left arm all the way in the wall! Both of my arms were soaking wet inside the sea—what fun! Then I felt something in my hand! I cupped my left hand over it in my right and pulled my arms out. A turtle, a little turtle was standing in my palm smiling at me. *Well, little turtle gift, you're coming with me!* I told him. I looked down at the soaking-wet mess I was all over my tunic and down to my sandals. I figured I may as well get what I came for, so I bent down and grabbed the shells from the ground. They were pretty—white with pinks and blues, sparkly and dry, as dry as the ground we were walking on. I grabbed as many as I could fit in my satchel and put the turtle on top wondering what happened to Mama, and oh boy, where'd Levi go? Just then, a big man, the one I saw Papa talking to, scooped me up in his arms.

He ran carrying me and said, "You're going to be okay, Little One!" He caught up to where my family was, set me down right next to Levi, and he vanished! The slow motion feeling went away, and I heard all the water noise and the people trying to shout to each other again. I saw Mama. She couldn't reach me because she had the donkey and Levi, who I was supposed to be watching, and the crowd was forcing us all forward. She saw my wet tunic, too, but she just cried. Her face smiled even though she was crying. What's all that about? I thought I'd help her, so I grabbed Levi's little hand. He smiled at me and squeezed my hand tightly. He's a pretty good little brother. I smiled back at him. Wait until he sees what I got for him! We started walking a little uphill, and my legs were getting tired. I guess it was steep going up out of the seabed just like it was steep going down into it. Mama made me hold the donkey and Levi with my other hand, while she and Papa got behind the donkey and helped to push him up the steep slope. Poor donkey carried all our stuff pretty much by himself. When we got up out of the seabed, the elders were spreading us out along the shore to make certain that everyone behind us had room to get out. For a while all the people were on the left side of the dry bed or on the right side of the dry bed. We were looking at the sea, watching it slam into the invisible wall and churn back again. When all the last of the people came across, the last of the elders came with Moses. He was still holding his rod up in the air. I bet his arms were as tired as my legs! The elders helped Moses up the steep bank because he had to keep the rod up in the air with one hand. God's fire-cloud pillar was behind Moses. It kept the army on the other side away from us. When the fire-cloud pillar rose straight up into the air, the pharaoh's army ran down into the seabed to follow us. I guess they wanted to make us march all the way back into slavery. I sure didn't want to go back there. God didn't want it either. He took away the invisible walls that held the seawater back, and it went crashing down onto the soldiers in the seabed! It was frightening because of the noise of the water and the screams of the soldiers. Our people were screaming too. Everyone was scared, but we were safe.

We got to rest for a little while. The sea quieted down, and the wind went away finally. Mama and Papa grabbed me. They weren't even mad at me for running off. They just hugged me and cried. Papa, too, he cried. Mama wanted me to change into my dry tunic, but I didn't want to. I wanted to feel that Reedy Sea water on my arm for as long as I could. It was the best thing ever! The army that tried to follow us into the dry seabed drowned, and that was pretty much that. Everyone on our side was really happy and sang songs to praise God. I pulled the seashells out of my bag and showed them to my parents. Mama just cried. Papa said the little turtle had to go back to the water where he'd be happy. He took us to the shore, and I let Levi put the turtle back in the water. He thought it was pretty great! I'll never forget what God did, and neither will he.

A few days later, all the people who were so happy started complaining to Moses because they couldn't find water. I keep saying, *Just listen to Moses because he listens to God*, but grownups make things way too complicated. Moses brought us to Elim. Lots of water to drink there! I have a seashell for Moses, but I don't think I'll ever get close enough to give it to him. I guess he's really busy, and I'm just a kid.

After a while, we left Elim and got to a desert. People started complaining again and said they wished they were back across the Reedy Sea where they had pots of meat and all they could eat. Not me! I remember where we came from, and that place wasn't good for me! Anyway, Moses asked God, and God gave us some kind of food that fell like raindrops from heaven. No one had ever seen anything like it. They kept saying, "What is it? What is it?" So that's what we called it, *manna*. It came from God, and it tasted pretty good, if you ask me. Way better than any pots of meat I ever had on the bad side of the Reedy Sea.

So this is how we live now: God does something pretty awesome for us. Everyone's happy for a little while and then they turn around and complain. It's as if they forget everything God *just* did! I'll never forget the Reedy Sea. I'll never forget the place we came out of. It wasn't good for me. Someday when I'm grown and have little kids of my own, I'm going to give them my seashells and tell them what God did for a little kid. I'll tell them how I stood right next to the invisible wall. Sometimes I wondered if God would march us right back across the Reedy Sea since the people complained so much, but Mama said that God made a promise to Abraham, and God keeps His promises. "He's faithful," Mama says. I wish grownups would be faithful back. I wish they would just listen to Moses because he listens to God. Things would be way less complicated. I trust God. He parted the Reedy Sea just for us!

The Ayes Have It!
(Num. 13, 14)

Part 1

"Oh, out with it! Come on, now." Morushe slung a very worn and faded saddle blanket over a stall wall. The donkey, content with abundant hay and a respite from the hot sun didn't need to be tethered. Morushe turned from the barn and started toward the small workshop. "I can see you from here! Something's wrong. I know you too well. If I don't know you, then I know nothing. You're up to something, Del. What is it?"

Delmez focused on his task, never making eye contact with his accuser. Neither did he utter a word.

"How do I know? You wanna know how I know? I know you, and I'm telling you that when you get a real scheme in your head, you do *that!*"

"What?" Delmez broke is gaze, finally looking up. "I do what?"

"Look at you. *That.* That's that thing you do when you're up to something. You're not even working on any of the many job orders you have. You start sanding, and you sand on your worktable like that! See there on that side, and now this, you're sanding a depression right into the table itself! You're going over and over *something* in your mind."

"Well, well, maybe so!" Delmez couldn't hide his irritation. If a man couldn't find privacy in his own work shed, no, in his own thoughts in his own work shed, well, *what* then? "I just need to think a little more." His thoughts wandered to prestige at the village gates and over everyone between here and there, then the opposite—a horror of public ridicule for causing a false alarm. Which eventuality would it be? Maybe this was just nothing, but, no, there had to be more to this thing. And maybe, just perhaps, one of these days, *he'd* be sitting at the gates. Him, with lots of money and people calling his name, looking for wisdom, advice, friendship. *Why, Elder Delmez, what do you think of such and such. Oh my, what wisdom you impart. How fortunate we are, indeed, to have you presiding over our village matters.* "Yup, one of these days, it's gonna be me," Delmez dreamt aloud.

"And what sort of knowledge trinkets do you think you might have that would be of value to anyone?" Morushe unfolded his arms and folded them again betraying the impatience he'd been trying to conceal. This was his second trip he'd make to retrieve a repaired plowing tool, and it still wasn't ready. "What do you know besides smithing which you don't seem to do much of judging by the backlog of your work orders! Half the village is waiting on something from you!"

"Well, what if I saw something?"

"Like...?" Morushe was getting a little irritated, but if he couldn't get what he came for, at least he could get a good story for amusement's sake.

"Morushe, what do you think of spies?" Delmez cast a brief look to the ground. "Yes, and I'm sorry about the plow. It'll be fixed and better than new shortly, but deft secrecy is key. I've been busy observing. It's a matter of public security. Something may be amiss, and if it is, our whole city could be endangered. So what of it, man? *Spies...*"

"And what of it?' Morushe taunted, "*Spies...* What spies? Do you know any about?"

"I..."

"If you do, brother, then we must tell the counsel at once. Can't have anything like that, but if you're mistaken, oh, this will be a joke for the ages!" Morushe could not contain the delight anticipated at the humiliation of Delmez, all in good fun, of course, but this blunder would go straight to the city gates! It's not that Morushe had it out for Del, but it would be a payback of sorts for some of Delmez's misguided antics. There was, for example, the falling star, which Del convinced Morushe to have the city's army standing guard all night for an invasion of unknowns, which never occurred. Morushe took more of the ribbing for that one than Delmez. Everyone knew Del was not all that levelheaded after all. Morushe threw his lot in with Del and was made the fool. Not the only time either. Paybacks would be sweet. *So now we have spies, eh?*

"What if I do know…something. Not *know* something but *have seen* something. But not something of an ordinary nature but something extraordinary. I should want to share it with my closest friend…"

"Delmez, I'm you're *only* friend."

"But are you a friend capable of keeping a confidence for the things that I have seen…"

"Well, you'll have to make your mind up about that, Del. But we've known each other always, and through all of your hair-brained plots, I have only suffered the consequences alongside you as a brother."

"Oh, come on now, I'm solid like a rock."

"Stolid, perhaps."

"You hurt me with such words! What have I ever done to make you—"

Morushe let the sack of grain, which he had brought as payment for the plow, fall to the ground. Left hand out, fingers extended, his right pointer finger began the count. Pressing it against his right thumb, Morushe began, "Well, just *this year*, there was the time you tried to sell that horrid pack beast to me—"

Delmez took offense. He leaned forward such an acute angle that he was nearly nose to nose with Morushe although standing two feet away. "That was a prime pack animal! It had only to be broken and trained for the yoke! That animal was a fine bargain, which I got from a caravan trader passing through the market!"

"Delmez, that animal was broke-en! It was lame, ill-tempered, and way too old for the plow. I nearly got cornered and kicked to death just mucking the stall! Of all of the lame-brained ideas—"

Delmez stepped back a pace and looked around, finding no consolation. "Yes, well, perhaps, it is true that one gets what one pays for. Morushe resumed his count, right-hand pointer finger matching that on his left. "Then there was the time you convinced me to open a merchandizing shop with you—" Delmez had clearly been thoroughly castigated for that enterprise before.

With the palms of both hands toward his former business partner and shaking his head, he simply said, "Enough, enough…"

Morushe, satisfied that his point was made, ceased the count. "So out with it, brother Del, your secrets, if you have any of value and which you could scarcely keep although you'd swear me to bide."

Delmez struggle for a bit of self-dignity, "I might have some secrets still which I haven't disclosed…"

"Have you, really then?"

"Well, no but… I *could* have if I had chosen to…in any event, Morushe, I've seen *spies*."

"Well, I might have guessed. Is this what keeps you from your shop, Delmez?"

"I have other businesses that do well…although I don't deny having an idea or two gone amiss."

Morushe offered a hard consolation, "Well, Del, you're the only one who shoes horses and makes oxen yoke and drinking vessels of any quality, and you may as well know it. And you are backlogged—*everyone* knows that! You'll soon have complaints owing to your waiting list, if you don't get back to work and pick up your slack. No one wants to go all the way to the next village. Belmur is a horrible craftsman, but he will fill his orders, at least. So now I can guess that this new spy occupation is what has taken you from your shopkeeping. So tell me what it is about this…spy business, which has you out when you ought to be in."

Delmez felt vindicated by his friend. Morushe didn't really understand his level of genius, but Delmez was willing to work with him anyway. And Morushe could be terse, but, well, isn't a friend supposed to tell you all, including the warts? All in all, Delmez counted Morushe a worthy friend. The fact that he was Delmez's only friend was a trivial aside. Excitedly, Delmez began his story. "Well, brother, since you asked, I was returning the widow Elkanan's donkey to her barns and it's stall, as she had no one to retrieve the beast that day—"

"What day?"

"More than a full moon ago," Delmez continued, "when I saw two fellows moving suspiciously about the neighbor's barn house. It's a shed, really, in which are kept harvesting tools, barrels, baskets, feed, and the like. So I cautiously moved to investigate—"

Morushe was still in a mocking mode, "You went to spy on the spies?"

Delmez, accustomed to his friend's skepticism, ignored the slight and continued, "Well, I had not yet established their activity or identities. I first thought them to be thieves, but they didn't steal anything. There were two men, which had jammed themselves into a large basket. Tangled upon each other like unwound hemp strands, they were. Hours passed and—"

"And this is why you haven't finished the poured statue to be placed inside the village gates? The old man Shenir has been waiting for you to build a new yoke for his plow team. The old one is so splintered and about to fall apart."

"And my curiosity heightened, so that I took a comfortable posture to wait them out. 'How long can two men remain inside of a basket?' I asked myself. Presently, being passed about four hours, each emerged from the basket with caution. I was not close enough to hear them, but it was apparent that they were waiting to move with cover and darkness. When it seemed to them that no one was about, they made a cart in haste from scraps around the barns. In it, they carried off only a pitiful smattering sample of what could have been removed from the premises. For this, I suppose that they are not thieves, for wouldn't a thief take all that could be had, if opportunity availed itself? These two did not, but only a few fringe bits of produce, a bit of soil, and what they could hastily eat. Having taken the night to build their cart and fill it, they remained hidden at the edge of the field until the next night, when they made away, and I followed them."

"Really?' Morushe was thoroughly intrigued, "Go on…"

"They travelled south until they crossed out of our land. Going not much further, they reached their camp. It's massive. There are millions of them! I saw thousands and thousands of tents and an enormous fire in the center of the camp. As the dawn turned into daylight, the fire just vanished, and in its place appeared a cloud! A huge cloud not in the sky but in the center of the encampment! Like it was a column of cloud."

"Del, there's no such thing as a *column of cloud*."

"I know! Exactly my point!" Delmez continued excitedly, "Morushe, you won't believe me when I tell you who these people are!"

"Well, that's pretty likely, Del, but why don't you go ahead and tell me then, brother."

"Morushe, do you remember when your cousin's employer had interests in a certain convoy some months ago?"

"The caravan with traded goods from Egypt. Yes. So what about it?"

"And some among them had spoken of a wild band of people on the march out of Egypt?"

"Uhmm…yes, but what of it?" Morushe was feeling an on rush of sarcasm.

"It was them! Them that I saw! It was them!"

"Oh, of course! Ha, ha! And did they lose upon your pestilences and curses like the stories have come by the caravans?"

"No, actually, they just look like a tired bunch, wearied of their journey, but more interestingly, there are some among them who are not of them, merely travelling with them. Of these I chose and spoke with and they who have verified all things. The pestilences scorched the farmlands. They left out of curiosity about the God who could do those things, and since their crops were ruined, they figured they didn't have much to lose. You know, Ra is their sun god, but the God of these travelers turned the day to night, defying the sun god! They said the God of the travelers is more powerful than any of the southern gods. The stories about the pestilences, the Reed Sea parting, everything all true!"

Morushe bent over to hoist the sack of grain back onto his shoulder. "So…no doubt you are going to tie all this together so that when I leave in a moment to *get back to work*, which you might also consider doing… I can have the satisfaction of knowing that we had a coherent conversation when last we spoke…"

THE AYES HAVE IT!

"I said the wild tribe was here! Their people…were *here!*"

"Oh, you did say that… Tell me, Delm, did you get a sense of peace or trouble about them?"

"Well, both! They were a restless bunch, but from what I gathered, I now being the spy, they have been on the move. I also learned that any tribe who would not let them pass peaceably through their land, they smashed! But here's the thing: it's not them. It's this *god* of theirs."

"What do you mean?"

"Delmez, where did our gods come from?"

"What? What do you mean?"

"I mean that! Where have any of our gods come from?"

"Why, from *you*! If you would get back to work, that is! From your father's metalworks, of course! What kind of question is that?"

"Exactly. And my father, no great honor, simply a man given too much drink and the craft of shoeing horses and beating out silver."

"He makes fine goblets."

"The best around admittedly, but he'd beat out a goblet or a god, just the same for a gold coin. Don't you see, he makes those images, as you would like them. You pay him handsomely, he bangs out the thing and then you go home, put it on your mantle and pray to it. If it rains, you say your mantelpiece god favored you. If it is sunny, you give it to the mantelpiece god again. When things go sour, you come back and buy a different idol whom you suppose has been neglected and brought ill upon you to benefit by attention. And so you, and all of us, have a mantle full of gods of various *imagined* capabilities of benevolence. But just as my father bangs out a piece of metal over the fire, he melts another."

"So you're saying your father can kill our household gods? Pah!"

"I'm *saying…are they really gods in the first place*, is what I'm saying. My father is no priest, and I am not the son of a priest—"

"That is certainly true…"

"But in contrast, I, now the spy, go to this camp, the camp of the wild tribes, and their god is this massive cloud floating in the air. Not high up in the sky but just right with them. When it moves, they follow. And guess what—"

"*What?*"

"At night, their god is this giant flaming fire—"

"Yeah, you mentioned that, Del," Morushe said with disbelief.

Undaunted, Delmez continued," Fire…just *suspended* in the air! It lights the entire camp, too, and when it moves, they break camp and go with it. When it stops, they stop. It's the most unimaginable thing. I tell you it's an extraordinary sight! This god of theirs, it's real! It's not something hammered out. They don't even have a statue of it."

Morushe knew Delmez was off track. "Nonsense, Del! That's nonsense. Where would they put it? And how could they have brought their god with them if they really did come out of Egypt? And Egypt is the most powerful nation on the earth, how could they just walk out of there in the first place, this 'tired bunch'? Oh, these are all just stories, Delmez!"

"No, it's true. And they say *He* is a spirit, and they're not allowed to make an image to worship."

"You don't say."

"And they've left a trail of eyewitnesses to all the facts, if you'd only investigate. And I'm glad you're here because I can say my good-byes early. I'm going to finish up these projects and then I'm leaving, I'll come 'round your home to to say goodbye.

"What's that now?"

"I'm moving. I'm leaving to go live among them."

"What's this? This is madness! Delmez, what are you saying? I won't have it. I won't hear of it. This could be dangerous. You don't know these people. They could kill you. I'm telling the elders right this minute, Del, do you hear me? And you know what they'll do. They'll take your father's farm, his shop. Your shop. If you turn traitor. They'll burn it to the ground. You should have told them from the beginning if you truly did see spies. By now you've aided them, in all this time…"

"So if you chose not to believe me, not to see for yourself, not to come with your old friend, my only friend. Then I must ask you to turn and go as if we had never met, never spoken…"

"Oh you are preposterous, Del, and you have your will exactly. I am going…oh well, I can't, can I, you fool. You'll get yourself killed."

He sighed. "I'll come along this one time to see your *fire god* and then we're coming back home to our businesses. And maybe you can hammer this one out."

"It's not possible…"

"Oh well, then, what's to be done! Hold on and I'll go pack for a moon—"

"It's already done, friend. I have two packs. Yours is right here."

"Oh, you do presume too much, Del! Give me that!"

"This way, my friend. My only friend. We turn south now."

Part 2

On some days the sun was outdone. So it was that day. Hard as it toiled, a line of heavy clouds ran interference, blocking it from our view. This gave no reprieve from the swelter. Make no mistake, it was hot. It seemed as if the heat was trying to melt everything. Heavily laden clouds made sure that it stuck thick and humid like an invisible coat. None of this mattered, though. I felt the rolling sweat careening from the top of my head, sliding down the hair it plastered to my forehead. Sweat clumped on my eyelashes, making me squint to see while trying not to move. Still it streamed down my face, neck, across my shoulders, jumped off the shoulder blades to surf down my back. It all ended in a pool around my waistline, but I couldn't care less. The discomfort heightened the excitement. We'd been inside this basket for what seemed like hours. A hasty escape to get cover, and a tight spot at that, but it sufficed. Cramped in, Ro's elbow pressed my left cheek right onto my teeth, but we dared not move. A rustle might give us away and compromise the entire sur- veillance mission. There were twelve of us in all, travelling in cohorts of two, we went as far into the land as possible and scheduled to return in forty days' time. We came in from the south, of course, having left Egypt. Investigating this place, Canaan, we moved into its midterritories between the sea on our left and the mountains, which hide the sea on our right. There are many cities and settlements in this land. Many of the people work in metal, building strong char- iots, weapons, and decorative items. We had about eight days left before we were expected back at main camp. When we split off from the ground team, Ro and I had continued due north, later moving west along the coast. To some degree, we were able to travel by day, provided we keep distant from locals. We can make out some of their speech, but their tongue is not ours. We gathered that this people come from an island in the western Mediterranean Sea, wherein a volcano erupted some long time ago. They left that island and inhabit a great stretch of the coastal areas of this land, Caanan. But God—the great God of our ancestors Abraham, Isaac, and Jacob—has given this land to us. The twelve of us here now have come to find out this enemy's strengths, weaknesses, of course, and see the lay of the land. These many cities, which Ro and I had seen, were dug in and well-established. We moved quickly by day or by night passing through cities—Gaza, Askelon, Ashdod, and Joppa. We crossed the brook of Kanah and looked over the plain of Sharon. With eight days left, we turned south, heading back for base camp passing briefly through even more settlements—Ekron, Gath, Lachish—and then due south again. This land is incredible. The farmlands are huge and spread out. The crops have given a bountiful produce. The pasture land is hilly and thickly carpeted for grazing. There is some of everything—rugged mountains, highlands and lowlands fitted with sea breeze. Existing crops report the fine caliber of soil. The fertile delta down south in Egypt showed off fine yield, but this, these harvests are of another quality. And it's ours! God has given it to us!

We've come north from Egypt and the Sinai. Egypt. I said that as if it was my home. In a way, it was. But truly, it was not. We had been there for generations, but not as we started out when our forefather Joseph brought us in. Back then, we were welcomed. The way you are when you know someone influential, someone "on the inside." For us, that was Joseph. He was a powerful administrator back then. He brought our people there to live in Goshen, and we did well. We prospered and grew into a great people. Some years later, a new pharaoh came to power, and he turned the tables on us. Virtually overnight, he changed us from a prosperous population into slaves by the clap of his hands and the stamp of his signet ring. In that instant, everything that we had made was taken from us, and we were treated as less than the cattle. We were foreigners there; it wasn't our home but we became trapped, unable to leave. We continued to work even harder than before, but we never saw the profit. But even in that low place, our God was with us. During four hundred years of low, He heard every lash of the whip, every injustice, every abuse the pharaoh put upon us. There I was, forty years old, thinking, *This is my lot in life—to be born and die a miserable slave under the whip in a foreign land*. What could I do about it? There were a million of us, but we were weak and surrounded by the most powerful army on the earth. So what does one do but live to the best of one's ability? So there I was, living my routine and then... Moses. And then Moses! Somehow, something changed for him, and he became one of us! He went forward as God's spokesman before the pharaoh. Then God just walked us out of there—and loaded down with wealth, at that! Those people wanted God to stop the plagues; they just wanted us out of their country, and they gave us all kinds of valuables on the way out—gold, jewels, and the like! A small payment for the last four hundred years of enslaved labor, I'd say. And this story gets sweeter. God's giving us our own land; that's why we twelve are here. But there is this population here, and they worship some foreign gods. God told us the land is to be ours. That's good enough for me. Moses sent out dispatches to explore the land. I was one of them. It was covert action, of course, and something amazing to see. Mountains, hilly country, farm plains, grazing pastures. The water is clear, and the air has a cool breeze built in, not the unforgiving, heavy blaze of sun we were accustomed to in Goshen. I'm putting that word out of my mind, *Goshen*. It's the past, and we have a bright future ahead—so promises God!

Anyway, as soon as we can break away from this spot, me and Ro are continuing to make our way south, back to base. We have six days to make the distance, and barring any major incidences, we ought to make good time. I give Ro a gentle jab in the gut and point through a crack in the pile of woven baskets and rush covering us. We can see several of the foreigners moving into the nearby house and one mounting a horse now leaving the area. These people are living very well, like kings, every one of them. Especially compared to the way we used to live in, ha! Caught myself! It's in the past! Me and Ro have seen all we need to see. "But, Ro," I say, "I feel like a snack." Ro, whose real name is Jarel, son of Shimren, got the nickname, The Rotator, because back in—caught myself again—back in the old days…he could carve a perfectly round pillar from any mass, any chunk of wood or mountain, just all by himself, and we cut a lot of stone back then. It was in the way he worked his material. He would continually move around it as he chipped away, like some slow-motion dance. Moving, moving, cutting, now cutting, rotating around the stone chiseling, coercing it until a sculpted figure emerged from the core.

"A wheel of cheese, perhaps?" A gray cat positioned itself just over the "surveillance port" we were peeking out of. I felt a playful swat on the tips of my fingers that stuck out of the basket. Ro asked me again, "Would you like to have some cheese?"

"No," I said. "Well, yes…a wheel of something for later, but just now…"

"Look at the carrots, that basket of apples over there. Squash right next to it, onions in that far corner. We certainly fell into the right barn, didn't we?"

"Idea!" I said.

Ro replied, "I'm all ears."

Safe to emerge from hiding, we scavenged materials and worked quickly to modify a cart into a lighter traveling wagon with four wheels, which could be pushed by us; a pack animal would move too slowly. By day, we would simply appear to be merchants travelling. By night, we could move our evidence quickly back to camp. Six days to tryst. We packed our cart lightly, with a good variety of product, bid goodbye to our feline companion, and moved out to the field's edge. From here on, we travelled mostly by night. We could stay on the road without having to engage passersby on the premise of looking out for our own personal security. After all, travel is dangerous nowadays.

The field was plowed horizontally (relative to what, I don't know). An adjacent field was plowed vertically, with respect to the horizontal field, I guessed. Corn stopped, wheat started. Barley started adjacent to spacious rows of squash. "Grapes! I have a craving for grapes!"

"Sorry, partner, our cart is full," Ro advised. "Besides, look at those clusters, they're massive. That's a two-man carry!"

"Well, I'll just pluck a few because they look delicious, and ummm, they are! Anyway, the grapes are just right. The vines are massive for putting out so much fruit. It'd take a sharp axe to cut. And a two-man carry!" I smarted back. We took enough grapes for immediate sustenance, but we stuck to the plan. Robust movement south by night, casual movement by day.

Part 3

Home base was in a bustle as the search teams returned in twos. Some of the pairs had parted paths partway into their routes to cover more territory. I wouldn't have advised that. If one got hurt or captured, who would know? Where? How? No, this assignment was from God. Ro and I thought out our approach and execution in order to finish well. We started out and finished the assignment together. The hum of so many voices all at the same time grew louder as the teams trickled in. Loved ones were relieved to see their spy return safely. Stories recounted to rapt audiences. All of the team members brought back a few small samples to illustrate their claims. We, too, began telling the tales—what we saw, how green, how blue, how lush and who we saw, how many, how big, how tall, how well armed. The last two members of the teams arrived by midday. At the sight of them, Ro and I exchanged big grins; those two guys did it! They cut the vine and brought back the prize, the two-man carry payload of grapes! Well done! "Gath," they said, catching their breaths.

"From the fields of Gath!" They sampled a vineyard in Gath. Beautiful, delicious grapes, so dense and plentiful on the vine so thick that it took an axe to cut and two to carry it back. Good take!

We were surrounded. We, the "spies," stood in the arbitrary center encircled by the tribes, the nation. Elders and such up front, of course. We all gave our reports. The people were gripped; it was our dream at hand. Everyone agreed it was a wonderful land, but then I don't understand what began to happen. The other teams began talking more about the inhabitants. *They were big. They were giants.*

They had armor. They had swords and spears. They had, they had. If you could have seen the faces of the elders and everyone behind them. Their faces paled in terror just listening to these men. Why?

"Who cares what these people look like or carry? God just brought us twelve men forty-day passes, and we're all back to a man without a scratch! God had just walked us across the sea, pushing walls of water aside so that we could walk through with dry soil under our sandals! Then God let it fall on the soldiers who meant to drag us back to slavery. That wall of water may as well have been a wall of stone. It crushed and buried our enemy in one swoop! We left that place, not by the hairs on our chins but fat with wealth because of God! He is in our favor! So who cares who stands in our path? The LORD is our banner. God goes before us!"

I didn't realize I had been yelling this aloud. The crowd had grown loud and uneasy. Rumbling turned to shouting and shoving. Some listened to the reason of my argument. It wasn't a hard case to present: every one of us, over a million men strong, had just experienced God's favor. Who could deny it? *But...* that's what I don't understand: BUT! Other men kept saying *But.* "But the people of the cities are enormous. But they have metal weapons, but they have strong, well-fortified cities, but they have great numbers." But, but, but!

And those few of us, four of the six spy teams, turned the entire crowd away with their fear and apprehension.

Where's the sense in that? We had just experienced God, big time, and they're scared about some people! Ro shouted over the din, "You are afraid of the people of the land? God just destroyed pharaoh. Wasn't he the most powerful man in the world? Didn't his army have swords, shields, and chariots? Some of you built them when we were his slaves! *But* now, here we are, one million men among us, plus our women and children. Who of you sustained even a scratch through all of that exodus? Has not the LORD God delivered You? YES, HE HAS!"

I chimed in, "Tall, armed, strong, *whatever*—they cannot stack up to GOD! Have you just lost your memories? Only some days ago, we were in our slave hovels, which had been our father's and their father's. God has let us taste freedom—"

I was interrupted by a heckler, "Did He let us taste it only to take the plate from us? Back in Egypt, we had leeks, cukes, onions, and rooves over our heads!"

Ro and I briefly glanced at each other. Some of those among us were not of us, so that as we left Egypt, we left as a mixed multitude. Some among us were not of Jacob's stock but opportunists along for the ride. These continued to spread seeds of doubt into the community. Then the best thing happened.

The other surveillance team on our side—it was Joshua, son of Nun and Caleb son of Jephunneh—countered my heckler, "Leeks and onions? Seasoned with the whip of a slave driver! I would sooner eat the bread delivered from God than the finest meats in the land of slavery! We are free men now! Thanks be to God! We are free to worship our God! We worked sun up and past sun down! When did you have time to enjoy your leeks? There are some among us dissuading you from trusting the God who *just* delivered you! Some of you were not made slaves like the rest of us who are of the blood Joseph. *You* can go back and bake bricks for the Egyptians. Perhaps in our absence, the burden would have fallen to you so you came along with us in the exodus. Our God is still God, the true and living God."

The other teams interrupted Caleb again. Their first word, *but*.

"But these people are giants. They're so big, we looked like grasshoppers in comparison!" That sent the wave of fear rippling through the crowds once again. Fear, negative talk, lack of faith—a trifecta of failure.

"Grasshoppers?" Joshua shouted back. "Then let us be an *army* of grasshoppers! You saw what God did with an army of locusts! You saw what God did with an army of frogs! Then let us be His army of grasshoppers!"

I mean, what part of "God is our salvation" are these people not getting? There were a few who stood with us, but not many. Moses tried to quiet down the crowd. His clan and Aaron's had formed a ring around me and Ro, Caleb, and Joshua. This crowd was getting aggressive, pressing in, fists in the air, promises of violence. Seriously, this is what we get for making the most amazing terrain surveillance? I looked over in the direction of my clan, for my wife and children.

People were getting jostled about. I had a confusion in my head of people shouting, cursing, and babies crying. I couldn't find my wife or my parents. Me, Ro, and the other guys weren't the least afraid. I just found myself getting more angered by the people for their lack of cohesion, short-term memory, lack of vision, and what about all the evidence like the cart of goods we brought back in demonstration! The hasty cart itself was of fine wood. Moses had grown tired of their balk and angry with their discrediting God. Good night! This people just saw a river turn into blood. Who could ever forget what *that* smelled like? Locusts, darkness, the Passover, need we continue? This was really just days past, not even some long ancient history ago, if that mattered.

Ro said, "The part that bothers me most is how someone can say just anything. No matter how groundless or how it must fly in the face of facts, yet another will run to it and latch on to it. Pull it in like a prized fish, then let it be their latest handicap, their *but*." I was still trying to find my wife in the crowd. This crowd had surely turned into a mob, moving and shouting in every direction. The center of the circle was us twelve "spies." Then it became a big oblong and a small circle. In the circle stood only Ro, myself, Joshua, and Caleb. We were insulated by Aaron, his brother and their clans. Moses tried to quiet the crowd, but his voice was drowned out in the din. Aaron's clan was moving us out of the center of the crowd, away to a quiet area.

Joshua was thinking aloud, really loud. "Me, I was glad that God chose my generation. My father never saw a day of his life as a free man. Neither did his father. They lived on a string of hope. On a story passed down that God had met Abraham in the desert and made a promise to him, that was all they had in all those years. And now, now we are *living* the day of that promise's fulfillment, and some of you don't want to see it. Well, go on back, if you want to!" Joshua shouted to the crowds. "Let the man who wants to take up his tent and go back to the bricks!"

At that, some of those closest lunged at him! Aaron's "guards" cut Joshua a look for making their job more difficult. But Joshua had to finish, "But God made a promise to our forefathers, and this is the day! The LORD is with us! We are able to take this land! What do you want to do? Swim back across the Reed Sea and go back to slavery? That's insane! God is moving us forward. He's let me live to see the day of my freedom. He just destroyed the Egyptian army. Not one of you lifted a finger to do it. Why would you doubt Him now? Why would He bring us through all of that—the locusts, the frogs, the darkness, the Passover, the sea, everything! Why would He have done all of that if He was just going to dump us here to get waxed by a bunch of idol worshippers? Not. My. God! Whatever He's doing, He's got my good in mind. He's stuck by us, and I'm stickin' by Him. If God says we can do it, we are well able to do it!

"Who is with us say, '*Aye!*'"

The long oblong of naysaying spies riled the crowds with help from the dissenters within it. The majority swayed with fear and continued trying to grab at us. Some of these men seemed very rough types. Maybe it was just because of the way we were living in the desert continually on the move. Next they talked about stoning us to death, we four! This meeting turned completely into a rumbling mob action. Phineas walked me and Ro to my tent. My wife and children were not there. I stood in the door, my eyes darting, then scanning the mess of swirling humanity turned mob. Where were my little ones? Ro looked at me, knowing my thoughts. His tent, closest to mine, was also empty. He could see it from where we stood. From there his gaze hung down. *Defeated!* "So they want to kill us?" he said. "For telling the truth?! For believing in our God?! For reminding them of what God just brought us through? I wonder which of these *offenses* they want to kill us for."

Unbelievable. I see myself go from being worthless, whipped regularly slave, to free landowner in our own sovereign nation, and it slips away, sifting through my fingers like hot sand.

I sat down, the floor of my tent was covered with a colorful woven rug. My wife made it. She could make anything and out of anything. She'd make it beautiful. She was beautiful. And she was missing. My little children, my world. My tent was empty without them. I stared across to the wall, unwilling to say what was on my mind. No matter, Ro did. "I can't do this. They'll kill us, and I'm not afraid of them, but my wife, my children. What'll become of them? Who will raise my sons? That's *my* job. *My* sons..." Ro was sitting and staring opposite from me. When our eyes met, we both nodded.

"We can't do this."

And so began the worst day of my life—when I abandoned God. I didn't think of it that way. Well, I did, but I didn't want to, so I tried to stop thinking, and I moved by emotion only. My emotions desperately needed to find my wife and children. I got up to leave the tent. Phineas had set a guard and left to return to other matters. The guard tried to stop me, but I said, "I give up. If they want to cower, so be it. I just need to find my wife." The guard let me pass. The guard looked at Ro, who indicated that he would follow me. The guard threw up his free hand, returned his knife to its scabbard and walked away. I guess, the same way I had just walked away from God. He melted into the crowd making someone else's safety his concern.

So I left God. It felt predictably empty. I walked through a sea of people hearing nothing. I heard, as if as well as one could, say, underwater. I didn't hear words, only noise. I just wanted to find my wife. My mind saw splotches of colors as if stars that had melted, their insides oozing outward—yellows, greens, all colors melting together onto a dark palate. Senseless. I heard myself tell someone, "Fine, fine, if that's the way you want it then. You'll hear no more from me." From some direction, my wife stood right in front of me, my three children grabbing my waist embracing me. She looked at me, just stared at me. She never said a word aloud, but I knew what it was. All of our lives we'd known the legacy of our God, who had promised to deliver us. Here it was, and I had just backed down.

Why? Her eyes asked. *What are you doing? How could you?*

My answer was foolish, I knew. *There are too many of them against. I can't do it.* I couldn't even say it aloud; it was so wrong. I felt ruined. I walked past her. Ruined. I walked past the tent where Moses, Joshua, Caleb, and a few others conferred. They who would move ahead with God. They were champions. I was in ruin. I collapsed under the weight of the fists in the air and the call to stoning. The pierce of my wife's eyes confirmed my error. I made her my objective. Once found, her deflection told me that she should not have been my primary objective. I knew that. I had shipwrecked myself, and I was floating, lost at sea. My whole life had just gone wrong in the last half hour, but I didn't turn around. That's the curious thing. I could have. Matter of fact, I still can. If only I had found the courage to stand back up for what I know is true. There's no sense in that—to know what's true down to your bone and be too cowardly to stand for it. But here right now, that's me today.

Part 4

A guy grabs me from behind, my shoulder, and beckons me with a finger over to a quiet spot. Know what he says? "Ha! Ha!" He says. "I saw you!"

"What?", I said. I could have been nicer. Should have been but I was struggling just then. He said he's watched me ever since the barn, me and Ro hiding cramped up in that big basket, his neighbor's barn. His friend stands watching but doesn't speak. He says he didn't blow our cover because he knew something was unusual, so he and his buddy followed me and Ro all the way back to our camp to our mayhem here. He said, he'd checked out all the stories and found people of different places that we'd passed through in the exodus. All the stories were true about our God. Well, *I knew that*. But he had to find it out, I guess. He asked me why I backed down and went with the majority "with a God like that," he said. "With a God like that—you can do anything! That God doesn't sit on the mantelpiece. That is *The Outside God!* He's real, He's alive, and He's all powerful! Believe me, I know gods!" What is he, some kind of "god" expert? This guy held out his hand to me. 'Come on, come with me. I'm going to Joshua and Caleb's tents. They're sticking with *The Outside God*. He cannot be defeated. Come on!

Ha! This stranger stood with his hand out to me. He was from the land we had just spied out. He left everything to find out about the true God, and in finding the truth, he stuck with it. I just stared at him. He had no family, no nothing. Surely he did, but he'd left all behind to follow God. He called Him *the God who lives outside, not on the mantel piece—the Outside God!* This fella doesn't even know His name, but he left everything to follow the God of Israel. I just stared at him. I didn't mean to stare. I was just thinking, *Look at what I've come through, and look at where you've come from. How is it that you've come around while I've blundered so badly?* But on the outside, I was just staring, so eventually, he walked away. He turned and walked to the tents where Moses, Joshua, and Caleb conferred to join the champions of faith and courage. I stood outside, watching.

Back in my tent, stretched out on my pallet, I rolled my tunic up as a pillow and laid my tired head upon it. I sat up for a moment to pull a small splinter out of the roll. It was from the cart we had rigged to bring back samples.

My life keeps turning corners that I never would have guessed. God pronounced judgment on a foolish people who rejected Him. So they said it's better to die here in the desert than to go up against the inhabitants of our promised land. God said that He will grant that request. The men who spied with us and came back spreading fear throughout the nation were struck down with plague. The rest of us are to remain in the desert for the next forty years, a year for every day we spied out the land, until those over the age of twenty, who stood against the LORD die. So we move from place to place in this scrub, living in tents, packing, and relocating. It seems as if we bury some from among us at every juncture. In His mercy, the LORD has spared those who stood with Him. Joshua, son of Nun, and Caleb, son of Jephunneh, stand to carry out the work of the LORD. Every man must choose for himself. I chose poorly and now must walk the path that I chose until they must bury me here. At least my children will make it in. After all that I've been through, why would I make the wrong choice? I put my family before my God. Even my wife is ashamed of me. Then I put my life ahead of my God. True, I didn't get stoned, but now this is my life: to my core, *miserable,* because I turned my back on the One who didn't turn His back on me. Here's what I've preserved—a life of misery, and for my children, a legacy of shame. I closed my eyes and breathed in much needed sleep.

Part 5

Morushe picked at the campfire. The tip of his long thin branch was a glowing orange and crumbling the more he poked around in the flames. "Delmez, you've taken me on a lot of wild rides, but this is by far…well, this has made everything else that I've endured at your hands, worth it. I feel like I have a whole new life ahead. I've never really thought about a god being interested and active in the lives of humans. I guess because I've never believed in all those other ones since I knew you made them…"

"Wait a minute, are you insulting my craftsmanship?" Delmez had made use of an overturned wooden cart, a byproduct from the near uprising, and leaned his back against it. He cast small pebbles toward the crackle of the campfire. "Now my smelt work isn't realistic? Is that it? Not good enough for you?" Delmez tested his friend. He felt safe. He felt good and safe. No other way to describe it— excited for what would be coming next but safe in the fold of the outside God whose name he still didn't even know.

"No, not a critique, I'm just saying. I've seen you take a lump of metal or a scrap of wood that anyone else would have thrown in the fire. I've seen you beat and carve it into something that someone would pay for and the people's imagination do the rest. But this God is all historical fact. I'm in awe, but that fellow you were talking to—"

"I can't make it out, Mor. He's holding the bad decision in his hands, knows it and won't let it go. All I can say is we are all free to choose, in fact, we must. What comes along with the choice, the consequence, is what may be hard to live with, and that is the thing which we cannot choose."

Landslide
Joshua 5

*W*ho'll win a race, a camel or a rabbit? The camel can run, and it has long legs. But the rabbit has speed and cunning. Aaiii...we are the camel.*

Suddenly the man on the dias stood up! With an angry growl, he grabbed an attendant's sword and flung it, sending guards scattering! It stood standing, stabbing the soil for a moment until it fell over and lay quietly in the grass.

He'll kill me. I'm only a messenger.

"Speak slowly, and tell me again *plainly*, exactly what you saw." Demanded the man.

Breathe...focus...you can do this. Oh, goodbye, Mother. Goodbye, my father. I'm only seventeen, and today, I die in the service of an angry king...because...because he's afraid! He's afraid of the rabbit! The little one come out of nowhere, who will win...

Senoweh took a deep breath, doing his best to fill the lung cavities to their utmost. *Steady and be ready.* "My king," young Senoweh began, "it is indeed as I have said. The captain has sent me to report what we have seen. The band of peoples that which came out of Egypt devastating the great pharaoh's army. They have run through two Amorite kings east of the river, and they are now upon our door. They have been camped at the Jordan River these three days—"

"Yes, yes! We know all of that! Get on with it!" the man on the dias, the king, snapped at Senoweh impatiently. For a moment, he turned, giving a nervous look to the army general sitting to his right. Again calmly, he quietly said, "Get on with your report, boy!"

Breathe…be steady now and live. Live! If he hurls his sword again, I'll run. There to the left around those guards, then over that way! I'll disappear. I'll run to the rabbit! But it's no rabbit! It's a lion! A lion running through the desert and now ready to pounce. I'll run to the lion, plead for mercy…steady now, be alert, get ready to run…

Senoweh inhaled a great gulp of air as he continued, "Well… they…they carry a box wherein dwells their God. At least, we think so! And it is their priests who carry this box. On poles…and…anyway…the priests and the box of the God stepped into the river and… and…" *Ooiii…steady and be ready to run* "And the river waters began to move!"

"Water moves, boy! That's what it does!" The general made himself and several of his attendants chuckle. Would he be intimidated by a god who lives in a wooden box? The reports about this god must have been erroneous, and besides, he desperately needed to diffuse the king's fear, lest he make some poor, snap judgements. All of the seven nations around had become fearful hearing that the band with the powerful God was near. But the nations were many and had many gods; surely, they could conquer this one band simply by sheer numbers. Even if they weren't always best of friends, in their mutual best interests, leaders of Canaanite, Hittie, Hivite, Perizzite, Girgashite, and Jebusite nations had gathered to discuss the approaching band. Some knew their lands had been spied out.

"Well," Senoweh said, "water doesn't move like this!" General Kauw raised an eyebrow to a youth who dared snap back.

Senoweh made his case. "The waters collected themselves and left a dry bed riverbed a mile wide! Go yourself and see the town of Adam where it just piles up and rolls upon itself! It's like a waterfall. The water falls down and then goes up and falls down all over again!"

The king glared at his hapless general. "Anyway," Senoweh continued, clearly indicating that the most important detail was yet to come. "Anyway, as I said, as soon as their priests stepped into the river, with the box, the water moved, and the Israelite band had begun crossing to this side! That's when the captain sent me back to you to report what we've seen!"

"Not possible…" the general muttered. "These things cannot be…the river is at flood stage this time of year. What fools would try to cross it at the worst time of the year?"

The king flashed anger at his army general. "Enough of your arrogance! Are all of these reports, even going back to those of pharaoh, to be disbelieved to assuage your pride? The Amorite kings, Sihon and Og, were completely destroyed by this band! Attendant, call the council at once! We must decide what can be done. We cannot prevail against the God of the box who controls the earth, wind, and sky! With Him, those people are more powerful by a landslide!" The king turned to young Senoweh who was beginning to sense that he didn't have to run for his life. "Well done, young man. We'll soon have an answer for you to carry back to your captain. In the meantime, you may rest in the general's quarters." General Kauw, caught off guard and outranked by the decision, squinted his eyes at Senoweh with some message not meant to be taken kindly. To his Captain, Kauw barked, "See to it—most comfortable!"

Captain Meshuroai understood completely. The young soldier was to be taken to the soldier's tents, furnished rations, and rest. "Come on, boy, let's see if we can find you some water that moves!" It would have been a hardier laugh enjoyed by all had the king not been gravely concerned about the God-of-the-box. Senoweh was handed off to yet a lesser rank, and led to the rear where soldiers of all ages, mostly conscripted, mostly for life, encircled him to hear fresh news of the unstoppable band.

The king stepped off the temporary dias. As he moved, an entourage moved in concert to the tent of counsel where field decisions were planned. Sifting through a crowded tent of attendees who would rather have been elsewhere, the king searched each face to find a surprise he didn't know he had. He found none, but an answer was desperately needed. "Sihon *and* Og? *Both* of them?" He looked down at his lap pensively and quietly said, "Smashed…and they were the Repahim, the terrible ones." The king spoke aloud, locking eyes with each listener. "And all they asked for was to pass through the land unmolested? Now those fools have lost their land to the wild band. How could this happen? What are we to do? We are many bands. They are only one. They can only draw themselves so thin. Do we let them pass? Where are they going to? Does anyone know the objective destination?" Now everyone spoke and all at once, which caused some confusion, but it was better than the silence of defeat.

"Win back Heshbon! Win back Bashan! Fight as one! Surround them as many! My lord, we need only furnish continual watch to see what direction they move. Yes, we strike as one and drive them where we want!" The king listened to all input until the chatter died down.

"Well, where *is* that, 'where we want'? One thing for certain, they won't go *backward*. They may have destroyed the pharaoh, but they won't claim that land, or they'd have done it in the first place. No, they're going somewhere, and we need to find out where that is. Then we can set up defenses and fight to eradicate them."

One solemn lord spoke softly as if he held the scales of reason in his right hand. "Defenses? Defenses? You do not know your foe! What defenses did pharaoh have against a billion frogs? Twice that in locusts? Rivers of blood? You speak as if you are fighting men, but I am telling you that none of you alone or as one with any or all of your gods are a match for that God and *no, He does not live in a box!* The wisest thing that you can do is concede. There are no gods in any of our regions alone or combined that are able to match that God. I have seen with my own eyes how He smites their enemies and protects them in the very midst of the tempest. I was there in Memphis the night that the angel of death passed over their homes yet smote the firstborn of every uncovered home. You do not comprehend the magnitude of the God that champions these people. He goes before them in battle." He threw his drawn sword into the dirt. "Resign and submit yourselves. Perhaps we will find Him to be a God of mercy as well as strength. He moved toward the door of the tent, attendants in tow.

"Where are you going?" the king asked in frustration.

"To find the boy. I, too, saw the water move."

Senoweh was escorted to wait in an infantryman's tent. While the counsel debated, Senoweh laid on a mat, making his decisions as well. It would be dark soon. He would run fast, fast as a camel. He would run home, get his parents, and then return to the front to dispatch his message. From there, he and his family would slip away and become people of the lion.

Hours later, evening turned into night. A strong arm frightened Senoweh from his sleep. A thick hand covered his mouth. Senoweh tried to jump up, but a dark shadow pinned his arms down to his shoulders. "You will not leave this camp." Despair gripped Senoweh. The king would have him killed after all. How terrible this life is. *How unfair to kill the messenger. I am only the messenger. He means to put fear into the soldiers on the frontline by returning my body to them.* His strength gave up the impossible task of fighting this strong arm. His back went limp onto the mat.

The strong arm sensed Senoweh's compliance so he continued, "You will not leave without me. I know what you say is true because I have seen it myself." He released his grip. In the darkness, Senoweh could make out the face, the eyes, the single scar along the upper jaw, the voice! It was the one officer in the commander's tent who dared to stand up against all the others. "I am Heshnowen, formerly lord vassal to the king, but the king speaks madness and certain death. I choose life. I know you do as well. You are a good soldier. I have a plan, and it is already in place. I have dispatched my family members to collect your entire family. As I speak, they are on their way to our meet point. Once we deliver the king's decision to the captain on watch at the Jordan River, we will break away. We will all cross over and submit ourselves to the people of the real God."

*****

"God of the box? God of the box?" Joshua's officers found a lighthearted moment in their acceptance of this band of immigrants during their preparations for war. "God doesn't live in the box! God created the universe and everything that you see. He created you! Why would He live in a box? God isn't a god made by human hands. He wasn't carved from wood or stone! He forbids us to make images. We only worship Him! He is the Great I AM, the beginning, from everlasting to everlasting!"

"Aaahhh…," Senoweh said as he sat on the floor of the tent learning about the true God. He ate of the camp's rationed provisions, which seemed better than the fine food of the general's camp. Yesterday Senoweh

179

thought that he was about to die. Now his spirit felt assurance as he never had before. This night was the beginning of a whole new life. This God of love and life wanted him to live. This life was better—by a landslide!

Maybea
(Num. 22; Rev. 2:14)

My name is Maybea Bray. You may call me *Maybea*. Don't give me any nicknames or jokes, bet you a million, billion sheckels I've heard them all! Just Maybea. I live in the center of the earth, and that, my friend, is *not* where you live. It's where *I* live. Cool Mediterranean breezes; lush pasture; beautiful rugged mountains; and cool, clean water to drink—I was born here in this land. Somewhere around here. I guess. Now hold on to your pine straw, and don't get to thinking what you're thinking. Your species is so judgmental! You start waving that almighty opposable thumb and discredit everyone else's worth. The equine species is not as dumb as you might think. We nonspeech creatures just might know a lot more of what's going on than we let on to. We are very observant, and we pay attention. Close attention. You think we're just out here eating all day long? Well, that too…but we see a lot of things in the physical and spiritual. Your 'higher' species just run right past the obvious and bungle everything up!

Take me for example. My life started out great, just wonderfully—a nice field of grass, warm climate, no predators in lunging range, life was good! Then the wretched human who lives on the land *sold* me! Sold me to his wretched neighbor who had an even more wretched little human son. Oh, the trouble that one caused. And that little one, everyone must have known that he was trouble because he never had any friends. Not a one. That's how I came on the scene. The human father gave the boy a dog, but it ran away. So I was abducted! Dragged from my lush field and fine life to grow this…*human* boy. But immediately, I refused the job. I could tell he was more work than I could put into him or that I wanted to. I mean, sometimes a Jenny's gotta stand her ground. Nevertheless, I was inducted into the service of this…child.

From the beginning, his father, Beor, showed an egregious lack of discipline. So what more would you expect of the child? And he'd been a creepy kind of kid, just always. Here's what I mean: One day I was minding my business being the territorial creature that I am. I patrol my fields and keep the *us's* in and the *thems* out. If you're not one of us, I'll run you off! That's what we Jennys do. Anyone who doesn't belong here with our horses, sheep, and other creatures is gonna hit the road! *I* make it happen! Anyway, it was a quiet day, early in the afternoon. *She* was in the kitchen making some kind of food like a soup. It was smelling rather good! Leeks, cabbage, celery, carrots, potatoes—I could pick out each smell. The boy went in when *she* wasn't watching and grabbed the whole pot! He sneaked to the back door with the pot, ate a bowl or two, and left the rest sitting on the door step. And so what was I to do? I don't have this God-given sense of smell for nothing. I meandered over to the stoop, and the lovely smell wafted past my nostrils. It tasted even better, and before I knew much, I had slurped the entire pot. Boy, did I get a flogging for that! Not only that. Then the little wretch would take things from his parents, play with them, and leave them outside, incriminating me—missing sandals, woven clothes, oh yummy linens and cottons, freshly baked loaves of bread. I have a fine and widely appreciative palate, so somehow, I had gotten into a thing or two. Well, that's not fair! Would you flog a dog for wagging its tail? Oh boy, did I get it again and again.

I've never even been on the inside of a house, but they are jam-packed with things to eat, and food too! Well, I still have scars from those days. Getting me in trouble was fun for the miserable boy. I suppose he had to do something; he had no friends. I mean, not a one.

I used to have to walk him to the village markets. He was a lazy one. I carried everything and sometimes him as well. And the narrow streets are so crowded with vendors and shoppers you can barely walk. He'd be on my back just beating me with a staff till I'd drop to my knees to get him off. The last time, I'd just had enough! I was going to stomp him to death, but I felt compassion for his crusty heart. I often think that I should not have let the opportunity pass.

So the mule-headed boy, Balaam, grew up to be a miserable and friendless adult human, always contrary to what is good. What did he do for a living? He classed amongst the most despicable of your species. He was a conjurer of sorts. One who used divination and false words in "prophecy." I mean, how do you fall into that line of work? Why couldn't he just be a farmer?

So one day a king, fella named Balak, king of Moab, sees the Israelite nation coming, squashing everything and everybody in its path. This Balak is scared, so he tries to hire Balaam to curse the Israelites. He sends a delegation of important types to bribe Balaam. Interesting that Balak recognizes the superiority of the Israelite God but he doesn't have enough respect to submit to Him. He tries to treat the Almighty like the false gods of his own nation—some kind of power to harness and manipulate. I told you that you "higher species" run right past the obvious and bungle things up. So Balak has heard about what the Israelite God has done all the way from Egypt, but all he thinks about is how to manipulate God. What a bungle! Why does *he* get to be a king and I get to carry a loser on my back all day? How did that work out? But anyway, back to Balak. He's scared of the Israelites, and here they are camped under his nose, ready to plow him and his little kingdom under. Balak doesn't understand what "God" means or the nature of the true God. Seems like he only thinks in terms of magic tricks. Humans have a special kind of logic that can miss a forest for all of the trees, but hey I'm just a donkey thinking out loud…anyway…

When Balak's people arrived with bags of stuff to bribe Balaam, Balaam told Balak that he first had to consult God to see what God would allow him to do. That night, God told Balaam *Don't do it.* God said, "Don't go with those men or try to put a curse on Israel because the nation is blessed." So in the morning, Balaam sent the men back home.

Then Balak sent another delegation of even more important people, with even more stuff and a big pile of money to bribe Balaam.

Ol' Balaam had a hard time turning his eyes from the pile-o-stuff. I'm just sayin'. He was liking the fancy clothing, trinkets, and all that gold bullion way too much. Me personally, I got no use for it, but Ol' Bale's eyes got so big they liked to pop out! He wanted that money so badly he wanted to figure out a way around God. Now, *how're you gonna do that?* Go around God? That's not gonna work out—any donkey knows that! But Ol' Balaam decided to keep asking God until he could find some loophole. Do you know what I mean? Until he heard what he wanted to hear or figured out a way to twist circumstances so that he could get all of that shiny stuff. Balaam told the men to stay overnight, like the first group did, and that he would ask God again. Now, I've just gotta stop here for a moment. *Why?* Why does Balaam find himself in this very spot? God already gave him an answer about this situation. *It wasn't the answer Balaam wanted to hear.* So now, God is angry with Balaam because of his disobedience and greed. So God gave Balaam up to his own greed. See, sometimes God lets a thing happen so that *you* can learn something about *yourself*, and you need to ask God to help you change it for the better. Balaam should have said, "Sorry, guys, but God already said no, so I can't do it. Sorry you came all this way! Have a safe trip back home…" That's what he *should* have done and repented to God for his selfishness. But Balaam was unrepentant in his heart, so God told him to go on with the men from Moab but only do what God would tell him to do.

In the morning, Balaam saddles me up. Now, number one: as big as he is, he ought to be walking. After all, I'm not a horse; I'm a donkey, and he isn't a small boy anymore. Number two, why is it that your species always has to take so much stuff with you everywhere you go? Why can't you just *go*? When I see a nice green patch of fescue, do I try to take the rye I'm standing in with me? No! I just *go*. I leave the rye and go enjoy the fescue. Why? There'll be more rye when I get back. Your species always drags around pockets, purses, garments, coins, oh so many things to weigh the packs on the backs of hardworking nonspeech creatures. And by the way, why don't you make the streets wider? So many people crowd the marketplaces that one can hardly pass…and well, anyway that's my point so I'll pick up the story.

So I'm walking on the road with this huge man on my back, and there in plain-enough sight for a *blind man* to see, stands an angel of God. He has a very large, very sharp-looking sword drawn, and he's right in my path, so I get off the road and turn into a field. Balaam starts kicking me in the side, *very annoying...*he tries to get me back onto the road, but there's no room for me, him on my back and the angel all in the same space, so I just stay off the road until the angel leaves. Common sense, eh? All the while, Balaam is beating me with a rod. The angel moves on ahead up the road, so I started walking again. The angel stopped in the road again, and the man on my back is kicking me in the side and beating me with a rod. Unbearable this man. So I think, this is a narrow pass between two walls. If I just suck it in a bit, I can get by because I'm really regretting that day I didn't beat him to death as a child. So I try to pass closely to the wall. Balaam's big ol' foot got smashed against the wall, *a little smashed*, but he starts beating me again. I am *reaaallly* getting tired of this fellow. Once the angel moved away, I was able to walk again, but as the first time, he only moved up ahead on my path. This time the spot was so tight there was nowhere to turn. I am tired, I ache, so I lay down to rest, and the wretched human beat on me a third time. That's it! Enough is enough! I am just fed up with this human. I am a creature of great patience, but this was too much. I should have kicked him to death back in the day. I let all of his shortcomings go, but this was too much. I had to confront him. As much as nonspeech creatures loathe breaking the barrier between us and you humans, augh! I just had to, so I snapped at him.

"What have I done to you to make you beat me these three times?" I mean, *explain yourself*, Mister! Do you know what he does? I'll tell you what he *doesn't* do! He *doesn't* even notice that I'm *speaking!* I tell you: your species is *so* unobservant. And he's still sitting on my back; he just starts yelling at me. I roll my shoulder so that if he doesn't get off me, he'll just topple over. He finally gets up, walks right in front of me, and he's still yelling, "Blah, blah, blah... You've made a fool of me, and if I had a sword I'd kill you right now! blah, blah, blah, blah, blah!" Isn't that a nice treat—what I get for a life time of commitment and service? There's a fine lot of ingratitude, which has been the hallmark attitude of this human all his life. I mean, I looked at him and then I just looked away. Take a deep breath; think before you speak. That's a free bit of good advice for you, by the way. So I'm calm, collected. I look back right in his miserable face, and I said, "Am I not your donkey, which you have always ridden to this day? Have I ever done this before?"

What I'm saying is *Thiiinnnk, man!* But no, Ol' Balaam's not much of a thinker.

He says, "Well, no, you've never done anything like this before."

Well, no? Well, no? That's the best he could do? Genius of a man, that Balaam! So God had to intervene and open his eyes so that he could see the angel who's been blocking my path all this time. Boy, you should'a seen him jump! Know what he did, that coward? I thought he was gonna go from heart failure right then and there, but the coward jumped up when he saw the angel with the sword and ran behind me! Oh, man alive! That was worth the trip! Then the angel, *he* says to Balaam, "Why have you beaten your donkey these three times? I have come to oppose you because your plan is reckless. The donkey saw me and turned away. If she had not, I would have killed you by now, but I would have spared her."

So now Balaam is starting to get the picture. I'm sure I could almost hear his little brain parts scraping together. *Maybe, I'm soooo sorry. Let's just go home and get you a big basket of apples and maybe a kettle of soup or something.* No! Nooo! That's not what happens! He says to the angel, "I didn't see you trying to oppose me, but if you're displeased, I will turn back."

Oh, what? Now, Mr. Nice Guy? *Now,* you're willing to turn back? Now I have to comment on this bit of insincerity. In my modest opinion, he was scared to death of the angel with drawn sword, yes! But if he really was interested in obeying the word of God, why did he let these Moabite priests stay overnight when God had already told him *no* in the first place? He had already received God's answer about the situation. God said don't do it. I'm a donkey, and *I* understood that! Why does he find himself here on this road at this time going to aid the Moabite king? I think he pursued the matter so that he could hear what he wanted to hear so that he could get all of that shiny stuff. Anyway, even I could see through this thin veil of sincerity to his true motives, and remember, I've know this human for many years.

So, the angel of the Lord says, "Go ahead with these men but only say what I tell you to say." What a greedy human, this Balaam. He wanted the money and prestige that King Balak was offering to him. So, God released him to his depravity.

So, on we go to Moab, and I'm feeling pretty good about what God is gonna do. I know it's gonna be something good! I wonder what's scraping around in Ol' Balaam's brain. Wishin' he hadn't gone too far now? Shiny stuff doesn't seem so shiny anymore? Why didn't he just listen to God and let Balak the king get what was coming to him? Why'd he drag himself into this mess? Well, I'm never in a hurry, so that walk gave Ol' Balaam a lot of time to worry about a lot of questions. I figure, if I'm going to walk a lot, I may as well enjoy it, so I did. When we finally got to our destination, Balak built seven altars and sacrifices a bull and a ram on each one. What was that all about? Trying to manipulate the Israelite God, perhaps? Then Balaam received a word from God:

Balak brought me from Aram, the king of Moab from the eastern mountains. "Come," he said, "curse Jacob for me. Come, denounce Israel." How can I curse those whom God has not cursed? How can I denounce those whom The LORD has not denounced? From the rocky peaks I see them, from the heights I view them. I see a people who live apart and do not consider themselves one of the nations. Who can count the dust of Jacob or number the fourth part of Israel? Let me die the death of the righteous, and may my end be like theirs!"

Well, I guess I was the only one laughing at that point, but it sure was funny to me! Ol' King Balak was in a fit! He screamed, "What're you doing? I told you to curse them! Curse them, don't bless them. Man, what're you doing? You've blessed them!" Balaam wasn't exactly sure how the words came to be in his mouth 'cause he wasn't planning to say any of that, but all the same, he knew it was God, so he just begged off, "Hey, all I can do is say what God puts in my mouth."

Now the next part of the story makes no sense, but I'm talking about humans, so… Balak doesn't get the hint. Instead, he says, "Let's try another spot!"

Huh? What's that supposed to do? But off we go to another field. Balak builds seven more altars and offers seven more bulls and rams. That's a waste of time, but what do I care; I got to rest awhile. And Balaam gets another word from the Lord:

Arise, Balak, and listen: hear me son of Zippor. God is not a man that he should lie, nor a son of man that he should change his mind. Does he speak and then not act? Does he promise and not fulfill? I have received a command to bless: he has blessed, and I cannot change it. No misfortune is seen in Jacob, no misery observed in Israel. The Lord their God is with them. The shout of the King is among them. God brought them out of Egypt. They have the strength of a wild ox. There is no sorcery against Jacob, no divination against Israel. It will now be said of Jacob and of Israel, "See what God has done!" The people rise like a lioness. They rouse themselves like a lion that does not rest till he devours his prey and drinks the blood of his victims.

King Balak yells, "Don't curse them or bless them!"

Balaam again says, "Man, I gotta do whatever God says."

Okay, here's the part where only humans can understand.

King Balak says, "Let's try another spot!"

I mean, what *is it* with your species? Really? So off we go again, another high point to overlook the nation of Israel, ready to plow through Moab, another seven altars, seven bulls, and seven rams. Balaam would have resorted to sorcery, but even he knew that God would not tolerate him, and he looked at the Israelites camped tribe by tribe, and God's Spirit came over him: The oracle of Balaam son of Beor, the oracle of one whose eye sees clearly, the oracle of one who hears the words of God, who sees a vision from the Almighty, who falls prostrate and whose eyes are opened: *How beautiful are your tents, O Jacob, your dwelling places, O Israel! Like valleys they spread out, like gardens beside a river, like aloes planted by the* LORD, *like cedars beside the waters. Water will flow from their buckets. Their seed will have abundant water. Their king will be greater than Agag. Their kingdom will be exalted. God brought them out of Egypt. They have the strength of a wild ox. They devour hostile nations and break their bones in pieces. With their arrows, they pierce them. Like a lion they crouch and lie down, like a lioness, who dares to rouse them? May those who bless you be blessed, and those who curse you be cursed!*

Balak finally gets it! He's not gonna get any curse on Israel like that. He's done. He jumps up on his horse about to go his way, but Balaam, did I mention he was greedy? He sees his payoff walking away, and he knows he can't outright curse the Israelites. "Wait! I...know," Balaam shouts, "I know how you can get them..." He lowers his voice as if it would lessen his treachery, his culpability. Balaam says, "I know how to get them to curse *themselves.*" Balak stopped his horse in its tracks, head down. He slowly turns back around to Balaam and gazes intently into his eyes. Yeah, he did it: Balaam once again circumvented God's will. I mean, he'd done it already; that's why he was even *in* Moab in the first place. Now his plan is just sinister but completely "Balaam." He tells Balak how to tempt the Israelites so that they sin against God. That would compromise the covering God put over the people. Now, again, explain to me your species: how could someone who seems to know a few things about God, who even speaks to God and *God speaks back,* I mean, does God have conversation like that with everyone? No! You have something. Why wouldn't you want to seek Him out to have an amazing, beautiful communion with the Almighty Creator? Why would you just be trying to manipulate Him to get a nice smock and a pocketful of gold bits? Only a Balaam. He knows God is against him cursing Israel, so Balaam gets the Israelites to do it to themselves. Is that supposed to square with God? I mean, what *is it* with your species? Really! So anyway, Balaam tells king Balak how to set a trap, which the Israelites fall right into. While at Peor, the Israelites mixed with the Midianites committing idolatry and more sins before God. It causes a huge plague, and thousands of Israelites die before it's over.

Ol' Balaam got his money, but he didn't get to keep it for long. He was killed in revenge for inciting that scourge in which twenty-four thousand people from Israel and Midian had died! Never got to wear his nice smock. A fat lot of good all the gold bits did him. I guess he lived up to his name—*one that ruined a people.*

So ended the life of a wretched man who chose to be so.

I'm only a donkey, but take my advice: God is good. All the time. *Seek Him while He may be found!*

Have I Got a Story for You!
(*Judg. 6–7*)

"Aaauuggggghhh! Late! I'm late! I can't believe I overslept! What a disaster! Nobody does this!" Rofie jumped up, rolled up his cot, grabbed a cloth, and headed to the creek. After a quick wash, Rofie wrapped his tunic around his waist, all the while running in the early-morning darkness, back to his tent. At least it was still so dark that no one could see him or at least how unprepared he was for the morning roll call. Rofie hung the wet tunic inside his small tent, suspending it from one of the poles that constructed the tent's frame. His other article of clothing, a working tunic, lay ready for the day. He slipped it on quickly, tied a belt around his waist, and strapped sandals on. Weapons. Rofie had several knives. He chose a longer one with its sheath, sliding it at the waist between the tunic and belt. Finally, he grabbed a sword, which had been gifted to him by an uncle. It was a handed-down item once plundered from some great exploitation the details of which had grown muddled over time. Rofie thought he had some idea how to use it, but in truth, he had no practical knowledge. He brought it figuring that it would be useful in a time of war, as this was, and he was glad of it. *We're making history—tales which will be told to our children's children's children. And what will they ask me? "Great grandpa, what did you do in the battle?" And what will I say, "Well, children, I missed the battle because I overslept!" Augh, no!*

Out of the tent, across the maze of other soldier shelters, Rofie made his way toward the assembly point. Darkness now lifting past dawn, he noticed two, four, groups, now more soldiers walking in the opposite direction. *Oh no, what's going on? Nothing worse than being late and missing instruction.* He was too embarrassed to stop and ask why so many men were going the wrong way but now woefully sure that they had new instructions, which he had missed. *There's Alban. I can ask him what's happening.* Rolfie motioned to Alban to step aside out of the southbound procession for a moment. "Alban, what's going on? Why is everyone going the wrong way?" Alban was indifferent to the obvious fact that Rofie had missed the role. Didn't matter.

"They said we could go home. They said we could go on home." Alban started to get back into the southbound lane, but Rolfie had his left hand fastened to Alban's left bicep.

"Wait, what do you mean, 'They said we can go home'? *Who* said we can go home? What's going on Alban?"

Alban's right hand pried Rolfie's grip open. "Look, man, stay if you want to, but I'm just not... I mean, these Midianites are a tough lot. Besides, I'm from Asher. A lot of us came from Zebulun and Naphtali's tribes, too, besides your own. We were called up, and we came a long way. Look, I have a farm and a family... Purah said we could go home if we're..."

"Afraid?"

"Well, yah, afraid. And that I am, so see you another day." Alban threw off Rofie's hand and went back to find his tent and others who would be travelling with him.

Rofie continued on, and as he got closer to the command post at the spring of Harod, he passed great numbers of men going in the opposite direction, inquiring until he found Purah, Gideon's assistant. "Well, we have too many men—"

Both of Rofie's eyebrows shot upward at the same time. *Too many men* and *Fight the Midianites,* just don't go together in the same context. Purah, noting the young man's overt expression and knowing God was up to some more greatness, just smiled. He put a hand on young Rofie's shoulder, and they began to walk just a short distance but in the opposite direction of the great column of soldiers in the right direction. "*God said...*we have too many men! So He has graciously allowed anyone who is afraid to go home. You can go, too, if you like—"

What? Let me figure this out: The LORD, Himself, told Gideon to fight, so that's a win! The LORD knows how tough the Midianites are, and even though Gideon called in three more tribes to help, God said we don't need them? That's gotta be a win! This is gonna be something good! Something epic! Something I can tell my children's children's children when I have them. And when I do, and they ask me, "Great-Grandpa, what did you do in the battle?" I'll say, "I went forward while twenty-two thousand went back home…" I'm in!

Rofie suddenly stopped in his tracks. The triumph on his face erased, and his eyebrows tried to meet each other at the bridge of his nose in doubt. "Wait, did I just say twenty-two thousand? Twenty-two thousand? Purah, did you say that twenty-two thousand fighting men just went home?"

"Yup!" Purah rubbed his hands together, enjoying the brisk early-morning air. "Samuel! Take twenty men with you and see that the camp is evacuated quickly and quietly! Go now!" He turned back to Rofie, "Look, young man, you are free to go or you can stay, but I have a lot of planning and coordinating to do right now. May the LORD be with you, whatever your decision!" Purah walked quickly toward the command tent. Rofie caught Samuel before he'd gotten far on the southern trail.

"Who is that Purah, exactly?"

"Gideon's second in command!"

Wow! Never seen anything like this! See how this man trusts the very word of God and that's enough for him. If I go home now, for sure I'll miss something big that God's about to do. It'll be a story for my children's children's children. When I have them.

"Lirion!" Purah popped out of the command center. "Take five men with you—Yigal, Ofer, Shai, Ze'ev, and Raviv. Of all the men who have elected to stay, send them to down to the water. Have them take a drink. There the LORD will direct us. Of whomever I say, 'Send him to the left,' your men will keep them to the left. Of whomever I say, 'Keep him to the right,' your men will keep them to the right!"

Lirion took charge of his men, and at the appropriate time, they sent the men either to a group on the left or a group on the right. Rofie stood his turn in line, and when he with a small group were sent to drink from the spring, none of them knew what to expect. Perhaps it was a fighting drill, and "enemies" would spring from the tall grass with batons and pretend to spear them. *Did the Midianites have some fighting style we needed a speedy training on?* Rofie was not about to be ambushed by anyone, but he was thirsty. He approached the spring with suspicious caution, and having briefly surveyed the area, Rofie cupped his hands, filled them with water, and drank delicious water. In a moment, Lirion pointed, sending Rofie and one other off in a group to the right and the others of their group off to the left. *Well, what was that all about? This is the army. Hurry up and wait!*

About two hours later, Rofie's small group was led by Lirion back to Purah, now a familiar face to Rofie. The men were reissued fighting gear. "Well…," Purah began in his familiar satisfied tone, "it looks like the LORD wants Israel to know that this victory is by His hand. So He has sent most of our fighters home, and most of the remainder will be back at camp while we three hundred will be sent to destroy the enemy."

This is gonna be a story to tell because as I hear it, there are Midianites, Amalekites, and a huge mixture of other people in that valley down there…so that means…ummmm roughly…ohhh, I guess four hundred and fifty of them for each one of us. But… Purah seems to believe that what God says He does, and actually, I know that to be true myself. I guess I never really thought to put it in my own life. It's always been a story in the past or in someone else's life, but now, here I am, one of three hundred. The enemy has more camels than we have soldiers, but I'm gonna get a good night's sleep so that I don't miss the excellent story of whatever God's gonna do tomorrow…

"*Great-Grandpa Rofie, what did you do in the battle?*"

"*Well, little one. Your great-grandpa was just a young man back then in Gideon's army.*"

"*Great-Grandpa, did you carry a sword?*"

"*No, little one. I carried a horn in my right hand, a jar with a torch inside it in my left hand, and a great shout for the LORD of lords in my heart! When Commander Gideon signaled, we three hundred, all blew our horns, smashed the jars which held our torches, and we shouted, "For* the LORD and for Gideon," God caused such fear in the enemy camp that they turned on themselves. Many slaughtered each other, and the rest fled. We fought them all the way to Beth Barah, and that was a very long way. That was the day that the LORD defeated a great, great army with just a handful of faithful servants. My prayer for you, little one, is that you chose to be a faithful servant of the LORD, and let Him do great things in your life!"

The Volunteer State
(2 Kings 5)

Liman pulled the burlap sack higher up on his shoulder. The rope that tied it shut on one end draped down the length of his torso until its other end was wrapped around his left hand. He opened and closed the hand to make the prickly feeling go away and inhaled a deep breath to inspire him on his task. One more time, he asked his companion, "He was the *what? Of who?*" He hadn't decided if it was a question or an exclamation, but if he declared it a question, he could perhaps get some clarity. With that, he added, "I can't believe it! I can't believe it! How do you know that?"

Rigsier, feeling the wiser for bringing his pack animal, gesticulated with his free hand while holding the donkey's lead with the other. "Believe it or don't, it's still true. I know it with my own eyes!" he said, pointing with emphasis to his eyes.

"How could he be here?" Liman continued with his indeterminate exclamations. Not that he didn't believe his friend. It was just that the truth was such a huge story, and Rig just mentioned it so incidentally and matter-of-factly. Liman didn't have a heavy load, but he did wish he had the foresight to bring along his donkey. He made a mental note should this occasion happen again.

"I don't know all about that. I just know what I know. Why don't you ask him yourself? You may see him soon enough."

Sometimes you want to know something but only if someone else is willing to get the information. That was mostly how Liman felt just then. He didn't need to know such that it would put him in personal jeopardy. He was just extremely curious. "I'm not asking nobody nothin'! I'm already too close. How'd we get stuck on this detail anyway?"

"There's nothing wrong with helping needful folk," Rig commented. "I've done this plenty of times. I'm all right, aren't I? It doesn't take all that long. It's something different, and it's helping people. We have to help each other. People are supposed to help each other. Come on, this is where we turn, right at that hill over there! Then we'll see some houses and caves."

"Sure," Liman thought aloud, "helping the next guy's all right, but running stock to a leper colony? I don't exactly remember volunteering for this—"

"Well, someone's got to do it, and there's no shame in it, man. And look at me, healthy and solid as a spring buck! No fear! All right, well, this is the drop-off point here, so see, we don't have to go any further. Help me unload the supplies." Rig loosed the load tied to the donkey cart and unloaded bundles of foodstuff, medicines, clothing and miscellaneous articles, assorted tools, and tanned hides They were locally donated items, which helped ease the sting and complications of being separated from the rest of society. Leprosy was feared. It was loathsome and minimally managed at the end of a long stick. It was fatally contagious, and it was to be avoided at all costs. Anyone contracting leprosy was necessarily isolated from the general population, thus the leper colonies. Those afflicted lived in a communal setting. When one left the commune, he was obliged to call out quite loudly so that anyone in his vicinity could move away a safe distance. This call is exactly what Liman began to hear. He heard the shake of a bell and the call: *Unclean! Unclean!*

The drop-off was routine enough that either side could vaguely predict the arrival of the other. Rig and Liman unloaded and removed themselves a comfortable distance from the supply drop.

"So...how'd you know he's here?" Liman pressed.

"I've already told you."

"Well, tell me again. This time I'm really listening." Liman sat on the edge of the donkey's cart, tired legs dangling. Each time he swung his legs in the air, he showed a mark of impatience, and the old wooden cart responded with its own creaks of exhaustion. Rig sat next to Liman on the cart knowing that in a few moments, several members of the colony would be at the drop-off to receive the goods.

The one they spoke of might show today. If he did, maybe Liman could ask the leprous man himself rather than continue pressing Rig with his many questions. Rig tired of the story but went about it one more time with a sigh of exasperation. "My uncle, the merchant, the one that travels a lot. He was on the highway. All of the sudden, they nearly got run over by some foreign army general's men."

"An army general? Foreign, you say?"

"Stop interrupting. Turns out it was a Syrian man called Naaman—"

"Naaman... Naaman...NAAMAN!" Liman snapped his fingers. "I've heard of him! He's quite famous in—"

"Syria, like I said, now quit interrupting. So Naaman, had—"

"LEPROSY! Yes! Naaman is a famous general, and he has leprosy? Isn't that odd? Such a powerful man but as frail as the rest of us, when you think about it...odd...but anyway, what does all of that have to do with this guy here?"

"If I could only tell my story..." Rigsier commented dryly.

"Oh, yeah, yeah. Go ahead!" Liman adjusted his sitting position to demonstrate full attention given to Rigsier, who was, not at all impressed.

"Sooo... Naaman. Oh, for the love of a good story, there's Gehazi now! Ask him yourself!" Rigsier threw his hands up, this time definitely done with storytelling, for sure.

"Really?" Liman was fascinated. "How'd you know which... oooh, that fellow there, I bet!"

"Toldja you'd pick him out easy. Best dressed outcast anyone ever saw!"

"Yeah..." Liman continued to stare in fascination. "His clothes look worn, but you could tell they were expensive at one time." It wasn't that Liman had never seen a person stricken with leprosy before. Unfortunately, leprosy was common, but this incident had been acquired in a most unusual way, if his friend's account was to be believed. He supposed there was only one way to really know. Liman cleared his throat and spoke loudly, "Excuse me there, sir, no, sir, him...over there, that gentleman, umm uh, yes, sir. I...ah, well, I err..." Rig's eyes rolled about while he hung and shook his head.

He came to Liman's rescue, "He wants to know if you're Gehazi, *the* Gehazi!"

"Rig!" Liman was done embarrassing himself, and now more embarrassed that his associate could be so brash.

The man moved slowly as if weighed down by sorrow. When Liman waved his arms about to get the leper's attention, he stopped and put down his bundle. Another member of the colony carried it away, leaving Gehazi empty handed in his once fine garments, looking at the two young men. Nothing surprised Gehazi. He had seen God at work close up so, that these two should single him out and inquire of his history seemed nothing exceptional. "I am Gehazi, and yes, I was once the servant of the great prophet." Liman's jaw dropped as the man continued. Perhaps he was unprepared for such a fluid confession. "No doubt you have heard that I was stricken with the leprosy which once plagued the great general. It is true. Naaman had a servant who showed a faith for him, which God honored, and cleansed Naaman. What I showed God was greed. I was privileged to serve and see up close the wonder of God, but I showed him how perverse, selfish, and deceitful I could be, and so, the sickness of leprosy fell upon me." The leper's gaze settled on some point, which Liman couldn't determine, but it seemed to be an anchor that gave him courage to continue on in his confession.

"'What was he thinking?' you ask? I have asked this of myself many hundreds of times since. I sit for hours and contemplate what I was then and what I am now. Then I allowed myself to be blinded by things, which appear fine to the eye—"

"H-how…" Liman stammered out a word of his question, but it was enough. The leper had asked it of himself so many times, it was easily recognizable. "How could I forget how great our God is? How omnipresent He is? How all-powerful and loving He is? These things cannot be forgotten, but He gives us the freedom to make decisions, including the poor decision of choosing other things ahead of God. I guess the best answer is that I allowed myself to not care just long enough to commit the act." Gehazi let his eyes go from the anchor, swinging them in another direction. "These clothes that I wear, what I put ahead of God, decay with me a little at a time. A little every day."

The leper dusted the front of his garment, grabbed a fistful of its faded weave in each hand at chest level, and walked back toward the colony with his head erect.

"Well," Rig said, "there you have it from the horse's mouth. The man admitted his downfall and guilt. What else can you ask of a person?"

Liman, still confused by what he just witnessed, answered, "Rig, the man admitted what he did, but did he repent? We all sin, but I didn't hear a moment of repentance in his confession. He looks like he's volunteered to be the example of what happens when a person makes such a mistake. Yes, we have to claim our mistakes, and our actions have consequences. I wonder if he's still here because he hasn't asked God to forgive him."

"It could be that he *has* asked forgiveness but still has to live with the *consequences* of his choice. Maybe…he thinks that his sin is too great to be forgiven, or… he simply hasn't asked God."

"Rig, What a mistake! That's an even bigger mistake than the one that got him in this mess. We serve a big God. Our God is loving and forgiving. He's an awesome God! We have to tell him—"

"Now hold on there, partner! This is as far as we go. If you want to talk to him again, you'll have to wait for the next volunteer run. Goodness, you didn't even want to come on this run, but you've had a change of heart." Rig took the donkey's lead and turned for home. "Sometimes you have to see up close the plight of others, and it puts your heart in a different state. Next time we come out, perhaps you can minister to him, but remember, it might be that he has to live with the consequences of his choice. It seems like Gehazi is already resigned to that fact."

"But he worked for the prophet…how…"

"I can't answer that," Rig said, "but Gehazi made the choice in his heart. God teaches us, but He gives us the freedom to make decisions. Look at Namaan. He chose to humble himself and God brought him to a whole 'nother state."

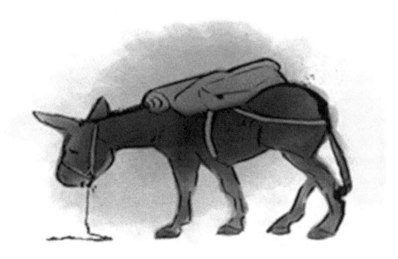

On Research Methods
(1 Sam. 17)

Here's what happens every day: I get up early. I mean early. *Before the birds,* early. I scrub myself. Then I start polishing the stuff. Armor takes a long time to prep. A lot of moveable parts. I assemble weapons, polish and stock ammunition enough for thirty days of siege. Around three hours into my day, the big guy is awakened by the other soldiers who are up and about. He dresses and gets mess. Later we suit him up in his armor. From the minute he is woke, he is talking. He's a big trash-talker and a nonstop one at that. Convinced that he has a sense of humor, his antics border bullying of the other soldiers. Of anyone. Even of me. He has no respect. He is no general, only a foot soldier but a very large one. It's the best thing to make of a thug of a family of thugs, five of them, there are, all conscripted to the army. It's the king's best way to keep peace, protect the nation, and do something about this clan he's misfortunate enough to have to claim. Does Big Trash Talker know it? Doubt it, too busy talkin'. Thinkin' ain't his thing. Just trash. He's our main weapon, the number one deterrent, put up front to protect the borders. No special training. Just let him do what he does naturally—rant. He's so big that he can't miss you. Arms so long you couldn't get near him. Voice so thunderous it would make your heart weak. He's a preemptive strike. Does he know it? Doubt it. He ain't smart. Just loud. He's impervious. Kings would sue for peace: acquiesce land, goods, money, slaves—whatever we wanted. Our economy ran on coersion. It was easy, and fun money.

Somehow, someone negotiated a showdown between us, and them. It was probably us. Probably him. I suppose it was inevitable.

They were moving in to our territory doing their own kind of domination. Talking about some God-given right. I did a little reconnoitering and research. Caravans say they just walked out of 400 years of slavery stacked to the gills with wealth and that they crushed Egypt's army back at the Sea of Reeds. Well, that can't be right. Further intelligence says that they have some kind of invisible God who does all that smashing stuff for them. The God leads them around by a cloud in the daytime, and by fire at night time. Well, that doesn't seem likely since (1) Egypt is unbeatable (we tried), and (2) how could anyone be invisible? So, so much for the research method.

Our prime point man initiates a one-sided shouting match at the enemy camp to begin his program—the instillation, and reinforcement of fear and doubt. Every day he rants. He hurls expletives, insults, and poorly crafted jokes that serve to entertain our infantry. They are delighted because this promises to be a skirmish, which will want minimal investment and turn maximum yield. They sit behind him as if attending an entertaining performance. The Big Rant has four big brothers, all in the front row. They laugh and shout so loud their saliva falls like rain upon the unfortunates bonded to them, as I am to this center of attention. His antics work. The enemy is silent. Previous experience tells us that they are being consumed by a paralysis fed by fear. Our nearly victorious army is in uproarious delight. The standoff will only last so long. One side or the other will have to give. The giants do not plan to buckle. It seems both sides vie for the title of *crusher,* and that's a big ticket to cash. The wanderers think that their God is gonna gift them a whole country? We have lots of gods, and to think of it, not one of them has ever given anyone I know a single thing. All the same, if we're gonna talk about gods, we've got bunches, and they've only got one who won't even come out and face us. I personally don't put any value into the whole god thing. I've seen how hard a craftsman or two worked to come up with some fanciful appearance carved out of a wood stump. Especially the fishy one. Never quite sure why anyone thought that up. What good would a god who looked like, and or was a fish do for a human being? I have given up on all of that, but notwithstanding, it doesn't look good for the wanderers and their invisible God. Behind me, there are five giants in the first wave, and if there's any life left in the wandering army, our second wave will stomp it out. We have five, nine-foot-tall weapons who can't lose. We will win whatever the wanderers have taken and themselves as slaves without so much as lifting a finger. It is a soldier's dream. Meanwhile, it's all fun, games, and lots of jokes. The soldiers sit at ease, off guard, as if entertained by some one-man show, laughing, chatting, passing merriment and liquid spirits about in early celebration of the impending victory. It can only go one way. Big Rant vollies the spear effortlessly up, and over toward the pallored enemy camp. The shaft lands a nearly perfect vertical, the beautifully polished tip entirely embedded in the dirt. This is my cue to fetch. He looks at me with a grunt. "Go get it, Little Man." *Little Man.* I realize that I am part of the entertainment for, although I am not small, compared to him no one is big. I struggle to dig the spear's tip out of the earth. Behind me, I hear the laughter of the entertained audience in full amusement. I manage to free the shaft and hoist it over my shoulders. Before I return to my duty, I survey the enemy camp. I see soldiers dutifully guarding their king's tent, but he does not come out. Perhaps their priests are performing some ablution, for it would take another worldly hand to rescue them, indeed. I trot back to the bothersome giant, who is in fits of uproarious laughter—him, his four brothers on the side lines, the entire army. I am as a dog fetching bones. I consider the impossible for just a moment—that I could outmaneuver this cumbersome fool, and be free of him with one volley of the great spear. Then again, there are four more just like him, lined up, sitting at the ready, and I do have a family to concern myself with. So growing tired, I continue to retrieve the baluster spear at his whim. *Little Man.* It flies up into the air only to return, point downward, piercing, and burying itself into the earth deep behind the weight of its shaft. I dig it out again and return it to the showman. He grunts at me without words as I head out yet again. For encouragement I think to myself—this job is better than prison guard duty by a very great margin. The squalor, darkness, and vermin in the prison is unbearable for me. At least here, I am out on the plain in fresh air. So, with that consolation I do what men all over the world do: I go to work, to a job I do not love, to provide for my family.

The valley is, or would be beautiful were we not gathered here for such a morose occasion. I scan slowly, taking in the vista as far as I can see in every direction. Grass, flowers, soil that could probably be coaxed. What's this? The heat waves distort a small figure cutting across grass nearly up to its waist. It is a man coming toward us. Perhaps it is time to begin negotiations, and I might get home by the end of this day. No, if I believed in the gods, I would swear by them, but I do not. Stuff, nonsense, and wood carvings they are. I see not a man but a boy! A boy approaching me as if he intends to do what I want to do to the oaf. I stand in shock nearby the oaf who can barely stand up straight for laughing so hard. He is mocking the enemy's representative. He's not sure if he wants to be offended or amused, so he utters expletives to both ends. The boy astonishes everyone with his own assertions, determined to bring the giant down. I confess quiet doubts despite how I wish it could be true. The boy has come weaponless. I feel remorse for his young, foolish soul but at least, this should be quick. I see a few of the enemy soldiers move forward only a few paces as they dare ready to pull back the carcass of their brave boy once he is felled. Then I hear a whistle, and see a small rock catapulting through the air. It is so sound, so solid, so driven, and dedicated as if it has one mission in all of its existence, and this is it: the big oaf sees it but cannot think fast enough. There is a knock like that of a bird digging through a dead tree trunk. *Knock!* Then a sort of *squoosh*. The projectile crashes through the oaf's forehead, stopping somewhere inside of his enormous head. The large eyes cross, the baluster spear falls with a thud at my feet and the giant follows suit. Silence follows for what seemed like an eternity, but in fact, it is only a moment. The defining moment, and then both sides begin to whoop! The tormented are now empowered, the overconfident vanquishers jump up to a man, screaming shamelessly, and in flight for their lives.

I stood there beside the enormous body. I was not saddened in any measure, not even to see my entire army take flight. The boy came up to the giant, loosened the sword, and severed the giant's head from its neck. He yelled something about their invisible God. The rest of their army shouted praises to this God, and took off after our army, effectively crushing it. The boy took the sword, and the head. I offered him the javelin. He declined. I quietly asked, "How did you do that?" I am not sure why I asked that way. I only know that there was many a time that I wanted to silence the fool, just as this boy had done. Felling this walking tree was a recurring dream for me but one that I could never have accomplished.

The boy answered me, "In the strength of the Lord!" I helped him carry his prizes back to his king's tent.

I crossed the valley of Elah that day with David, and went back only once for my family. This God, *the Lord,* I have got to get more of. I have got to know. The caravan reports didn't tell the half about the invisible God who could do things like this! So much for the research method…

The Daily Times

The best story...hmmm... It's hard to pick out just one after thirty years of producing *The Daily Times*. I've seen a lot of good reporters and some mediocre ones best retired to a life of sheep-herding. Old Maccarus was a sight! Three days out of the week he'd come hightailing it back to the office at a full clip with some angry warlord or other hot on his heels. He brought us a lot of action, a lot of near disasters, but we sold a lot of news because of him! Rizen, a stouthearted fellow, also game for action and a little jolly fun. Tezren, Relnor, all good men, brave hearts and great reporters. But to pick one, well...well, I guess it'd have to be that old Jonah. Jonah Ben Ammitai. Steady as a beam, that fellow! Oh, and his "right arm"...what's his name? Goz. Goz-mel! Gozmel! Always looked like a runt next to Jonah, always following behind at the double step, but he thought the world of Jonah. Jonah treated him like a little brother, taught Goz everything—tried to, at least. Gozmel didn't truly have what it takes to be a reporter in his blood. He never stopped trying, though. He followed Jonah everywhere like a puppy. Jonah was always levelheaded. I mean, you knew he wouldn't blow in the door and duck and hide in a closet because he'd just fast-talked some wealthy foreigner out of a carriage full of gold in exchange for some local sham. No, Jonah was as "steady as he goes," for twenty-five years. Then he sort of fell off a cliff, so to speak, at the end, so I retired him. Retired myself shortly after that! Hey, ya gotta know when to roll up your tent and call it quits. A smart guy knows, anyway. I wouldn't say that Jonah had any major vices, but he did have a soft spot for the underdog. Always with the stories about someone lost in the desert for three days, given up for dead, comes home! Or troublesome kid turns around and makes good. That sort of thing. Maybe he just spent too much time in the big city. It can wear on you, and being away from home for years at a stretch… Maybe, I should have taken him off that beat long before. Anyway, there was that day when Jonah hit his "enough" point, and he quit. He and his entourage of one. I didn't see it coming! Do you know how hard it is to keep the news comin' in fresh from all directions, and provide stimulating reading for whoever can? It's not easy, and you can lose track of your best man at these distances. I didn't really worry about Jonah though, because Gozmel was always with him; those two were as tight as two fleas on a tick! When Jonah went off, Goz was determined to bring him back to *The Daily Times*. You want to know what happened? Well, the story is known well enough.

Jonah worked here. His desk was…there, that one, just there but he never spent much time at his desk. Jonah was always on assignment—foreign correspondence and all of that, you know. When he had first arrived in Ninevah, local politics were interesting enough, but as time passed, the city grew more dangerous. All sorts of crime escalated. You know, any culture will suffer in such conditions. There were fewer and fewer good things to report on—no public arts, no volunteer programs, tourism decreased, the markets lost diversity. The whole state was failing because crime and war were on the increase. Jonah began to hate his assignment. Ever have a job you didn't like? Well, that was Jonah. At least, that was the predicament Jonah found himself in. Reporting on the big city of Ninevah had lost its appeal. Then the sandal dropped; Jonah wasn't the only one who noticed! God himself had put Jonah on assignment, but Jonah didn't want the job anymore. So he quit. Yep, that simple. Done with reporting, done with Ninevah. "Simple," except that, well…there are obvious profound complications associated with walking out on God, which we need not belabor, but for the sake of my story, I will state the obvious fact that one cannot hide from the Almighty; therefore, I cannot purport to know exactly what Jonah was thinking when he tried.

Narrator arranges himself more comfortably in his chair. No longer attentive to his audience, his mind and his line of sight drifts to events of

a time some twenty years prior. One sees his mind's eye Jonah and Gozmel
conversing on the back deck of Jonah's house.

JONAH. You see, my dear Gozmel, when the Word of the LORD is placed upon your spirit, you have two choices. God always gives you two choices—to live or die. You can live in obedience or chose your own will. Inevitably, it will lead to death. Why? Because choices come with consequences! They're attached! The stick is that you don't always see them immediately, but sure as the sun rises in the east, consequences follow actions. Take for example, when we were boys. Remember the chicken that you—

GOZMEL. Did not steal! It followed me home.

JONAH. Goz, we lived halfway across the village from that farm.

GOZMEL. It followed me home...

JONAH. Maybe you should have stolen a puppy. Puppies follow. Chickens...not so much.

GOZMEL. It followed me home. What could I do?

JONAH. Ummm...return it? Because things got awkward when the owner came to your father's door that night.

GOZMEL. Yes, yes, I remember the crime. I remember the punishment. I only don't get why we're bringing up twenty years ago... Oh, yes, consequences...and your point was?

JONAH. Freedom of choice! That's what God gives to us, but it comes with a price.

GOZMEL. The consequences.

JONAH. The consequences! I spoke His Word to the house of Israel, and what has Israel done? Has the country listened to God? No! It continues to follow the ways of the nations who do not know the LORD. But now, even worse. God sends me to foreigners!

GOZMEL. You never minded working Ninevah before.

JONAH. I never had this special assignment before. Before was just, you know, *The Daily Times*. I reported this town same as I'd report the next. This town is on a downward spiral. Left to itself, it will self-destruct. Now, now this is different, life-altering.

Gozmel: So you quit your job? You quit writing for *The Daily Times*? You just left?

JONAH. Quite.

GOZMEL. You're nuts! What's that supposed to do? You had the best assignment. Any reporter here would give anything to have that assignment! You got it handed to you and you quit?! I would give anything to have your job!

JONAH. Well, friend, now you don't have to…

GOZMEL. I'm telling you you're out of your mind. Don't be a fool going off this way. And you know I follow you on every assignment. So, you're going off the deep edge and gonna take me with you. Know what? *I'm* a fool—I'm following you! Why am I trying to talk sense into you? Here's what I should do: I should forget about you, run back to my desk, find a crisp, neat copy of my resume, and knock ten guys down trying to get to the editor's office first so I can get your job! That's what I should be doing right now, but I'm wasting time standing here trying to save your life! This is not a plan! Here's a plan: get hired. Do a great job. Get noticed by the boss. Get a promotion. Do a better job. Get to keep your job until they give you a pension to go away. That's a plan! That's about thirty years of *plan*. This, what you got, is not—a—plan! Notttt a plan. But! If you want to go crazy and you won't see reason I should just—

JONAH. I put your resume on the boss's desk with my recommendation before I left. Surely he's expecting you as we speak. You should go back now.

GOZMEL, turn around right now, and go back to the city, and—what? What?!!! You did what?

JONAH. You're the best replacement I could imagine. And you will enjoy the assignment. You're a good match. I've just lost the luster for news coverage, I guess. I lost the heart for it.

GOZMEL. Why would you give your job away. You'd never get it back! Not from me! There's a hundred guys waiting for that position at all times!

JONAH. The dead have no need of this world's trappings.

GOZMEL. Dead, what dead? Who's dead? You're not dead. I'm not. I'm not dead! Am I dead? No, not. Not dead.

JONAH. My dear Gozmel, God has given me an assignment, and I have refused it…

GOZMEL. You're a dead man! Ohhh, you're a dead man! Biiiiggg trouble, man. But I mean. But what! What! Why? Is that why you quit? What! Tell me what!

JONAH. Look, Goz, we're writers, right? Write books, write sonnets, write prose, write news, write copies, write transcripts. Scrolls upon scrolls—you name it—we do it. But reporters go a step further. I go get the stories. Sometimes I go places I don't like. I sometimes I see things that I don't want to see, but my job is to tell the truth. God has sent me to this people, the Assyrians, of all people. These people are violent like no other. They're so brutal that people kill themselves rather than be captured by Assyrian armies. And these are the ones He sent me to preach to! To warn them! If they don't change their ways, they'll reap judgment.

GOZMEL. Sounds…like…a lot to write about…

JONAH. Gozmel, I hated them! The whole lot of them! I wanted them to die. I wanted them to die with the violence that they inflicted on others so that their godless culture would implode upon itself. This people does not have the love for God that makes a human sound and whole. Best that they were left to kill themselves, it would give relief to the fathers and husbands of nations all around. So I figure, if I don't warn them, they don't change. If they don't change, they earn—

GOZMEL. The consequences!

JONAH. Right, you are. See, I know this about the LORD: He is merciful and forgiving. I know He'd forgive them, but I didn't want forgiveness for them, so I left with the message undelivered.

Gomez: Ooohh. This story is getting bad, very bad…

JONAH. He said go north, to Ninevah, to warn the people of their approaching judgment. I wanted them to meet that doom—

GOZMEL. So you went south! And I'm following you south! Ooohhh no, Jonah! Nooo!

JONAH. I am heading south, but I don't know why you're following me. Where in particular I'm going, I don't even know. What I know is, I'm not going north, not to Ninevah. Not to warn those people. It'll save them.

GOZMEL. Oh, you are a thickheaded block of old wood! You don't save anyone! Salvation comes from Him...

JONAH. South...

GOZMEL. And lemme tell you something else while I have your attention. You think you can manipulate God? You know, you can choose your actions, but you can't choose the consequences! You think you can manipulate God's hand? Make Him do what you want? That's beyond, well, I never thought you could be capable of such poor thought. It's foolish, presumptuous, inane, arrogant, and just plain wrong—all in one fat wrapping, and it'll explode in your lap.

JONAH. I left you my job, my house, and field.

GOZMEL. Suicide? You know it's a suicide mission—wait, no! This is not a "mission." This is a misguided, self-absorbed act of pseudo heroism that *you* think will result in you giving "the bad guys" what you think they deserve! Call it whatever you want, but the fact is that you're putting your own will above God's and it won't work! Can't! You listenin' to me? It's not your call to make. You've appointed yourself judge, jury, and executor! Hey! Remember this: you're just a writer. A little news reporter of little news bits, mister! No more!

JONAH. Please feed my dog. And he gets an extra helping of beef jerky with his meals twice a week.

GOZMEL. Well, Mr. Bar Ammitai, you're grossly mistaken! How dare you put your agenda above God's. He made this universe and put you down right here in it. Put you in, and He'll take you out! Put His finger atop your head, turned you east, and said, "Go." And you're saying no?

JONAH. I didn't ask anything of anybody. I didn't pack anything. I carry nothing. I just stepped out the front door, walked out of the courtyard, and locked the gate behind me. I can't do it anymore. I can't bear to hear *The Daily Times* from this city anymore. So I wandered through the streets, past the stone synagogue with *No!* in my head. Through the market quarter, past the vegetable vendor, the spice store, the butcher of meats. *No!* Past sellers of garments, rugs, and dyes. Past the jeweler and potteries. *No!* Past the farrier, tanner, carpenter, and smithing shops. Winding between a shepherd and his flock of sheep pushing out to the pastures beyond the city wall. *No!* was still in my head.

GOZMEL. *No!* in your head? Ask God for a new head! *No!* in your heart? He'll give you a new one! Friend, I smell ego, and it's yours!

JONAH. I reached the city gates and stopped for the first time. I know that inside, my head is still shouting *No!*, and I know that you are still following me although I still do not know why. This is not part of your assignment. I take a long collection of breaths and a longer look around at a people who have suffered interminably at the hands of a ruthless tribe. I think I'll go to the sea.

(Narrator adjusts in his seat. Fidgeting, he moves a few items around on his desk, which was Jonah's desk at one time. He stares at a small wooden box. Inside are a bit of sand, seaweed, and a few tiny shells. Narrator appears to be dreaming, but he is fully cognizant as he continues telling his story.)

NARRATOR. And he did. Jonah went to the sea, and Gozmel was, of course, right behind him. He walked as if in not a trance but such intense thought so as to lose track of all else. Thusly, Jonah made for the port with Goz following like a hapless pup. Jonah had a faraway look, like he didn't hear the sheep bleating, the vendors hawking, or the carts and donkeys pulling across dusty stone streets. Goz knew what he was doing. Jonah was trying to let everything go and just walk away. Quit. Goz kept rattling on trying to engage him, and finally, Jonah wouldn't slow down, but he did start talking again. Goz couldn't tell who Jonah was talking to, but at least he was talking. Jonah spoke clearly.

JONAH. I heard the battering ram beating, beating…beating at the city gates until the massive wood and iron-laden doors gave way, throwing great splinters through the vanguards who stood to defend their city. Shards speared men, piercing those who stood three and four deep. Behind the batter ram poured in the violent ones like locusts, sparing nothing. I heard men falling from the watch. Great blocks of stone displaced from the wall crashed into flesh. Fire flew over what was left of the walls then the vanquisher poured in. Over the walls, over the fallen gates. Over the fallen men. They killed the old and the very young. Mothers screamed trying to hold onto the babies pried from their arms. Children were lead off into slavery. I heard the horses and soldiers that swept through the city. It swept me from my sleep. So I told God, *No. No!* Will a man say *No* to God? I said *No!* and tried to close my mind and turn my back, even to God. Why? (*Sighs*) Because He is good. Does that sound strange? Think a little further then: He is so good that He would give them, even them, a second chance. They who have been an enemy to our nation, a plague, but He would let them live! Oh, and not just that: He would tell us to love them! Love the murderers? Love the ones who reduce cities to rubble; set fire to rooftops; carry off our gold, silver, the sweat of our hands; murder innocent men and enslave children? Yeah! That's my God! I said that I know Him. I mean, I know what He'll do, but the why? Well, now that's another matter! I was angry and tired, so I just said no. (*Sigh*) I love this port. I love the ships, the sails, the winds. They are what it means to be completely free.

GOZMEL. They're not free. They can't be. The ships are tied to the ports, the sails tied down to the masts by thousands of lengths of rope. Then the lot of it is driven across the water by men tied by chains down below, forced to row. Do you know a worse master than men? But... I think I do get your meaning—a sail stretched by the wind. Nothing seems more clean, more crisp. Things seem pure and right when you feel a gentle briskness across your flesh. Your eyes try to balance the shimmering line out there that you never get to where the water meets the sky.

JONAH. I admire most the working man's toolbox, the modestly handcrafted family fishing sloop. That is a boat with heart, a man will go far in such a tiny cup to feed his family.

GOZMEL. Sure, but for a trip in some reasonable comfort...

JONAH. I select the merchant ship. Shipping agents of great treasures yet room enough aft the mast for the captain to share a traveler's tale with a passenger. In fact, I would pick this one...

(Narrator shifts restlessly in his chair, wears a vacous stare in his eyes and recalls)

NARRATOR. Jonah did just that! He picked a ship out of ships. He seemed enamored by it. It's lines, depth, the carving on the mast-head—everything about it, but it wasn't really the ship; it was the ship's direction, westerly bound. This was not the largest of ships but respectable enough to host a fair cargo. Still, against the backdrop of sea, it seemed minuscule. Gozmel had no desire to leave the port waters of Joppa to find himself bobbing about on endless waves on a mission, which he was sure had to end badly. The ship jostled about as if it was a child's toy in bathwater. Waves rolled up to the piers as if they had all boldness and authority but then slid back discreetly to its vast center beckoning the tethered craft to follow. At a short distance, the waves stood off against the quay but broke up into less harmful constituents before each collusion. Jonah continued working on his self-delusion.

JONAH. There's so much of it, the sea, it can swallow you up. But with this ship going west by northwest, perhaps southwest, by any means, west. I will put a distance between me and Ninevah and the whole matter. I will breathe deeply on the sea—clear my head, relax a few days, perhaps. Think...yes...that's what I need, an impromptu getaway of sorts. I will think about things which I had been putting on hold for some time. I could see some new places, not new but new to me, perhaps consider negotiating a reassignment. Whatever. I will stay until my rest-lessness permits sleep.

NARRATOR. Having negotiated his fare, Jonah went below deck and found that his assigned quarters amongst crowded accommo-dations was merely a hammock. Despite the rabble and bustle surrounding him, he soon fell into a heavy sleep, and sleep he did! Meanwhile, dear Gozmel, unwilling to let Jonah out of his sight, bought a ticket, for the adjacent hammock and melted into it. In this time, the ship's merchants sailed many miles and made three port stops, loading and unloading along their route. Hours later, all other passengers gone, they were heading due west in open sea. Quickly, a storm wrapped around them with deadly intent. The ship's hands were terrified. All hammocks rocked violently even as the boat went round in a swirl. Captain Amirek shouted orders to steady the men but could not be heard above the angry sea. Shortly, everyone was shouting in half a dozen languages, but the sea swallowed them all. She spoke the loudest. This was the bad feeling Gozmel had felt before leaving Port Joppa. He tried to shake off the sleep and looked over at Jonah in his hammock. He never stirred. Jonah was swaddled in sleep. His face was at peace knowing nothing about all of the mayhem that was about to devour the ship. Sleep weighed on Gozmel like a coat of iron. When it fell off, fear quickly wrapped about him. Now standing, he stumbled topside, immediately awash in seawater from the pitching boat. The fear in Captain Amirek's eyes confirmed that their situation was grave. The captain directed men in various directions desperately trying to keep the masts pointed up and the water bailed out.

CAPTAIN. All sails down! Lieutenant, rudder, twenty degrees on my mark!

LIEUTENANT. Aio, Captain, sailsss downnnnn! Twenty degrees on your mark!

CAPTAIN. Yev, cast all cargo on the port side!

YEV. Captain, we can't lose the cargo. It's all our profit!

CAPTAIN. Do it now! Mark!

YEV. Aio, Captain, twenty degrees! (*Shouts*) Get thoosssse saaailssss downnnn.

CAPTAIN. Cast all cargo. Mister Omir, I told you to cast the larboard caarrgo! Do it nowww!

MR. OMIR. But, Captain, we'll be throwing away all of our money! We cannot cast the cargggooo...whaooo! Helllp! Meee...helllp!

CAPTAIN. Man overboard! You there, over here, and help! You, man, throw the net over! Omir, swim, man! Come on, man! Catch the rope. That's it! Now give me your hannd… I've got you! Give me a hand over here! Pull, man!

NARRATOR. Both men lay on their backs for a moment. The captain raised his head, looking over at the nearly drowned man. He continued to speak.

CAPTAIN. Look, if we don't lighten this ship, we'll go down in this storm with the cargo. Now get up and go cut all the ropes. It's got to be now!

MR. OMIR. Aio, sir, aio, sir!

NARRATOR. A sailor, a boy, barely old enough to be away from home, slides across the deck belly down only stopping at the impasse which Mr. Omir had become. Mr. Omir rolls the boy over to reveal wide eyed fear and shakes his shoulder to bring him back to awareness.

MR. OMIR. Boy, throw all cargo fore and aft, overboard now. And go below. If you find any crates, get them up here and over-board—go!

BOY. Mr. Omir, I went below, and there's a man lying in his bunk, I think he's asleep, Sir.

MR. OMIR. What?

NARRATOR. Jonah was hardly woke when his hammock upturned and he landed face first on the wet deck floor. Wiping blood from his nose and seawater from his cheeks, he saw three men standing over him, yelling in a language that he did not speak. Jonah's blank expression caused one sailor to try different tongues until he hit upon Jonah's. The sailor translated for the Captain.

CAPTAIN. Who are you, how can you sleep now? Why have you not called upon your gods? We are about to die in this storm!

NARRATOR. The seamen decided to cast lots because this storm was so sudden and so violent. No surprise to Jonah, the lots and all eyes fell upon him.

CAPTAIN. Who are you? What is your nation, and who are your gods? We must pray to everyone's gods because we are about to die in this storm!

JONAH. I am Jonah, a Hebrew of Joppa. I worship the Living God, the God of Abraham, Isaac, and Jacob, the true and all-powerful God who created all things.

NARRATOR. This whitened the pallor in their faces even more.

CAPTAIN. It's you. What can we do for you to calm the sea for us?

GOZMEL. Jonah, you're the only calm person on the boat. You know something that the rest of us don't. We're on the same team! You've got one of those looks like you're seeing something the rest of us are not.

NARRATOR. For a moment Jonah heard the LORD within his spirit. He paled as the next words came to him heavily but he knew it was from God. Jonah didn't want to think—but who can stop the mind? The men mused over his words only for a moment.

JONAH. Cast me overboard and the storm will abate.

TRANSLATOR. Captain says, we go back to land.

NARRATOR. Those honorable men tried to spare Jonah. They went topside and tried to row back to port. Just then, the storm surged into daggers, which nearly broke the ship apart. They could make no headway. They returned below to Jonah.

TRANSLATOR. Captain says, throw you overboard, now!

NARRATOR. Reluctantly, three men ushered Jonah up to the deck. Jonah did not resist. Two hoisted him up; one by the arms outstretched and the other by the ankles. They swung twice.

TRANSLATOR. Captain says, 'Oh Hebrew God LORD, please no kill us for throw this man over!'

NARRATOR. With another swing, the third lad helped shove Jonah over the port side ledge. He was already chilled by his garments, wet from having been turned out of his hammock onto the deck floor. The wind for those few seconds as he fell, was even more chilling. Jonah hit the water's surface with a hard smack to his back, barely audible in the raging torment. As Jonah's weight broke the surface and began to sink, frigid and silent, his eyes were glazed but open. Jonah held his breath but didn't try to swim. He wasn't going to try to live. He was remorseful but too ashamed. In those moments, he knew that he wanted another chance so that he would not have to go before the LORD in such shame, but it was too late.

GOZMEL. "His face told me everything; he felt ashamed. Like an unbelievable failure, and for what, because he made his own choice, the wrong choice when the Word of the LORD came to him. But it had been his choice. But I couldn't bear it. I knew I couldn't stop them from throwing him over. Indeed he wanted it so, at least, it was by his word that they did so. I wanted him to live. I wanted him to wait through the storm and work everything out. I dove in. I wasn't sure where because the water rolled at the boat in swells two hills high. It seemed as if each one that hit pushed us another latitude away from the last spot. Everything was motion. There was no non-motion. I thought I looked for him in every direction, but it was too dark to see, and even if it wasn't, everything was so stirred up the sea was the color of mud. Everything floated past me—wooden plank, fish, some land animal, human skeleton, crates everywhere, the precious cargo. Mud sullied my hope of visibility, so I went with the currents as if I had a choice, hoping by some chance to find him. It didn't take long to know that I was making a fool's move, so I worked back toward the boat.

I breathed air, salt, water, mud, whatever else was in my path. With all limbs past exhaustion, I knew there was no resting, if I didn't get aboard, I would likely give out soon, and the next wave would be my undoing. Looking right, left, or anywhere didn't matter. My eyes were overwhelmed with the movement in the darkness. Everything was moving, everywhere was darkness. I raised my hands to move upward but they would not go. Was it a rock? Surely I wasn't that far down. I slammed my hands against it. Flat, smooth. Intervals. The strake! I had been swept across the underbelly of the Merimede. Not much left in my lungs, I walked my hands along an interval, a plank of siding. Widthwise until it curved. My palms rounded the edge up toward a side. I grabbed a hold as best as my cold fingers could against a new launch of swelling wave intent on dragging me deep. I heaved with the last cache of breath in my chest after which felt as if one side had pasted itself against the other side. My feet pushed against water until I could see the mottled angry sky. An arm went up, and I should thank it for doing so, flailing about for attention. I had not the senses to speak, being overcome by the sea. The sailors onboard the *Merimede* were standing about staring at the weather. Indeed, a worthwhile look, they stared hard before deciding I was worth the *Man Over-board!* Alarm. First presuming me to be the man just cast from the ship, they wondered at the anomaly which I would not recognize for a few moments yet. Those men saw that the strangely violent storm had quickly abated with the sinking of the man. A ladder of woven hemp affixed in along the portside rail was thrown over. Longish, it's bottom dipped beneath the waves but quickly surfaced, floating perhaps ten to fifteen feet out from the ship. Exhaustion had convinced me to surrender. The boatswain's young boy, eagerly intent to recover me, gave me sufficient shame to resume the battle for my life. With a few more seconds, I found a knot of the rope net floating as if it was reaching out to me. Waves pushed me toward it. I grabbed the rope, looping my arm around it while I breathed air, saltwater, mud—whatever else was in my path. With all limbs past exhaustion, I knew there was no resting. If I didn't get aboard, I would likely give out soon, and the next wave would be my undoing. I pulled for all of my worth, dragging heavy legs alongside the hull. A sailor helped me heave onto the flat of the deck as wet as the sea itself, still, reassured to feel something solid under my belly. No one assisted me further as water oozed and choked out from my lungs, negotiating for air. The ship's mates, fully engrossed in the anomalies of the oncoming and cessation of the storm, yanked me out of the wet as an afterthought. Within moments of casting Jonah overboard, the tempest, which threatened to take all of our lives left the sea. I, not yet realizing the connection, lamented the ill timing. I thought that had Jonah managed to hang on for but a few moments more all would have been at peace. Only later would I piece together the hasty disembarkation with the quieting of the sea.

On the deck floor, I lay next to a tangle of fishing nets. The deck was dryer than the sea but still very wet. So were my insides,

I coughed out the sea. I'd gone out looking for Jonah, nearly killed myself and came back empty handed, almost not at all. I fought my mind's picture of him shoved sideways and downward by water and more water, dark muddied hands of water pushing him down. It must have been true, because he remained somewhere below and the sea was now picturesquely calm.

I cannot say that I missed my port exit, as I had never determined one at the outset. I didn't know whether Jonah had either. I stayed aboard for some days with the sailors discussing the storm and the departure of Jonah. Telling these men about God was more like just connecting the dots. So well-traveled were nearly all of them that they had heard much about God, about the extraordinary God who chose an ordinary people. We had pushed across the Mediterranean, putting in at several ports, all the while merchants, vendors, sailors, passengers—everyone had a bit to tell of the hearsay about this God. These shipmates became believers, tossing their pocket-sized carved idols over the stern with big grins.

I now disembarked in Joppa, and glad to have the firm earth much around me, lingered at the port. Perhaps the smell of a familiar wind of freshly caught fish held me, but I never returned to the news agency. Foolish, eh? I had the job of jobs bequeathed to me, thanks to my deeply conscientious and departed friend. I knew that I couldn't spend more than a few minutes there, not after this experience, but what to do now?

NARRATOR. While Gozmel was finding peace, Jonah was still deep in the sea.

JONAH. It was very dark as I sank down into the churning water. A cold dark. My arms were out at my sides, hands cupping the saltwater as it hit each palm, sifting up in between my fingers. Down, down. Little air in my lungs left, bubbles slip from between tightly pursed lips. Eyes wide, why didn't I swim? This is what should be happening to me. I am in some foreign somewhere, where I shouldn't be, but where the consequences of my actions place me. My body felt heavy and cold. My head filled with pressure, my lungs emptied of breath, my eyes stared ahead at nothing. It was so dark. I felt a current of cold water moving toward me and made out a massive shadow in the darkness. A greater splash and disturbance in all of the turbulence hit me, from which direction, I cannot say. The push tumbled me over, and after a few minutes, the water left my head. I opened my mouth and gasped for air! Am I alive? How can I be alive? I have no more breath. I am not floating or sinking. I'm… laying, exhausted on something. Am I at the sea floor? I am in something? I have breath. Am I dead? I feeelll…not dead, I don't think. No, not dead but not normal. Seaweed everywhere! My head, my arms! The smell was strongly of the sea. My eyes had glazed. They came back to my senses to work with me. I sent them about to investigate and report back to me. The cave rumbled and hummed with the rhythm of breath. Inhale…now an exhale. I heard a gentle song from the cave of whatever creature this was, and I knew it was one by the rows of teeth I tried to step across, but poor idea. My eyes report that all of the sea seems to be just on the other side. So here I sit, I Jonah, son of Ammitai, son of truth, sitting in the bowels of some kind of sea creature. Now how did I come to be here? Didn't I say, "*God gives you choices, but the way of man leads to death*?" Yet here the Great God did not let me die. He used this great animal to preserve me! Didn't I say, "*The* LORD *is forgiving*?" yet when I rebelled against Him, turned my back on Him and esteemed my judgment to be above, His, oh, what an arrogant fool I am! If He gave me another chance, I would be His faithful servant again. I would never have the audacity to put my will above Him, the Almighty God. How did I get to that place, such that untempered arrogance ran through my head, heart, to my hands, to my feet? Little by little. How did I get to that place, which brought me to this place, somewhere in the bowels of a fish, deep in the bowels of the sea? The LORD had to bring me very low because I had made myself very high. It was simply arrogance. Praise the God who brings the haughty ones down low. The earth is just the footstool of God. I repent to the LORD because He is the Great Almighty. Because I want to serve Him and honor Him. The sickness inside of me—not my person—my flesh but my soul was from sinning against God, the very one who knit me together. I am prostrate down on my face and seek Him in repentance and sorrow. Oh, dear God, how I have strayed away from you. I can scarcely breath, even see, and my soul aches to return to you! Show me how to love as you love. Put my heart back on the path that leads to you, my LORD, my God. In the belly of a fish, I, Jonah, son of truth, rejoiced because the LORD is the God of another chance, or where would I be? He restored my soul and mercifully released me from that fish, which spat me out, right back at the port shores of Joppa!

Inhaling both air and sun, I peeled off the seaweed and began wading! I would walk to the ends of the earth for my God! So I set off, up to the port and beyond the markets, beyond the farms and pastures, scarcely stopping over the great distance until I reached the gates of Ninevah. I entered the western gate embraced by stone statues of their gods, cut stone images standing six-men high. Markets of thieves, vandals robbing the robbers, immoral men lured into doorposts of loose women, an unattended child. Oh, I would have told them, "This place is finished!" But God had just recently done a work of mercy within my own heart. So I told them that my God, the only true God, is all-powerful, will judge the wicked, and exact justice for all deeds. Of course, I wanted to tell them that He is forgiving. I moved through the busiest streets with a countdown: *Forty days and Ninevah will fall!* I called from my stomach with all of my breath, but the smell of seaweed and fish bowels—that's what turned heads! Then they heard the message. I counted down every day, moving through the streets, wide and narrow. I walked through alleyways and dirt paths, calling to every man in the city to repent because the sin of the city had become great, and God was about to call destruction upon the entire city. And then the unthinkable happened. Just what I thought might happen, just what I knew would happen: they repented! I mean, they really had a change of heart. From the king, down to a man, the city dressed in the sackcloth of repentance—sackcloth. They even expressed repentance for their animals, covering them as well. Yet, somehow, in my heart of hearts, there I was at square one again: disappointed, no, angry. Why? Because I knew God would forgive them. I mean, you just don't know these people, the evil things they'd done. And sure enough, He forgave them. So who could I say, "told you so!" to? Only God, and I did! In my anger, I did. Isn't that how I started on that *little by little* path which led me down to the fish? *I knew it! God, isn't this what I said in the first place? That's why I tried to go to Tarshish. I knew you were going to forgive them! Oh God, just kill me, I'm better off dead...* He said, "Do you have the right to be angry?"

I went out of the east gate of Ninevah, which was embraced with carvings of fiercely scowling griffins whose eyes were sightless. With wingspans three-men tall, homage to their dead gods was not wanting in effort. Still, I felt no pity on a people who chose to worship a piece of stone fashioned by their own hands. I found a small knoll with a few sparse trees and made a shelter, but the sun beat on my anger, which was going down that *little by little* path. God gave me a vine and grew it so that it wound all about the shelter frame and made a pleasant shade. It was beautiful with tricolored and fragrant blossoms that soaked up the sun's heat. It relieved some of my agony and discomfort, and I was able to rest into the evening. The following morning at dawn, a miserable worm chewed at the vine so that it died. Over the day, the sun cut into me and rekindled my anger, stoking it hot, making me just want to die. This was all too much for me, so I reminded God that I'd had enough and felt it would be better if I just died. He said, "Do you have a right to be angry about the vine?"

Of course, I did. I was well on the path of "*little by little*," which had already once led me down into the sea. It seemed like I didn't even care. I knew what it was like to almost die. I was ready. It was all too much for me. My merciful God wouldn't let me go down into the sea again. He said, "You're concerned about a plant. You didn't plant it, water it, nurture it. it sprang up overnight and then it died overnight! Just a flower! Ninevah has over 120,000 lost souls and their livestock! Shouldn't I care about them?"

I, Jonah, son of Ammitai, son of truth, I am here to tell you that failure is an event, not a person. In my selfishness, I condemned 120,000 people to die. God, in His undeserving mercy, allowed 120,000 people to come to the knowledge of the Living God and learn what life is. That's revival! And because God is the God of another chance, He has taught me to have mercy on my brother's circumstance. Aren't we all going through something? Better than hate, is the love of God.

*****

NARRATOR. And that's what happened to the great city of Ninevah. I never saw Gozmel again. And whatever happened to that old fellow Jonah? You know… I don't know!

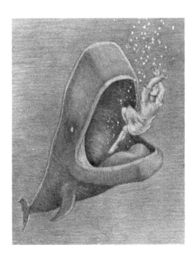

Hamsters. Sodium. Guinea Pigs. Chlorine.
Polonium. Sulfur. Blueberries. Argon. Navy
Seals. Beavers. Potassium. RNA. Begonias.
Calcium. Twins. Scandium. Frozen Yogurt.
Titanium. Carrots. DNA. Scuppernongs.
Pigeons. Vanadium. Mountains. Chromium.
Manganese. Knish. Strawberry Shortcake
Ice Cream. Iron. Cobalt. Rabbits. Current.
Peppers. Nickel. Owls. Copper. Zinc. Albelia
Shrubs. Blackberries. Gallium. Hawks.
Suntans. Geraniums. Cottage Cheese With
Pineapple. Arsenic. Periwinkle. Selenium.
The Ten Commandments. Dried Dates.
The Bible. Bibles with Commentaries. The
USA. Monkeys. Verbena. Tumeric. Valleys.
Boulders. Strontium. Wildflowers. River
Stones. Hafnium. Moose. Baby Birds That
Can Fly. Emeralds. Racoons. Raspberries.
Crepe Myrtles. Yttrium. Plankton. Double
Helices. Palladium. Islands. Silver. Blue Grass
Music. Cadmium. Baked Chocolate Pudding.
America's Armed Forces. Proteins. Squirrels.
Tin. Orchids. Mandolins. Cerium. Ice Cream.
Time. KINDNESS. GOODNESS. JOY.

Bears. SELF-CONTROL. FAITHFULNESS. Banjos. Irises. Tungsten. GENTLENESS. PATIENCE. Osmium. Morning Glories. Zinnias. Pea Gravel. Eagles. Picacho Peak. Baked Potatoes. Singing. Impatients. Animal Rescuers. Simon the Swan from Lake Oconee. Hydrangeas. Anemones. Lions. Walnut Trees. Lead. Forgiveness. Paper. Graphite. Topaz. Dirt. Buffalo. Bismuth. Boxwood Shrubs. Pistachios. Thorium. Tulips. Hippos. Buttercups. Uranium. Pansies. Neptunium. Water Lilies. Curium. Dahlias. California. Asters. Soil. Shoes. Chocolate. Deserts. Forests. Gravity. Constants & Variables. Fibonacci Triplets. Sparrow. Old Faithful. Slate. Waterfalls. Chipmunks. Memory. H2O Being A Solid, Liquid And A Gas. All Of Those Planets Out There Keeping The Earth In Its Orbit. Georgia (The State). Cashews. Zebra Fish. Fruit Juice. Draft Horses. That God Has A Plan For My Life. Self-Propelled Lawn Mowers. DMV Workers. Civil Service, Holiday, Night And Odd Shift Workers. That I *Know* That God Has A Plan For My Life.

About the Author

The author, a New York City transplant, loves rural living and helping animals. She currently lives in Virginia with a host of domestic animals where she enjoys gardening, reading and researching religious history and historical fiction.

CPSIA information can be obtained
at www.ICGtesting.com
Printed in the USA
FSHW011103230621
82607FS